THE OPPOSITE OF REMEMBERING

Other Books by Ian Gouge

Novels and Novellas

On Parliament Hill - Coverstory books, 2021
A Pattern of Sorts - Coverstory books, 2020
The Opposite of Remembering - Coverstory books, 2020
At Maunston Quay - Coverstory books, 2019
An Infinity of Mirrors - Coverstory books, 2018 (updated ed.)
The Big Frog Theory - Coverstory books, 2018 (updated ed.)
Losing Moby Dick and Other Stories - Coverstory books, 2017

Short Stories

Degrees of Separation - Coverstory books, 2018
Secrets & Wisdom - Paperback, 2017

Poetry

Selected Poems: 1976-2022 - Coverstory books, 2022
The Homelessness of a Child - Coverstory books, 2021
The Myths of Native Trees - Coverstory books, 2020
First-time Visions of Earth from Space - Coverstory books, 2019
After the Rehearsals - Coverstory books, 2018
Punctuations from History - Coverstory books, 2018
Human Archaeology - Paperback, 2017
Collected Poems (1979-2016) - KDP, 2017

Anthologies

New Contexts: 3 - Coverstory books, 2022
Making Marks in the Sand - Coverstory books, 2022
New Contexts: 1 - Coverstory books, 2021
Triple Measures - Ian Gouge, K.M.Miller, Tom Furniss, Coverstory books, 2020
Oak Tree Alchemy - Coverstory books, 2019
Play for Three Hands - Tom Furniss, Ian Gouge, K.M.Miller, pamphlet 1981

Non-Fiction

Shrapnel from a Writing Life - Coverstory books, 2022

Ian Gouge

The Opposite of Remembering

First published in 2020 by Coverstory books
(updated 2023)

ISBN 978-1-9993027-9-5 (paperback)
ISBN 978-1-9162899-3-2 (ebook)

www.iangouge.com

www.coverstorybooks.com

for Harry and Hannah

The Funeral

"Hello. I don't believe we've met."

She had been observing the woman from afar throughout the service, puzzled that there could be someone in the small congregation she didn't know. Now as she approached her - the woman smiling in a gently compassionate way, sharply dressed in a trouser suit not quite dark enough for a funeral - she wondered if there had been some kind of mistake.

The woman extended her hand confidently, with the certainty of knowing there was a bond between them.

"You're right, we haven't met - but I'm sure you know who I am."

"A one-way conversation"

How many people know exactly where they are going when they set off? Even if it's just to the shops or to fill the car with petrol, so much *could* happen between here and the supermarket or garage… You might not even make it. But you always assume you will. You have to. If you don't, what would you do? We're all hostages to fortune in the end.

Is that what Liam was thinking that morning - being a hostage to fortune - as he went down to the hotel restaurant for his breakfast? How far ahead was he thinking? That he had a plan of sorts was certain. It began with breakfast and went on from there, generally with increasing vagueness. Nothing very exciting nor, to be honest, particularly remarkable, but a plan nonetheless. In its predictability and lack of ambition, it was a plan much like his current life. Perhaps most of us have plans - and lives - like that.

If he was surprised by anything these days it was that he had become an old man. People - friends and family - dutifully objected to any assertion he made in this general direction, and perhaps on one level they may have been right. But when you came down to it, their opinion meant little to him. Even if the boundary where you tripped into being 'old' was an indistinct one, he felt it a threshold he had indeed crossed. There was no one moment nor single event that had seen him make the jump; it had crept up on him. If part of his surprise came as a result of this stealth, it was also responsible for generating a larger part of his anger. It had transpired without his permission, and even though he knew there was consequence in having had the luxury of time to do things, to live his life, he somehow felt as if the terms of the arrangement had not been stated clearly enough up-front. It was akin to a badly worded HP agreement. Yes, he had done a great deal, but the price he had paid - almost inadvertently and without any explicit contractual agreement - seemed to have been weighted too far in his adversary's favour. Until recently it hadn't been a battle, but it was now.

None of this has anything to do with his mental state as he pauses dutifully at the 'wait here to be seated' sign. If pressed, he might have struggled to identify when he had last consciously thought of himself as 'old'. Yet even so, there are signs - clearly visible from the elaborate restaurant mirror into which he finds himself looking - that age preys on his mind. His clothes look as if he has borrowed them from someone younger, a nephew perhaps. There is also something in his manner, the way he stands, to suggest he is a single man. And even that pose - a little too relaxed even for a man in his fifties - offers up the notion that not very far beneath the surface something vaguely inappropriate is going on. The occasional respondent in a vox pop might even have suggested that he was gay.

Such superficial analyses would have been wrong on all fronts. The clothes are indeed his, chosen because he likes them, picked out after careful deliberation with little regard as to whether or not they suited 'a man of his age'. And his nephew (had he one) would never have worn them nor looked as good in them as he thought he did. And what was wrong with weekend jeans that were a little faded, a shirt whose pattern verged on the indecent side of bold? The analysts would have been wrong because he was no longer in his fifties, but sixty one. Wrong because, even though he was now single, for the vast majority of his life he had not been. And most certainly wrong because he was not gay, had never been, nor shown even the slightest inclination in that direction. At least not as far as he knew. He wouldn't have said he was 'a man's man' - whatever one of those might be - but he was comfortable in his own skin; a skin that was beginning to feel a little thinner than it once had, a little more scale-like. In moments of fancy, he wondered if he might be turning into a snake who was just about to slough. If so, it would have been a re-birthing to which he would happily have subscribed.

"Table for one?"

As he follows the waitress into the open-plan restaurant where they are serving breakfast, he wonders just how long he'd looked like a 'table-for-one' kind of person. How was she to know that he wasn't the vanguard for an enormous family, or the leader of a group of high-flying executives about to start their day together with a breakfast meeting? He trails her through the sparsely populated main body of the place to an almost segregated section filled with small tables designed to take two people at a push. Breakfast apartheid. Virtually every table here was occupied. Liam glances back over his shoulder at the oasis of open and unoccupied space as he is shown to number forty-three. The waitress's gesture seems inappropriately grand, as if she were revealing something quite remarkable. He looks at what lay on the surface of the table and sighs. It seems hardly worth the trouble.

Having established that he has indeed had breakfast there before, she retires and he sits down.

"I'm sorry?" says a voice immediately to his left.

Liam glances across to where a woman, half-way through her own breakfast, is looking quizzically at him.

"Excuse me," Liam says, "I didn't realise I had brushed you when I sat down."

Instantly recognising how peculiar it had been to have chosen 'brushed' for that sentence, he goes to return his gaze to the distant horizon of the juice bar but is stopped by a burgeoning smile.

"You didn't," the woman replies, "I just thought you said something."

Liam's short-term memory has not deteriorated that far.

"I was just muttering to myself, I expect," he confesses. "All that space over there and they treat us singletons like lepers who have to be kept away from the normal people."

She follows his gaze and then laughs. No-one laughs at breakfast in business hotels; it just isn't the done thing. Bad form.

"Excuse me," he says again, momentarily thrown, then stands up and starts to make his way towards the orange juice. He can feel her eyes follow him for a moment and then he is in amongst the minor melee for the toasting machine which, he assumes, will most likely cremate the bread as usual.

When he returns with his dark brown toast, marmalade and a small bowl of fruit, the woman has gone. A utilitarian cylinder of coffee now sits on his table. It is an unfair exchange, he suddenly thinks, as is spending his time in this way. He feels out of control, nothing but a pawn in a machine that feeds him plastic breakfasts and limited professional stimulation as if such a combination should be enough to make him feel grateful. He doesn't. If he did once - and he suspects, sadly, that this had indeed been the case - then not doing so is something getting old bestowed on you. Or took away. He refrains from trying to give it a name.

The day proves unremarkable. Having, over the years, more or less accidentally fallen into the world of mergers and acquisitions, he is involved in providing impartial advice to a corporate heavyweight who is in the process of buying another business. "Right place, right time" he had told people in the days when it had all been fresh, an adventure, and seemed to matter. But once he'd cranked the handle a dozen or more times, it had lost its sparkle. "Same shit, different day" he thought to himself. It was a harsh and over-critical assessment, and not one to which he wholly subscribed. No two deals were the same; they each had their angles and nuances. The current transaction was progressing pretty much to plan; very little had arisen thus far to suggest complications or the likelihood of unearthing of knotty problems that would need to be solved. To that extent he was going through the motions. Knowing clients are paying good money for his experience and expertise, occasionally Liam feels guilty that he doesn't share the passion of his customers. He has a 'game face' which gets him through meetings; he knows the questions to ask, what to concede and what not to. People seem impressed. It boosts his bank balance.

The following morning, the same autopilot which had guided him through the previous day sees him standing once again at the breakfast 'wait here' sign. He wonders if it will be the same waitress as the previous day and, if so, whether she will bother to ask him where he was qualified to sit. When it proves to be a different young woman, he steels himself for the ritual.

"Table for one?" she asks, locked in her own autopilot.

Before he has a chance to reply, a voice from behind him.

"For two."

Liam looks around. It is the woman from the previous morning.

"If you don't object," she suggests. "It would give us a chance to put your theory to the test."

"And avoid leper's corner?"

She smiles.

"This way please," says the waitress as she turns on her heel.

"After you," says Liam, graciously, "the glory is all yours."

They are stopped in the sparsely populated area of the restaurant and offered a table comfortably big enough for four. The singletons' section seems miles away in the distance.

"Thank you," says Liam discretely to the woman as he sits down.

"For rescuing you?"

"Rescuing both of us."

They avoid looking at each other as the waitress pours them coffee. For some reason Liam had expected her to take tea and is surprised when she does not. As he watches the black liquid swirl into his cup, he feels somewhat off-balance. This is most certainly not part of the ritual. Feeling discomforted, he wonders if this going off-piste is to blame. It will be temporary, he knows, and that in about twenty minutes he'll resume his familiar tack. Yet even as he realises this, that his day is set, ready and lacking the promise of any real variation, he feels undeniably defeated.

"My name's Alison," his companion says as soon as the waitress has gone, offering her hand across the breakfast paraphernalia. "It's not a name I especially like, so feel free to play with it."

"Liam," he says, taking and releasing her hand. "Why don't you like it? Isn't it a perfectly acceptable name? I mean, it's not as if it's Marge or Bunty."

"Believe it or not, I knew a girl called Bunty at my school."

"You didn't!" says Liam, unable to disguise his surprise at the coincidence.

"No, I didn't actually. I just wanted to see how you'd react."

She laughs. It is a short, meaningful sound. Liam is taken with how it seems to escape with the velocity and focus of a bullet from a gun. And then it is gone.

"Shall we?" she says, standing up.

Following Alison to the buffet, Liam feels further off balance; suddenly his breakfast choices have been elevated from the mundane and unimportant. Whether she intends to or not, it is inevitable that Alison will judge him in part by what he now choses. Pile his plate high with sausages, bacon and hash browns and she will draw a different conclusion to that were he to return to the table with just a bowl of fruit or muesli. He tells himself it doesn't matter - that it shouldn't matter - but is unable to escape the sensation that it does; probably not from her perspective, but from his. Eventually he decides there is nothing intrinsically wrong with what he normally has: a little bacon, some scrambled egg, and two slices of toast.

"Did they have to cook those eggs?" Alison asks when he eventually gets back to his seat.

"I'm not with you," he says as he puts the plate on the table and sits down.

"You were so long, I wondered if they'd cooked them specially. Or perhaps the toaster was broken."

Liam notes Alison's own selection: granola, yoghurt and toast. So she knows the toaster is in perfect working order and is just playing with him.

"You wouldn't believe me if I told you," he suggests.

"They had to fry the bacon?"

He smiles.

"You wouldn't believe me…"

"…if I told you." She finishes his sentence and scoops up some yoghurt. "I think I get the picture."

They eat in silence for a minute or so, Liam taking surreptitious glances at his companion between mouthfuls. Even though he has always been a hopeless judge, he can't help trying to register age first. She appears slightly older when she glances away to the side, as if doing so catches her off guard and exposes something physical about her that she is striving to keep hidden. Confused, he can only come up with a guess that she is in her forties, give or take, and even this broad assessment is made with limited confidence. Her hair, a brown leaning towards a potentially enhanced auburn, is reasonably short at shoulder length and has about it a sense of the casual which could only have been generated by an expensive cut. Such a conclusion is supported by her clothes - a navy suit of some kind over the palest of pink blouses. He has already noticed the heels on her shoes seem perilously high. There are other touches of femininity: her earrings, and a large gold brooch with two blue stones inset. She is undoubtedly a professional woman.

"So what do you do, Liam?" She beats him to the punch. "What brings you to leper's corner in this miserably indifferent hotel?"

He laughs. He has never thought of it in those terms, but the hotel is, of course, entirely devoid of personality.

"Though thanks to you we're not entombed there this morning."

She nods but says nothing, her expression making it plain that she expects her question to be answered.

"I suppose I'm an expert in mergers and acquisitions."

"You suppose? Don't you know?"

"It's what I do. Or what I get paid for. I help people buy and sell businesses."

"But you don't like doing that," she suggests.

"I wouldn't say that; after all, there are worse ways you can earn a living." He pauses. "Let's just say it's not as entrancing as it once was."

"And do you wish to be 'entranced', Liam? To be magically whisked away into some kind of wild adventure."

Liam replaces his knife and fork on his almost empty plate, drawn in by Alison's jousting.

"I'm not sure I'm up to wild adventure any more," he offers.

She fires one of her short ballistic laughs at him.

"That's bollocks," she says. It is an abrupt appraisal delivered with a certainty that surprises him almost as much as the vocabulary she chooses to use. "Of course you are. You're not senile, are you? You still have your wits, a little vim and vigour, don't you? Please don't say that you've given up."

"Given up? On what?"

"Chance. Opportunity. You can't say that all this," she gestures to the room, "repetitive breakfasts in chain hotels, endless meetings, the shallow lure of filthy lucre, are all that you have to look forward to. That when you wake up in the morning, you've actually no idea where you are because every hotel bed's the bloody same. I don't believe that for a minute."

He is intrigued. What qualified this complete stranger to come stomping into his breakfast - no, more than that - with such brazen certainty?

"Why not?" he asks, attempting to be playful in return.

She ignores his question.

"When I interview someone," she says, "do you know the first question I ask them? I don't ask them about their last job, or why they're doing what they're currently doing; I ask them what they do when they're not working. What they do for a hobby, how they spend their time. *Their* time. It's a way of finding out what makes them tick."

Liam feels himself blushing.

"Ah," he says, not a little sheepishly. "So when I told you I was in M & A..."

"You failed the interview completely! Being 'in M & A' doesn't make you an interesting person. Almost the opposite, in fact. Tell me you're a weekend gymnast, or that you run a Sunday school, or do survival training, or bog snorkelling, or something else please!"

"Bog snorkelling?" Liam laughs.

"Apparently it's very - therapeutic."

As Alison allows a pause to settle on them, the realisation that he's playing second fiddle is reinforced on him. And it is a refreshing change not sitting tucked away having breakfast on his own and without laughter.

"Then, as an unsuccessful candidate, I should get my coat."

"Not so fast," she says, as if suddenly concerned that his words are about to be accompanied by his rising from the table, "I haven't quite given up on you just yet."

"I get a second chance?"

"You get a second chance, but," she feigns seriousness, "no-one gets a third where I'm concerned." She takes the last of her yoghurt, then eases back in her chair. "So," she says, inviting him to continue.

It was difficult to know where to begin. How far back should he go? If he trawled through his existence to relate to her those things that mattered to him - that had once mattered very much - then how relevant would they be if he had already consigned them to history? If they felt as if they belonged to a different Liam, were they still valid? Or was that exactly the sort of thing Alison would have been expecting to hear, to challenge, to dissect? He smiles.

"What's up?" she asks.

"I was just thinking, you sound like a therapist."

He expects her to laugh again, but she does not.

"Who's to say I'm not?"

The notion catches him up short.

"Are you?" He is unable to hide a nervous tone in his voice.

"You first, pal; you first."

Across the restaurant his attention is momentarily taken by a man in a tracksuit apparently talking to himself. Bluetooth headphones in his ears, he is on the phone. Liam wonders when 'on the phone' ceased to have any real meaning, to truly relate to telephones. He tries to recall his first mobile phone, an early Nokia. He feels old again.

The arrival of the waitress with a refill of coffee brings him back. Alison is still looking at him, intently. Her eyes are just on the green side of brown. Liam looks away. There is a coffee stain on the tablecloth in front of him. With a strange sense of being defeated, he begins speaking almost before he realises he is doing so.

"Travelling. Before Rachel and I became parents we travelled a lot. To some of the usual places, but we went to some exotic places too: La Paz, Chile, the Galapagos, Vietnam - before it became 'popular'. And I used to take photographs. Not just because of the travelling. Somewhere I have maybe fifty-thousand photos from over the years."

"But you're post-kids now, right?"

"Yes. She left home just a few years ago. And I'm not a grandfather just yet, so there are no liabilities."

"Is that how you think of them, 'liabilities'?" She delivers the question evenly, without any indication of judgement.

"Sorry, wrong word."

Alison allows a slight pause.

"So why don't you go travelling again?"

Liam was expecting the 'why?' question, if only because it is the one he would have asked. Or maybe the one he had once asked himself. If he has stopped the self-interrogation, he can't remember when.

"Now Rachel and I... There doesn't seem any point."

He knows the phrase is not entirely accurate but leaves it there, expecting Alison to probe. There is enough distance -

enough time - between he and Rachel for him to be able to deal with any enquiry in an untroubled way. It had been hard at first, of course. People meant well, but every time someone asked how he was coping, it was a little like picking a scab from an old wound; it became sore again. He looks up at Alison not exactly inviting the question, but trying to communicate to her that it is okay to ask.

"So you should go," she says, ignoring the invitation.

"Go?" He is thrown.

"Travelling. Take a road trip - and I don't mean up and down the M1! What's to stop you? Once your M&A deal is over, pick somewhere you always wanted to go but didn't quite get to because kids got in the way or whatever. Treat yourself."

It was a challenge he hadn't expected.

"Treat myself? In what sense?"

"In the sense of giving yourself some time. Right now you're wasting it on stuff you don't really want to be doing. You've earned it."

For a fleeting moment he wonders what it would be like working for Alison. It would be a challenge. He can see that she would be demanding, perhaps even ruthless, but her decisiveness could be inspiring for those who worked with her. And then again, might she be too much for them - or they not good enough for her?

"Like Route 66, you mean?"

"Corny and a little hackneyed, but that kind of thing, yes. Or walk the coast-to-cost, or drive Land's End to John O'Groats - but slowly, no motorways. Drive across Scandinavia. Pick up your camera again. Reacquaint yourself with it. Can you remember what it feels like to click that shutter and then see something you've captured so perfectly that you're truly proud of it?"

He knows he doesn't need to answer.

As if she has suddenly remembered something, Alison downs the last of her coffee and throws her napkin onto her plate.

"I need to be getting on, I'm afraid. And before you ask, I'm not leaving you because of anything you've said - or not said."

"But it's been a one-way conversation," Liam protests, "and an unfinished one at that. I've no idea what you do - or don't do - and that doesn't seem fair."

She bullets a laugh at him. He wants to duck.

"Isn't that the truth," she smiles. As she stands up, she puts her hand into her bag and pulls out a business card which she spins elegantly through the air so that it lands right in front of him. "Japanese style?"

Liam recognises the cryptic reference and takes one of his own cards from the top pocket of his jacket. He hands it to her and she drops it in her bag without looking at it.

"Give 'em hell," she says, then turns and walks away.

As he watches her leave, her heels clacking rhythmically on the polished restaurant floor, Liam feels like someone who is suddenly in the still quiet after a thunderstorm. And already he is missing the rain.

"What about Katy?"

If you were to press her for the moment when she first knew, Rachel would have been able to articulate it precisely. Sunday 3rd June, 2012. At approximately nine-fifteen in the morning; Liam sitting across the breakfast table, head buried in the *Sunday Times'* supplement, empty cereal bowl, plate dusted with toast crumbs, an almost empty coffee cup immediately in front of him though pushed slightly to the side. There was nothing in the news, nothing emblazoned across the front page of the supplement which triggered the thought; nothing unusual which had prompted the notion. Yet from somewhere, unbidden, the knowledge that it was all over came suddenly and profoundly upon her.

Perhaps it was the lack of change. The cumulative effect of the same scene Sunday after Sunday, week after week, that had - like a slowly dripping tap - worn her down. If so, she hadn't realised it was happening, deaf to its undercurrent heartbeat.

She felt herself redden, as if she had been caught out doing something wrong, like that time at school all those years ago when Mr Peters had found her and Josephine Wilson smoking round the back of the PE block. Then it had been colour brought on by anger and embarrassment, not shame. If she had been annoyed they had been discovered, Rachel felt little of that now - yet it was almost as if she were both herself and Mr Peters at the same time. She had caught herself out, and the fact she had not seen it coming was the aspect which embarrassed her most. She considered herself an intelligent woman, at one with herself, suitably self-aware; a woman who was mature in so many ways in addition to the simple fact of her age.

For a second she tried to persuade herself that her sudden colour might be menopausal, but she knew how that felt - had known for a little while how that felt - so was unable to accept such a transparent excuse. And then when Liam turned over a page, the movement for a moment exposing a little over half his face to her gaze, she was certain. Poor, innocent Liam. She felt immediately sorry for him; wanted to get up and walk round the table and cradle him and comfort him in advance of what she now knew was coming. But she did not. It would have been too obscure, too out of character; such an action would have given the game away. He would have known something was 'up'.

When he turned the page again, he glanced at her from behind his flimsy paper shield.

"More coffee?" she said, as if that were the most natural thing in the world to ask him at a time like this. And from Liam's perspective - blessed with only half the story - of course it was.

"Thanks," he smiled.

It gave her the excuse to stand and go back into the kitchen, a reorientation that was the beginning of the period of working things out. She needed to corral the facts, to understand the whys and wherefores of this sudden revelation. She needed to compile arguments and apply reasoning, to see if she could map out what was supposed to happen next - after all, it was not every day you decided to leave your husband. Not in her case. And in doing so, she felt a frisson of excitement. There would be action and activity; she would be embarking on a new journey, an adventure. She could look forward to one day soon having Sunday mornings without the barrier of the *Sunday Times'* supplement.

"You're trying to kill me," her father had said when she broke the news later that week.

"Dad!" Unable to immediately elaborate on her protest, Rachel had stood from the conservatory chair in which she had been sitting and stared out into the once immaculate garden.

"Not that I need your help," he had continued.

She knew her father's grumpiness came not especially from her news, but intrinsically, born from the unavoidable fact that he was dying and could do nothing about it.

"A month," he said after a short pause, "that's what you've cost me. And a month I didn't have going spare."

"Stop it," she said turning, unsure if he was joking. His decline had not merely been a physical one, and Rachel found herself unable to judge as well as she once had whether he was being serious or not. Indeed, in many respects she was becoming un-acquainted with the man she had known all her life. And without her mother there any longer to provide insight or be the arbiter on such occasions she was flying solo.

Ronald could see the tears forming in his daughter's eyes. He had no wish to be cruel.

"And what does Liam think of this remarkable notion of yours?"

Rachel turned to the glass again. Half-way down the garden, the dahlias were beginning to bud; large fulsome bulb-like shapes of promise. He had always been proud of his dahlias - as he was of the whole spread - but the borders were beginning to look as if they had been invaded under the cover of darkness and were, in consequence, partially dishevelled. The lawn needed cutting. She wondered how good a gardener she might prove to be if put to the test.

"I haven't told him," she replied, talking more to the dahlias. It seemed easier that way.

"Not told him?!"

"I decided over the weekend. I wanted to sleep on the idea for a bit. To try it out and see how it felt."

"To use me as a guinea pig?" Ronald waited for a reply that didn't materialise. "Well you know how I feel about it, don't you? You can tell. You don't need to ask." Again nothing. "It's a crazy notion. Crazy."

She had wondered if it were indeed crazy - but not in the way her father meant. The excitement and potential of it, that was what seemed crazy to her. Crazy that she hadn't thought of it until now; mad that she'd wasted how long - how many years? - in not thinking of it before. The dahlias nodded gently.

"And?" Rachel turned when she heard her father speak as he shifted, the wicker protesting beneath plump cushions. "How does it feel now that you've 'tried it out'?"

She walked back to her chair and sat down, the question about her potential gardening prowess unanswered.

"Good," she said. "Right. Liberating. About time."

"About time?"

"As if I should have done it years ago." She let a second or two trespass. "I feel as if I can look forwards again, Dad; as if I've got something to look forward to."

"Such as?"

"Change. Something different. Liam's a good man, you know that, and a large part of me still loves him for that; but it's just that we've become stale. Perhaps we've outgrown each other."

"Will he think that?" Her father asked, then answered his own question. "Of course he won't. He'll be knocked for six. There's no way he'll be expecting that. He's always been so happy with you."

"Happy?" She played with the notion in her head, repeating the word as if doing so would aid her contemplation. "I'm not sure we've been 'happy' for a long while; not really. We've been turning the handle on the same old routine."

Ronald waited in case there was more. When he spoke next, his voice was softer.

"And Katy?"

"Katy?" The word came as something of a body blow, as if she had been struck from behind. "What about Katy?"

"How will she take it?"

It was a fresh question, one Rachel suddenly realised she had not even considered.

"She's old enough to understand," she offered, resorting to a textbook answer.

"Is she?"

"Dad, she's twenty four! She's been living an independent life for years now. She's been through things herself, break-ups; she has enough experience of life not to be shocked by this."

"Not shocked, perhaps," he said, "but stunned. You and Liam have been her rock all these years; the foundation upon which Katy's built her life. You know how sensitive she is, how badly she took my news. But you and Liam got her through that. Who's going to help her get through this?"

"We will," Rachel offered, her voice betraying her uncertainty.

"If by 'we' you mean you and Liam, then I venture to suggest that you'll both be too busy sorting your own selves out to worry about Katy. Liam especially. And if you're including me in that 'we' of yours, then I think that's just a trifle optimistic, don't you?"

As soon as Rachel rose and walked to the window again, Ronald felt guilty at landing such a low blow. But assuming he would be dead before any divorce, he was suddenly desperate. Not just for Katy, but for his daughter - and perhaps himself too. Enough of his life had crumbled in the recent past, and now the last of his own foundations - the marriage of his wonderful daughter to someone who, privately, he considered a paragon amongst men - was about to be swept away. He would have nothing left to hold on to, just when he was scanning the horizon for anything which could keep him afloat a little longer. He wondered if Rachel could see that. Suddenly more deeply tired than he had ever felt, he found himself unable to ask that question. Or any more questions.

Rachel turned when she heard him get up, and watched him as he shuffled away back into the lounge. She knew she had his answer, yet it did not change her own, even if he had tried to play the highest card he held. If she possessed all the aces, they were backed up with more than her fair share of trumps too, and she felt as if she was looking at the best hand she had held for some while, as if the dealer had broken open a new deck and that first shuffle had left her with winning cards for the first time in years.

Not that she had recognised it right away. Perhaps her father had been right and she'd chosen to use him as a test, to try out her idea on him not so much to get his reaction but rather to see how it sat with her. And now she knew. Even the curved ball he had thrown - "what about Katy?" - had unsettled her for just a few moments, not because she had yet to consider how they should tell their daughter, but because she hadn't thought of her at all. And a part of her actually wondered why she should. Katy was her own woman now - albeit a not entirely mature or successful one. But she had been away from the nest long enough, she had her own life to chart. Did she involve them in every decision she had to make? Certainly not. Nor would Rachel expect her to. Yes, they were kith and kin, but the elastic was stretching, more so in her case than in Liam's, but it was stretching nonetheless.

Knowing he was now either locked away in his study (the converted dining room) or upstairs laying down, she collected her father's half empty mug to return it to the kitchen confident their interview was at an end. His protest that she had shaved a month from his life was uncalled for of course, but Rachel considered it again as she rinsed out the cup. It had been a figure of speech rather than an accurate assessment of how he felt, she knew that; and she knew he was upset, after all he had been such a fan of Liam since the first day the two of them met. But she was certain her news had no more shortened his life than her announcing they had decided to renew their vows would have lengthened it. In any event, she remained steadfast in her opinion that he was tougher than he looked, and when he talked weeks she heard months; when he said months, her internal translation played it back as years. It was both useful and practical consolation to be convinced of this, and when a few minutes later she shouted up the stairs that she would see him later, thought nothing of it when there was no reply forthcoming.

"What do you want?"

Finding the right time to break the news to Liam was another matter altogether. Rachel's instinct was to wait until the following Sunday morning at breakfast. Not only would there be a kind of symmetry about it, but they would have time; as much or as little as they needed. And she wanted to believe - whether blindly, or not - that the decision would, on some level, be a joint one. In the same way she had arrived at her own definition and calibration of her father's inner steel, she had convinced herself that she was merely being the catalyst for an inevitable conversation. Beneath the apparent comfort of their routine and mundane existence, she had convinced herself that, even if it were unrecognised, deep down Liam was also seeking some kind of freedom. He just hadn't found the means of expressing it.

Or perhaps he had been afraid to. This had been her second string to that particular bow. And when she manufactured a third - he was unhappy in his work - it became easy to pluck those reasons from thin air and play a chord on them.

As it happened, she had no need to wait until Sunday breakfast. On the prior Thursday they had planned to visit some friends, but claiming a mild headache - which was not totally untrue - it had been easy for her to get Liam to call the thing off.

"I didn't really want to go anyway," he confessed later, as they sat in the conservatory to witness the last of the light fade from the day. It was a favourite pastime; a ritual whose conclusion was often signalled by the trees at the end of the garden becoming a dark mass, lacking definition and individuality, a transformation backed-up by the switching on of the lounge lights and eventual abandonment of the extension. They had been less than half an hour away from 'lights on' when Liam had spoken.

"What *do* you want?" she had asked, deliberately open-ended, hoping the tone of her voice made it abundantly clear that she wasn't talking about not going to see the Morgans.

Liam lowered his newspaper.

"What do I want? What do you mean? I just said I didn't really want to go and see Geoff and June."

"Yes, I know what you said. I'm interested in what you didn't say; what you never say."

"About what I want?" Liam's frown told Rachel she had to help him join the dots.

"Yes. What do you want, Liam? Nothing about Geoff or June; nothing as mundane as that. You never say what you want, so I don't know" - she paused, for a moment slightly nervous, afraid of where the answer might lead; she worried it would steal away her initiative - "what *you* want." The emphasis seemed to float between the last two words, as if it had a will of its own, before settling on the pronoun. It was a tactic, of course; a means of providing her with the opportunity to tell him about her decision. She would be responding. Like batting second in a village cricket match, she would know the score she needed to beat.

"Why should I want anything?" He smiled as if she were fishing for compliments, for him to confirm his satisfaction with their life together, its completeness.

"Doesn't everyone?"

"Want something?"

Rachel nodded. Liam knew he was being given time to think.

"And you don't mean a lower handicap, do you? Or being able to grow better carrots?"

"You know very well that's not what I mean."

Even though he was trying to be funny - and not without some success - she permitted a mild note of dissatisfaction to creep into her voice. It would be a sign, she thought, that she wasn't messing about. She knew Liam well enough to believe he wouldn't miss a card she played so rarely, and so was not surprised when his smile began to fade.

"You're serious." And even though he had said it rhetorically, he waited, offered a pause, a space into which she could jump to help him out.

For her part, Rachel knew he needed rescuing. It was as if she had tossed him overboard and was now standing by the ship's railing, holding a lifebuoy, teasing him with it.

"And if I can't think of anything?" he asked.

"Then I simply wouldn't believe you."

"On what basis?"

"On the basis that we always want something. People *always* want something." This time the emphasis was certain. "Something else; something they don't have. We can't help it. Isn't it in our nature?"

"And I suppose," Liam's smile had vanished totally, "you're not talking about things like Ronald not being ill and about to die?"

"I'm not." She held him for a fraction. "Of course you want that - and I do too, obviously. But I'm interested in *you*, Liam. What is it that you want?"

"On the assumption that I must want something?" he clarified.

Her nod was silent, and with it she seemed to suck all other sounds out of the room too. It was suddenly darker, as if the sun had fallen in that instant, the trees at the end of the garden disappeared for the night. And the lounge lights were not yet on. It was as if they were both in limbo, trapped in an uncertain realm between two worlds. Rachel saw Liam shiver and instinctively knew it wasn't a sudden fall in temperature that had triggered it.

"Well, if you're disallowing the obvious - like wanting Ronald better or to see Katy more settled - then I have to say that I'm struggling. I can't immediately think of anything. At all. But you seem to think there's something there; something I've not told you about. You know me better than that." Liam, expecting protest at this point, waited a moment. "Haven't we built what we have based on years of accumulation, identifying all those things we wanted and then gradually putting them in place?"

Looking away, Rachel saw Liam's profile reflected in the conservatory glass now made into a mirror by the darkened evening. She couldn't work out if it made him look older or younger, but there was something in it, the aspect she saw now, that transported her back in time.

"I'm not talking about 'things'," she said, aiming her words at the mute replica of him.

"I didn't think you were."

She watched the lips of the second Liam move, but the sound came from the left. She turned to face him.

"Don't you want new things, Liam? New experiences, new challenges? Don't you want - even once in a while - something different to happen, an adventure to shake us out of this..." For the merest fraction of a second she tried to find the phrase but then let the effort go, knowing if it were found it would be too negative, too damning, too damaging.

"'Adventure'?"

Her word sounded foreign when it came from Liam's mouth, leaving Rachel uncertain as to whether that added weight to her cause or not.

"You know what I mean," she protested, "something new and different. We used to want that, didn't we? We'd go off searching for new experiences, things to add to our lives' larder."

"Yes, we did." There was an undercurrent of sadness in Liam's voice mingled with what Rachel could only read as an element of frustration. "But we were young then. It's what young people do. It's how you find out who you are."

"Before you settle for it?" An edge escaped which Rachel was unable to retract.

"'Settle'?" Liam played back the word. "You make it sound like a defeat; like we've lost. Is that how you see it? Really? And after all this time? I'd prefer to think of it as making choices. Good choices. And however you look at it, we're not young any more. We can't go gallivanting off somewhere at the drop of a hat."

"Why not?" Rachel knowing it to be the obvious trite riposte, was not surprised when Liam let it fall away. Part of her had hoped he would have said that he missed the adventure too, the doing new things. If she had longed to see a spark, something that might ignite them both, then she was disappointed; there was nothing.

"So what do *you* want, Rachel? Because you must want something otherwise you wouldn't have asked. It's not the kind of question - 'what do you want?' - that people pose just to pass the time. You only ask it when you've an answer of your own."

Rachel, looking at him in that moment, saw a man who was spent. She had wanted to see some sliver of the boy who had spoken to her in the bookshop, the young man she had fallen in love with, who had given her a daughter, in many ways a perfect life. Perhaps above all she had wanted him to give her the chance to rescue him. The one thing which would have transformed her plan into *their* plan; it would have given them both something new.

She dropped the lifebuoy onto the deck and walked away from the railing, the sound of the sea retreating with every step.

"You've got to be kidding"

He is convinced there is something else he should be doing. Standing in the dark at the bottom of the garden looking up towards the house, he feels the warmth of the lit cigar as it permeates through to his fingers. It seems absurd that he should be smoking now, especially a cigar; isn't it common practice for cigar-smoking to be an emblem of celebration, of victory or triumph?

There is a small stash in the garden shed. When he had made his vow to give up all those years ago, unable to throw them away he had re-located the few he had remaining, sealing them in an air-tight container just in case. It had seemed a practical thing to do, and one he persuaded himself he could defend from multiple perspectives. Discovering Rachel wanted a divorce was the antithesis of a cause for celebration, and his immediate retreat into the garden after she had broken the news gave him the distance he suddenly needed, both from her and the house. Deciding to rescue the cigars and then smoke one was impulsive and primarily about occupation, the need to be doing something different. As he lifts it to his lips, sees the glow, and feels the once-familiar warmth again, Liam wonders if there is also a psychological dimension to his doing so, as if both the action and sensation might propel him back to when he was a different Liam - perhaps the Liam that Rachel craves him to be once again. That had been a younger incarnation, of course. The Liam who used to smoke was an earlier model still climbing the professional ladder and who travelled frequently to Europe; the Liam still establishing who he wanted to be. As he confronts him now, this past version of himself feels more of a stranger than he might have expected, and he wonders where along the journey the two of them had become separated.

His eye is drawn to movement behind one of the upstairs windows; Rachel's shape, blurred and softened by the frosted glass, briefly traverses the bathroom, then is gone again. Liam wonders if she was right; if that prepared - if not rehearsed -

speech of hers about growing versus stagnation, about staleness, had more truth in it than he had initially allowed. He catches himself being kind. Fundamentally he knows she had been talking about herself, trying to draw him in to her logic, to get him to collude with her. It would be easier for her if they were co-conspirators. Do these new thoughts about the Liam he has left behind give any additional credence to her argument? Possibly. But if so, he still has no sense of what he has been unknowingly missing out on, even if Rachel feels she has. And why should he have - *how* could he have - when his present life is based on the premise that he has everything he has ever needed or wanted?

"And Katy?" he had said at one point, being immediately struck by Rachel's reaction, how his words had hit home.

"What about Katy?" she had said, the darkness folding itself around them. He sensed echoes from other conversations.

"Does she already know?"

"How could she possibly?" Rachel had exclaimed a little too vigorously. "Why would I tell anyone before I've told you?"

Knowing it was a rhetorical question, Liam had let it pass.

The heat from the cigar suddenly more intense, Liam looks down to where the ember-coloured ash glows perilously close to his skin. He takes one final drag and then casually throws the butt into the vegetable patch. "So what?" he thinks to himself; it hardly seems to matter.

As he regains the house, the phone starts to ring. Liam pauses on the threshold by the French doors, waiting to see if it is a call Rachel is expecting, if she is ready to intercept it from either the kitchen or the bedroom. Allowing it to ring twice, Liam finds himself wondering whether there is already someone else on the scene, whether Rachel's announcement was predicated on the basis that she already has another bed she might soon call home. He propels himself into the lounge as if doing so will dispel the thought, but all that happens is that another one crowds into his head: will she try to keep the house?

"Hello?" His voice is flat when he answers the phone.

"Daddy?" Katy's voice is another body blow. "Is there something wrong?"

"Wrong? Why do you ask?"

"I had a message on my answer phone from Mum saying I should call."

"Really?"

"And you sound - I don't know - preoccupied." She pauses. "I wondered if it might be Granddad. If there was news..."

Liam allows Katy's words to bounce around inside his head, hoping they will chase away his latest thoughts, even for just a moment. Recalibrating, he finds he has to dive into another painful place. Glancing around the room, his eyes settle on the small selection of spirit bottles sitting on top of the nest of tables in the far corner of the room. A drink would take away the taste of the cigar, now bitter in his mouth.

"Granddad? No, there's no news; nothing to report as far as I know."

"So why did Mum want me to call?"

This is no way to tell her. If Rachel was minded to do so over the phone, Liam decides he won't allow her the cowardly way out.

"We just thought it might be nice if you came over at the weekend. For a change. We could do lunch or something. That nice pub just outside Ludlow. You know, the one you like."

"Mum thought that?" Katy checks, clearly dubious.

"Well at least part of it." Liam tries to laugh, but fails.

"I've been invited out to a PR event with work in the afternoon on Saturday, but I'm not really needed, and to be honest I don't want to go. If you're giving me a lifeline, a chance to cry off, then I'll gladly take it."

"Consider it given," he says. Then hearing Rachel coming down the stairs, continues, "We'll see you late Saturday morning then?"

As Rachel walks into the room, Liam is replacing the receiver in its cradle. He looks up at her, noting the question formed in her frown.

"She's coming here on Saturday," he says, flatly, "you can tell her yourself then."

Allowing her no time to respond, he walks out into the hall, bending his body as he passes her to ensure the avoidance of even the slightest contact. Pausing as if momentarily lost, Liam suddenly wonders about touch. How does that work now? The game has suddenly changed, and the rule book - if there had been one - simply thrown away. How had he felt the last time he had paused on this very spot, when the world had still been rotating on a steady axis? He wonders what new strictures might apply, and feels lost not having some kind of guidance. Marriage has provided him with a set of mores and expectations, offered a series of behaviours he knew to adopt perhaps because he had been exposed to them through his parents. They had been quiet, conservative types whose public hand-holding had been a rare - and therefore notable - event. Later, as he grew up, he observed how other people - other *married* people - behaved with each other. The whole package is, he realises, a construct learned socially; he wonders how you *un*learn it.

As he makes his way into his study - the same room which years previously had been Katy's playroom - he finds he has, by association, landed himself with a follow-on question: how will he need to behave in future as 'an unattached man'? Not only is this a consequence of the discarding of another rule book - the one more willingly and consciously thrown away many years previously - it is also the beginning of a strange new phenomenon, one which will force him to think about himself again. Liam as Liam; not Liam as half of a married couple, nor even Liam as father (because that implies a mother, and for a second he wishes, somewhat cruelly, to banish that notion too), but Liam as a bona fide individual.

Absent-mindedly, he stands in front of the large floor-to-ceiling bookcase that dominates the far wall. Occasionally he has been known to sit in his ancient and impossibly comfortable armchair and just stare at the books. After a short while they usually begin to lose their definition, their individuality, and blur and wander. Almost transformed into the brushstrokes of an impressionist painting, this metamorphosis turns them from the concrete to the abstract, and they become mere suggestions of what they actually are. It is not the vague or hinted at Liam needs right now. In the last hour and a half he has been forced to commence the journey from being a well-defined man with a secure place in a family, to a role with no certain edges, no boundaries; he has both regressed into what he once was *and* been catapulted forward into a version of what he will almost inevitably become once age and infirmity finally catch up with him. If there is a sense of accusation in the glance he gives his books it is because now, more than ever, he needs them to remain steadfast to exactly what *they* are. More than that, he needs them to be able to answer these new questions he has spinning in his head, the most fundamental of which is "what do I do now?"

In the soft light of the standard lamp he scans the spines facing him seeking some reassurance, wanders through their titles and authors, each one offering a coded message as to what lay inside. Many he remembers well: *Far From The Madding Crowd* read and re-read for teenage examinations and, he suspects, never really understood, not as he would understand it now; *Ulysses*, attempted to be read on more than one occasion for a similar purpose - and also not really understood. He doubts either would be of much help in his present dilemma, though in a strange way he fears he might now comprehend them far too well. Name after name and title after title speed before his eyes until they inevitably smudge and merge.

The armchair, when he sits in it, is reassuring. It has moulded itself to him over the years until it envelops him. No question of degrees of touch here; the embrace it offers him is complete and bespoke and without condition. He sighs. He has sat down. That, at least, is something.

When he wakes nearly an hour later, it is from a fitful sleep. It takes him a few minutes to relocate himself not merely in space - which is relatively easy - but also in time. Liam checks his watch. The scene from the conservatory comes back to him as a fragment from a dream, as if it had stayed with him longer than intended and trespassed into the waking world. For the merest sliver of time he tries to reconstruct his exchange with Rachel as unreal, but when he raises his hand to his face, as if doing so would either prove or disprove the veracity of those events, he catches a trace of the cigar on his fingers and is immediately returned to the shed, the garden, the phone call from Katy. "Real then," he thinks to himself, and then wonders not how he could possibly have mislaid reality in the last hour, but rather how on earth he - *they* - have arrived at such a state of affairs.

That conundrum - and the intrusion of the single word 'affairs' - re-prompts all those unanswered questions which have assailed him between the garden and here. It seems as if each query was immediately usurped by the next in a cascade of uncertainty. And now there is a new foe come to the party: how have they brokered this desperate situation? If Liam glances up at the bookcase to divine the answer, then he is disappointed for a second time.

Books. The irony of seeking them as allies is not lost on him given it had been books which had brought he and Rachel together in the first place. They had been searching for answers then too, though at that time not personal ones but anything relating to interpretations - nebulous or otherwise - of Eliot's *The Four Quartets*.

"If only it wasn't so bloody difficult!"

She is standing next to him in the campus' Borders bookshop, both of them staring ahead, trying to decipher the spines of volumes of literary criticism and hoping to find one called 'All there is to know about Eliot' or 'The Answers to every "Four Quartets" question ever asked', it's font large, loud and undeniable.

He has seen her around; they are on the same course. But it is early in the first term and theirs is a large intake this year; no-one knows everyone just yet. She is wearing too-tight pastel pink jeans and a sweatshirt that has been cut short to reveal a tantalising inch or two of her midriff. If she has 'a look' she has cornered the market in this one and, for Liam at least, become a head-turning apparition. How can it not be so given he is new to this game of freedom and independence, his hormones raging?

"Eliot?" he ventures, not daring to look her way.

"Who else?" she replies, simultaneously stretching to take a volume from the shelf he had been examining just a few moments earlier. He knows he should tell her not to bother, that the book she is reaching for is useless, but her stretching offers the glimpse of another inch or two of flesh - so he says nothing.

Through the unreliable medium of gossip, Liam is aware that Rachel (at least he knows her name!) has something of a reputation. Gossip is, he has already discovered, the way to broaden your social circle without 'officially' meeting everyone. People have opinions about others with whom they have shared the briefest of contact, and suddenly free from the juvenile conventions within which they have been operating for years, many of the Freshers are happy to share conclusions drawn based on virtually no evidence. Liam wonders if this rumour-mongering is a fast-track way of establishing cliques and circles, to short-circuit the time-consuming business of *actually* meeting people; a mechanism which allows you to get over that practical hurdle and get on with 'living'. If what he has heard is to be believed, Rachel would not sit easily in his own modest coterie. The reputation delivered to him is one of an individual who is outspoken and fearless (perhaps to the point of recklessness) but also somewhat jealously recognised for being as sharp as a pin, and unwilling or unable to suffer fools gladly. Even after a few short weeks, some of his fellow students are already rising to the surface as the likely cream of their year, and Liam's understanding is that Rachel is one of those. All of which - allied to the fact that, to his eye, she is divinely gorgeous - puts her completely out of his league, and makes his single word utterance - "Eliot" - even more remarkable and brave.

For any individual who has not established a bias about her in the way Liam has, in most respects Rachel is not especially outstanding. Of just below average height, she might be best described as 'compact'; she is not especially slim, but rather 'proportionate'; and, as with most young women at university forcing themselves into tight jeans every day, her dress - apart from that cropped top - is verging on the mundane. She wears her hair in a somewhat severe bob; its cut, unfashionably austere, probably contributing to some of the personality traits she is perceived to have. Yet it also enhances her features, particularly in the way in which it draws attention to her eyes. On this particular morning however, it is neither her hair nor eyes which captivate him but her slender and elegant fingers. As she flicks through the book recently withdrawn from the shelf, he cannot help but watch as they manipulate the pages skilfully, deftly. Rather romantically, he feels they are the fingers of an artist.

When she stops flicking there is a momentary pause, then Liam, shaken from his reverie by her lack of movement, glances up to realise she is looking at him.

"You've already looked at this one haven't you?" she asks believing his focus to be on the book she is holding.

He can only nod.

"Am I wasting my time?"

"I suppose it depends what you're looking for, but I think so."

"Aren't we all looking for the same thing?" she asks, returning the volume to its space on the shelf and unselfconsciously flashing flesh again. "Something to unravel 'Burnt Norton'!"

Aware that he has been searching for nothing beyond a means to bluff his way through the T.S.Eliot module, Liam is hit but the sudden and rather daunting realisation that by shear luck he may have found something else, something special. Or rather someone special. As he watches her leave the shop empty-handed - and without saying goodbye - he finds himself plunged into misery and turmoil, the standard response of the romantic adolescent male who believes he has fallen in love.

When she first kisses him it is at a party a few weeks later. She is sightly drunk. Liam, bored and standing against a wall in one of the quieter rooms in the house, is trying to decide whether to leave when he sees her enter. Before he is able to react to her presence in any way (being rooted to the spot having become his de facto response under such circumstances), she has walked over to him, put her hands on his chest, then stretched up and kissed him. It is a brief and exploratory brush of the lips. Her eyes question his own as his hands, suddenly unfrozen, find her waist, and then she tries again.

"That's better," she says as they come up for air. "I was beginning to wonder."

"Wonder what?" Liam manages to ask, smiling so much his face immediately begins to hurt.

"Whether you liked me or not." She moves a little closer, now leaning against him.

"You've got to be kidding," he finds himself saying, as if how he felt about her had to be the most obvious thing in the world.

"I rarely kid," she smiles, and entwines her elegant fingers between his own.

Liam thinks he will explode with joy, and pulls her closer, hugging hard, burying his face into her hair, smelling her greedily as if in fear that someone is going to rip her away from him.

"Hmm," she says, as if weighing up the situation, "that's just as well then."

When he manages to focus again - it has been perhaps just a second or two since he has been, as his mother would once have said, 'away with the fairies' - his eyes are settled on his ancient copy of Eliot's *Collected Poems*, its fractured spine evident even from where he is sitting. The question as to whether this is mere coincidence or actually the catalyst for his recollection bothers him for a moment before he decides it doesn't matter. Replaying that memory has done nothing to help him understand how he and Rachel have arrived at the similarly fractured place they now inhabit, almost in the same way as he was never unable to unravel Eliot himself. If the thought is a parallel of some sort, Liam knows it is beyond him, so lets it go.

He sighs. It had been, on reflection, a quite wonderful beginning. He had always believed that. Indeed, it had been quite a wonderful life, the one he and Rachel had ended up sharing. Until this point. Until today, when his world suddenly caved in.

"Something beyond the little game you were playing"

His phone rings towards the end of the following afternoon.

"You didn't call." Despite Alison's voice being even, factual and strangely familiar, Liam is immediately thrown.

"I had the mother of all days yesterday," he says, buying time, "and I didn't finish until after eight. I was a little late for breakfast this morning, so assumed I'd missed you. Or that you'd checked out." He pauses, expecting something. Evidently he hasn't finished. "Were you expecting me to call?"

"I thought we had unfinished business," she says. Liam can imagine Alison, wherever she is, adopting that same pose from the previous morning, leaning back, a combination of relaxed, authoritative, challenging.

"In what sense?"

"In the sense of me wanting to hear the rest of your story. Wanting to know what you're going to do next."

"Do?"

"About your camera, your road trip. Isn't that unfinished business?"

He smiles into his mobile.

"I guess so."

"And," there is the slightest of pauses, "you haven't heard from my side of the house."

"Your what? I've not heard that phrase before."

"I know, sorry. I picked it up in Houston once. It's lazy. I only use it when I'm tired."

"Rough day?"

"I believe the expression is 'the mother of all days'." She laughs. Liam almost feels his phone vibrate, as if Alison has triggered the haptic sensors in it.

"I sympathise. Are you still in the hotel?"

"I check out in the morning. Why?"

"Can I buy you a drink later? You can unload your day. It's the least I can do."

There is a slight pause, as if she is working out whether he owes her anything. Liam is certain Alison will not have been surprised by his offer, after all she made the call; she must have expected something.

"You eat first," she instructs. "I'll grab something here before I leave."

Liam wonders where 'here' was.

"How about eight thirty in the bar?" It seems a reasonable enough suggestion; sufficient time to allow him to eat and for Alison to return to the hotel and freshen up.

"Order me a Manhattan," she says, after a moment. "I'm sure one of those will go down just fine!"

And then she was gone.

Liam floats into the last meeting of his working day in buoyant mood. There have been so many lonely hotel days that the prospect of doing something different - and with someone new, interesting, and not related to work - is refreshing. Knowing the bulk of the deal he is involved in has been finalised, he finds himself in a mood for conciliation and accord. When his client takes him aside to ask if they hadn't conceded ground too readily on one topic, Liam calmly suggests that 'they have one in the bank': "we'll be able to drag something they don't want to give away over to our side of the house". What he does professionally is all about give-and-take, about compromise. In terms of negotiation, there were many theories trotted out by 'experts' at convenient and profitable moments and, where they lack real substance, Liam despises the trite. That they have, in many cases, been born from an individual's practical experience is undeniable, and he knows it is only natural for people to try and repaint things in their own shade and style. For most, striving for confirmation of uniqueness is as instinctive as breathing. Liam assumes he has long since given up needing to satisfy himself with such trifles. He leaves that to those who still feel compelled to make their mark, preferring to believe his clients like his down-to-earth approach in part because he refrains from such showy shallowness. Yet even as he sits through the dregs of that final meeting, he finds himself wondering if this assumption is indeed true, whether he has in fact deluded himself that he is above superficial game-playing. In consequence, his buoyancy leaves him, retreating like a shallow tide. He arrives back at the hotel in a quieted and somewhat apprehensive mood; if he is not on his game, from what he has seen thus far Alison is likely to rip him apart.

Three hours or so later, as he walks into the bar, he feels less worried. Thirty minutes in the hotel pool have loosened him up, as have the two glasses of Pinot Noir he had chosen to accompany the steak which, remarkably, had been cooked particularly well. At eight twenty-five, he acquires his third glass of wine along with the pre-ordered Manhattan. Five minutes later - as precisely on-time as he had guessed she would be - Alison enters.

Having only seen her in that razor sharp dark blue suit, he had anticipated her wearing something similar, toned down a couple of notches. When she appears in a casual long black dress, high halter neck, sleeveless, he is surprised enough to catch his breath. Even though he can tell she is tired - something akin to resignation in the smile she offers - she looks younger than he remembered. He tries to introduce a mental hologram of Katy alongside her to see if they could be sisters. Not quite, is his conclusion. The young-enough-to-be-your-daughter objection is edging towards the negative, but it's still a split decision.

"Ah," she says, her eyes flitting from him to the Manhattan which occupies the low table between the two chairs he has chosen for them. Before she makes any attempt to sit down she lifts the delicate glass and drains a third of it. "You're a life-saver," she says smiling, returning the glass to the table and sitting down.

"You look like you needed that," he offers. "Needed it and earned it, it would seem."

"I can't deny it," she says, then allows herself to scan the bar.

Liam has tucked them partially away from main body of the bar where two televisions compete with each other in showing different sports channels, and where the general background noise is just a shade too loud. He hopes his choice of location is appropriate without being open to misinterpretation. The thought forces him to blush slightly - and then concern that Alison might have noticed his colouring only makes it worse.

"Warm?" she asks, unable to resist a mischievous tone. "Or just uncomfortable?"

Liam laughs, unsure if he sounds convincing.

"Neither," he protests.

"Neither? You mean this is normal behaviour for you, talking to strange women in hotels and plying them with sophisticated drinks?"

"It isn't - if only because I don't think you're strange, and if you recall, you were the one who initiated the conversation."

She laughs as he hoped she would.

"Touché."

He watches her take another sip from her drink, visibly relaxing a little more having done so, then they chat for a while about inconsequential safe things. She asks about family and he mentions Rachel and Katy in a non-committal way; when he does likewise, she purports to have none.

"So, have you put your big deal to bed?"

"Just about," he replies, "not that it was that big a deal. Some loose ends to tie up tomorrow."

"And did you win?"

"Win?" Liam wonders for a moment. "I'm not sure it's about winning."

"Really? Isn't that what you client would want, to win?"

"In one sense, perhaps. But what they want - or what they *need* actually - is a good deal. And most often a good deal doesn't involve one side or the other losing. That's how I approach them anyway. You never know what might happen afterwards

- during any period of transitional services, for example - and so maintaining goodwill can be critical."

"That's what you tell them?"

Liam nods.

"And they believe you?"

"Why shouldn't they?"

Instead of replying, Alison is distracted by a member of the bar staff clearing a nearby table.

"You'd like another?" She arrests the waiter before he can retreat. Liam nods again and she places their order.

"And what about you? Did you win today?"

Alison smiles.

"Winning's a little less tangible in my line of work."

"Which is?"

There is a pause as if she is trying to establish the best way to break some bad news.

"In some respects my job's not that dissimilar to yours." She weighs up what she has just said, then corrects herself. "But only a little. I'm a kind of facilitator too, in a way. I specialise - if that's the right word - in getting the best out of people. There are all sorts of fancy phrases and job titles I could use - Organisational Consultant, HR Consultant, Cultural Change Facilitator. Typical bullshit bingo job titles!" She laughs. "But in the end it's just trying to get the best out of people."

"So what are you working on now? What's got you tired today?"

"It shows?"

"Just a bit."

She finishes the last of her Manhattan.

"I've been engaged by a CEO - introduced to them by a mutual acquaintance - who has a problem with his senior team. He doesn't like their culture and doesn't think he's getting the best out of them."

"And is he right?"

"In spades! Individually they're all capable enough. I've run them through the usual sort of personality profiling models and the mix should be effective. But the issue isn't actually with them, it's with the CEO himself. He says he wants one thing but behaves in a very different way. His team are confrontational and dysfunctional because that's how he is."

"Tricky," Liam offers.

"And this afternoon I had to tell him so."

"Which, I assume, went down like a lead balloon."

Alison's reply is interrupted by the barman with their drinks.

"Put these on room one-one-seven, please," she instructs.

Liam watches the man retreat before being brought back round by Alison's voice.

"A major understatement. I gave him all the evidence, starting with his team. Then told him what I had observed, and my conclusions based on all that. He was with me for a while, but lost it as soon as it got personal."

"Does that happen often?"

"What?"

"People - your clients - losing it when you get near the truth."

She laughs, though for once it is a softer laugh without any recoil.

"Most of the time, it seems." She glances around the room, weighing up what to say next. "But they're just people, after all. Most people are logical and compliant when you're talking about business or praising them, but as soon as you cross the line into the personally critical - wham!"

"Doesn't it get you down?"

"I don't let it," she says definitively. "It's not in my nature. And anyway, the 'wins' make it all worthwhile - which is why I asked you about winning, I suppose. There's nothing better than when you *are* able to make a difference, to turn someone around, lead them from the dark side."

"Like me?" Liam is uncertain why he asks the question the way he does, and is treated by the sight of a frown blooming momentarily on Alison's face before she chases it away.

"You?" Her laugh this time is back to its normal volume. "You're a pussy-cat. I didn't even have to break sweat to uncover what's wrong."

"The travelling thing."

"If you like." Her reply is ambiguous.

"Am I that transparent?"

"Only if I'm right," she suggests.

"And are you often wrong?" Liam attempts to deliver his question in such a way as to not give her any clue as to how right or wrong she may be.

"Not often." She pauses. "Have you heard of Myers-Briggs?"

He nods.

"Did you know it was actually based on work by Jung?"

"Really?" Liam was unable to suppress his surprise.

"Really. Ever done it?"

"A while ago." He tries to locate it in his history, but can do so only approximately.

"You never forget what you are; isn't that true?" As he feigns uncertainty, Alison smiles. "Look, I bet I can tell you what you are - or maybe were."

"Were?"

"It's not unknown for people to change, morph a little over time, based on changes in circumstance. Usually I think people tend to get more extreme, more pronounced. But let's see."

"You're going to define me, based on the limited interaction we've had?"

She nodded.

"To prove that I'm good at what I do."

"Do you need to?"

She ignores his question, taking a sip of her fresh drink.

"Ok. First, 'Extrovert' or 'Introvert'? Easy one to start with - it always is. You're an 'I', solid gold." When he makes to reply, she holds up her hand. "Let me get through it first, okay? Now then, 'Sensing' or 'Intuition'? I think you're an 'N', but it's a little more marginal. In fact, it could be a really close call. 'Thinking' or 'Feeling'. You're a 'T' - but you've always wanted to be an 'F'. I suspect your Rachel is probably an 'F', and a really strong one. Maybe your daughter is too. It wouldn't surprise me if you've actually *tried* to force yourself to be an 'F'." She pauses, trying to divine from his expression whether she might be treading on dangerous ground. Liam's relaxed smile encourages her to go on. "And finally, 'Judging' or 'Perceiving'. This one's tricky. My guess is you *think* you're a 'P', but that the test said you're actually not - and you didn't believe it. So, gentlemen of the jury, my guess is that when you took the test you came out INTJ, or *maybe* INTP - but you really don't want to be that at all. If you were honest - truly honest with yourself (and most people aren't) - you're still an INTJ, however much you'd like to see that F or P or S in there."

Wanting to draw out the moment, Liam raises his wine to his lips and takes a slow motion slip.

"Well?" Alison is suitably impatient.

"You know your stuff, I'll say that much."

"I'm close, right?"

"Closer than I'd expected. The first time I took the test - it was years ago - I was an INTJ, but both 'N' and 'J' *were* almost too close to call. The second time I did it, the 'J' had become a 'P', probably because that's what I thought I should be."

"I rest my case."

"What's more impressive," Liam allows himself to carry on, partly knowing that doing so is just a little reckless, "is that you've seen the thing about sensing, about how much I wanted to be an 'S'. Rachel's off-the-scale 'S' *and* 'F'; maybe that's what attracted me to her. Opposites and all that."

"Maybe; but it doesn't always work."

"What about you?" Liam prompts, hopefully.

She pauses, looking at him intently, the smile slipping away. Her reply ignores his query. "There is a bigger question, though."

"There is?"

"And that's what do you want to be now? If you had the choice, what would Liam look like tomorrow?"

"Is that relevant?"

"It is if you're thinking of taking a road trip or becoming a photographer. There are some things you could try time and time again and never be successful at because you're simply not made that way."

"Such as?"

"Being an Extrovert. Either you are or you aren't. I don't care what anyone says, that's one thing you can't make yourself. And if being good at something demands you be an 'E', then you'll be rubbish at it."

"You must be an 'E'," Liam says, trying to sound definite.

"I'm a wall-to-wall Introvert believe it or not. The way I am, the way I behave, allows me to do my job; but I'm no more extrovert that you are. People often mis-read the 'E'/'I' thing. It's true." She bats away the protest beginning to form on Liam's face. "But the question remains, what do you want to be - because you're not happy in your INTJ world, that's for sure."

Liam weighs up the question, though not in terms of the Myers-Briggs analysis that has exposed him to Alison. He tries to imagine what he wants to do - and what kind of person he needs to be in consequence. Or as a prerequisite. He is unsure which comes first. As he looks up he feels suddenly and profoundly sad, but it is a sadness trumped by the sight of tears forming in Alison's eyes.

"I'm sorry," she says, brushing a hand across her face.

Liam reaches a hand towards her, stopping it in the no-mans-land above the table.

"What for?"

"Going too far. Seeing too much. Being a nosy bitch. You choose."

"But I did choose," he says, trying to soften his tone. "I wanted to see if you could work me out, and you did, perfectly."

Alison shakes her head as if trying to expel unwelcome thoughts.

"That was just a parlour trick. Often it takes just five minutes with someone to work them out."

"So the problem is what exactly? I'm confused."

She tries a smile but it is unconvincing, and as if to deflect his attention from her, addresses her drink again. She holds it for a few moments before taking a sip. When she looks back at him, she knows Liam's eyes have never left her.

"You can't do what I do and always keep it impersonal. Almost by definition you can't. There's a risk you run. Most people treat it all as a bit of fun, some are openly hostile; but you take those challenges as par for the course, what you have to put up with to balance out the successes."

"Neither of which sound like me," Liam suggests.

"And then sometimes there are people who are too open, too unguarded if you like. They *want* to know, to understand; they want you to delve beneath the surface."

"And that's a problem?"

"It can be, yes." She pauses to put down her drink. "Remember 'it's business, not personal'? Well in what I do there's a fine line dividing the two. It can be superfine. Sometimes someone crosses it unintentionally; most often it's the subject who, because they are so impressed that you understand them, believe that there's some kind of 'connection'. But there isn't. You're just doing your job, and they are so desperate or hopeful or grateful, that they invest something else in what's just happened."

"Again, that doesn't sound like me," Liam suggests, though even as he does so a part of him is uncertain whether he truly believes what he has just said. Alison raises one eyebrow just a fraction. It almost goes unnoticed.

"And then - very rarely - there's a kind of connection the other way when, in spite of my best intentions, I find I get to see too much; to know too much. I'm the one crossing the line. Then all that INTJ-stuff becomes just bullshit because you see something else, something beyond the little game you were playing."

There is a shout from the main bar which diverts Liam's attention. From the over-exuberant display of a couple of the drinkers there, Liam can only assume something significant has happened in the game they are watching on the big television. Before he turns his head back to face her, he senses her gaze has not wavered.

"What did you see?" Liam asks, his voice feeling no more than a whisper.

"Something of your past, your present; something about your future, and the uncertainty it imposes on you. I saw hope, and loss, and fear. For a moment I could imagine you as a lost little boy alone in an unlit bedroom and scared of the dark."

Liam smiles.

"Right again; I used to hate the dark!"

It is the perfect comment to ease the tension, but Liam finds he doesn't want to let the moment go. He chides himself for being an old man out of his depth, shipwrecked in a below-average bar in a below-average hotel. He had sailed into his week on a boat that had seem sturdy and reliable, only to find it torpedoed by an unseen force. He needs to know how long he will be deserted on the island.

"So," he says, nervously, a slight quaver in his voice. He is the boy in the darkened bedroom, the nervous student before his first exam - or before his first date. He is the uncertain groom, the expectant new father, the novice leader of men. In an instant he is transformed into one and all of those things he has already been. "What happens when both people cross the line?"

There is no answer offered to the question Liam has posed. Instead, Alison smiles and changes tack to speak about something bland and unrelated. This time Liam lets it go, helping her edge them back from whatever precipice they had been approaching. As he tries to refocus, to reassure himself he remains on solid ground, he can't help wondering if it is already too late.

When, a few minutes later, he asks her if she would like another drink, her answer surprises him.

"No, thank you. But you can walk me home."

Uncertain as to what she means and whether he should take her literally, his obvious inability to disguise his confusion causes Alison to laugh, a tired, late-evening version of her trademark. She stands, picks up her handbag, and waits. It is evident he should also move. Liam finishes the dregs of his wine and then rises, following her towards Reception.

She pauses at the lift and presses the call button. As Liam realises at least part of what her request actually meant, he is then bothered by not knowing how to interpret the rest of it. 'Walk me home' is a statement which, he knows from painful experience, can be translated in multiple ways.

As if sensing this, again she laughs, this time her doing so is accompanied by the opening of the lift doors and her briefly pressing his hand with her own.

They say nothing as they make the brief journey to the first floor, where, as soon as the lift doors open, Liam finds himself following Alison away down the corridor to the left. So uniform, so identical, it could well be his floor they are on.

She stops outside room one-one-seven. When Liam stops beside her, he finds himself again perplexed, not entirely sure where he should stand, what he should do, or what he should say.

Alison rescues him as she knows she must, leaning forward to kiss his cheek, her hand once again squeezing his own.

"Goodnight, sweet prince," she says, then swipes her card key and disappears behind the nondescript door.

Liam is frozen to the spot, his eyes focussed on the three silver numbers adorning the door's veneer, his hand still warm from the imprint of Alison's fingers. Unclear what he must do next and whether there is a denouement he should be expecting, he remains rooted, paralysed.

It is a full twenty seconds before he is once again capable of independent thought and motion, at which point he turns on his heels and retraces his steps to the lift.

"Apart or otherwise"

"So what is it?" Katy said, swilling the remaining ice cube around in her glass.

She'd sensed something was different almost as soon as she had entered the house. The abundance of bonhomie from her mother was the initial giveaway; that and the fact that her father seemed only a partially willing accomplice.

The day had broken fair and the temperature had risen to become unseasonably warm. "The last throes of summer" her father had suggested as they drove the handful of miles to the pub. He had been correct when he suggested it was one she liked, but by and large she was ambivalent; for her, public houses - especially 'gastro-pubs' - carried little merit in themselves, they were just places that sold food and drink.

They had each chosen a light salad and eaten inside in relative silence. Avoiding starters and desserts merely conspired to advance her feeling that for her parents even a Niçoise was a chore rather than a pleasure. Managing just a single drink while they ate added weight to the circumstantial case Katy had been building. Her mother had finished her wine very quickly and, so evidently in need of a second, subsequently gave a fair impression of someone parched and lost in the desert.

"Let's sit outside, shall we?" her father eventually suggested, breaking into one of their mini-silences. "I'll get another drink."

Her mother steered them to a corner of the garden far away from the small play area where young children swung and jumped and occasionally screamed. Neither she nor Katy spoke until Liam returned with the drinks.

"Something's up," Katy pursued, "I know there is. It's obvious. So what is it? Tell me. Is it about Granddad?"

"Up?" her mother echoed, trying to appear quizzical.

"It's not Granddad," her father said, Katy immediately noting he made no attempt at denial. "There's no news, nothing new - good or bad. You weren't expecting anything?"

"I wasn't sure. I mean, not really. At least nothing positive. Is that awful of me?"

"No, not awful," Liam said, "just practical, pragmatic."

"Grown-up."

Rachel's contribution surprised both of them, Katy unable to interpret the meaning behind the look her father gave his wife.

"I mean, that's very adult of you, darling," she clarified. "If anything's going to happen, that is. Although I think he's much hardier than we give him credit for; I've always said that."

"That's because you're hardier, Mum," Katy found herself saying. "Not everyone has the same streak you do."

"Streak?"

"Why don't we," Liam said, deliberately interjecting, "put Katy out of her misery." He glanced at his daughter in a way her mother never managed. Preparing her for something he knew she would not welcome, he had a look that proved strangely comforting and one which could be traced back to his guiding her through the challenges of childhood. Katy had always found her father's approach soothing, even when the words or actions that accompanied it were painful - and she knew this was going to be one of those occasions. "Your mother has something to tell you."

This time Katy could not fail to miss the look the pair then exchanged: there was an out-of-character hardness, a steely quality in her father's glance; a trace of anger in her mother's. Katy replaced her glass on the slatted wooden tabletop and rested her hands alongside it as if she were bracing herself for some kind of impact. She watched her mother finish her drink.

"I know this will come as something of a shock," her mother began, her voice calm and steady, "but your father and I have decided to go our separate ways."

"Your mother thinks we should divorce," Liam said, uncharacteristically choosing more direct language, his demeanour resolute and unwavering. "We have," he continued, "been drifting - apart or otherwise - and it seems it's time to put a stop to that."

The words 'apart or otherwise' - articulated deliberately and distinctly - were laden with meaning. Katy's eyes remained steadfastly fixed on her father, watching his mouth more than his eyes, and so she missed her mother's reaction to what he had said, a reaction which, in any event, would have required no special skills to decipher it.

"Divorce?" was all Katy had been able to say.

"I would prefer to look at another way," Rachel began.

"But divorce? I'm sorry, but what 'other way' is there to look at *that*?"

"You're not at home now, are you, all grown-up and independent? You don't need us any more, not like you used to." Rachel's statement ignored Katy's question as if she were intent on reciting memorised lines.

"I'll always need you," Katy protested, interrupting her mother but looking solely at her father.

"And *we're* not getting any younger," Rachel persisted, determined to make her point. "We've one last chance - while we're still able - to try some of those things we've always wanted to. What do you young people call it? Ticking things off our bucket list."

"You have a bucket list?!" Katy alternated her gaze - and therefore her question - between them.

"Well mine is more metaphorical than tangible at this stage," Liam said, trying to lighten the tone - but then, immediately "though your mother's is a little further developed it would seem. Adventures are on the cards."

"What adventures?"

"And she's right, at least in one sense." In avoiding the direct question, Katy sensed her father was unable to answer it and that his response was a peace offering of sorts, not to her but to his wife. "If we don't do it now - whatever 'it' is - then we never will. And we'll probably end up resenting it, the fact that we let the chance slip by."

"And resent each other," Rachel interjected, grateful for the lifeline.

"And each other, which could only be bad for all of us."

When her mother moved to take Katy's hands across the table, she pulled them away.

"We don't have the precious advantage that you have, Katy," Rachel continued, only marginally phased by her daughter's withdrawal.

"What advantage is that?" She kept her tone hard, harsh. Just at the moment she felt devoid of anything that might possibly be labelled 'an advantage'.

"Time," came the simple reply. For the first time, Katy caught a glimpse of desperation in her mother's voice. Her eyes had softened a little. Had she not known her better, Katy would have assumed her to be on the verge of tears. "You might laugh," Rachel continued as if Katy had, "but everyone grows up thinking they've got an inexhaustible supply. There's always tomorrow, or next year. And then one day you're suddenly not so sure. Or rather you're certain that there isn't. Or there won't be. That tomorrow might be the last day. Do you see? Perhaps what's happened to your Granddad brought it home to me, I don't know. But that's how I feel, and I'm not ready to be painted into a corner just yet."

Katy glanced to her father; his own eyes, also softer now, had remained glued to her mother throughout her little speech, and she had the sense that he was hearing something for the first time, as if it brought with it a new realisation. She understood what her mother was saying; understood the words, that is, even if she was unable to respond to them as her father had. And for a split second she caught herself wanting to weaken, to give in, to collaborate with her mother. But Rachel had chosen to use her grandfather as an excuse, a catalyst for her decision, and that was one thing Katy felt unable to condone.

When they had set out, when her father had said they should put her out of her misery, she had not known what to expect. The only thing she could possibly have foreseen was bad news about her grandfather, yet in the end it was all about her mother, selfish and not selfless. She glanced around the garden, fewer people sitting out now.

"So all this…"

"All what?" her mother asked, immediately sensing that her argument had fallen on stoney ground.

"This. The pub, the lunch. Just to tell me that you two had had enough of each other?"

"I wouldn't put it like that," her mother protested.

"We felt," her father suggested, knowing it was too late, "that somewhere 'neutral' would be best. For all of us. Somewhere where there was no pressure, no associations."

Katy felt something on the back of her hand, and looking down, realised that she had started to cry. She was not immediately sure why. It was not sadness she felt. She knew what that felt like: from when she learned of her grandfather's cancer; when her last boyfriend had left her; when she had watched television images of the latest refugee crisis. The latter two had been like watching re-runs of previous events, but not the first - which made it the saddest of all. Perhaps some of those tears had been the result of anger, and in her case anger was always accompanied by some manifestation of heat, and strangely, of silence too. At this precise moment, silent was the last thing she wanted to be. And then she wondered if she might, in some bizarre way, be happy. Why would that be? She rubbed her face with her hands, her eyes lighting on her mother. There was a possible answer. Could it be a combination; sadness for herself, yes, but deep down might she be glad that her father would soon be free?

She shook her head.

"Fine." She said, as coldly as she could muster. "Mission accomplished. Can I go home now?"

Perhaps for the first time, Liam and Rachel realised 'home' for Katy was no longer where the two of them lived.

55

"You've no idea what it's like"

To the casual observer walking by the edge of the lake, it may have appeared as if the rowing boat had slipped its moorings and then drifted unshepherded, pushed by a gentle breeze out into the centre of the water. Yet had they paused to check, perhaps before raising the alarm, they would have noticed a woman's dark blonde hair intermittently appearing as she raised her head to glance over the boat's gunwales. Hopefully before further and potentially more alarming questions surfaced, they might also have noticed the tell-tale shape of a camera as she held it to her eye for a moment before she, the camera, and her hair disappeared again from view.

She had decided some time ago that her photography needed to be defined and bounded by 'projects'. She was not the kind of person who took 'snaps', who wandered about pretending to be satisfied by banal, picture-postcard touristic images. Photography needed to be more serious than that; it needed to be about something deeper. She knew she harboured somewhere, discrete and buried, the vagueness of ambition. It would be nice to be 'recognised'; she fantasised about exhibitions and book deals, and how her particular slant on things - her 'eye' - was a unique talent to set her apart. In her wildest moments she imagined people describing it as a 'gift'.

On that basis, serious people - serious, gifted people - needed to treat their métier with a degree of process and structure and reverence. Hence the projects. Her current preoccupation was with what she liked to call 'Barriers'. In her ever-growing library of electronic images, a new folder had been created some three weeks ago. It was home to numerous pictures of fences and walls, of doors and windows. "Barriers", she had told herself "were the things that caused separation". Yet after two weeks or so, she felt her frustration growing. Such a definition - or rather, such a literal interpretation - she now felt to be naïve, immature, and so she had begun to consider other incarnations.

People would not normally regard a lake in a public park as a barrier; after all, you could simply walk around it. Other than forcing you to take a longer route than the direct line from where you were to where you wanted to be, it never really prevented you from going anywhere. But as she strolled up to it that Sunday morning seeking inspiration, she wondered if it might be considered a barrier if you were 'in' it. The water would cease to be something pretty to look at, a focal point for a holiday snap, but a blocker between you and dry land, between you and safety and security. Arriving at that notion, hiring a boat had been the next logical step. Once out in the middle of the water she began taking shots, but found the lake appeared not as she'd intended, but rather as a benign element in a landscape. She needed to elevate it in importance, to change perspective. It had been this chain of thought which had led her to ship her oars and lie down in the boat, to take her photographs from as low down in the boat as she possibly could, to try and make the water dominate the picture.

As she captured one last image - of a dog on the edge of the lake staring down into the water, where it stood transfixed, rooted to a false horizon high in the photo - she knew it would only be once she had uploaded her pictures into her computer and examined them on the screen that she would discover if the experiment had been successful. At this point you might, therefore, have been forgiven for imagining she would row back toward the boathouse with a degree of gusto, keen to get home as soon as possible. Yet she did not, for she had other things on her mind too.

She had not thought of her mother since she had entered the park. At least not consciously. She was tortured by the paradox that trying not to think about her actually meant calling her to consciousness in the first place. Katy was angry that she had been forced into such a dilemma, her sensibilities bludgeoned in a fashion that was inappropriate in all sorts of ways.

"You'll understand when you're older," her mother had said at one point, the parting shot one Sunday at the end of an exasperating attempt to make Katy see reason, to disabuse her of any naïve belief she may have still held in relation to how life was supposed to be perfect. She might as well have said "shit happens" for all the good it did.

"I'm not a child!" Katy had protested, her words accompanied by suitably demonstrative semi-childish actions: the turning away, a strangled cry.

"Maybe not," her mother conceded, "at least in some things. But you've no idea what it's like."

"What what's like?" She had turned to face her again, cheeks red, eyes redder still.

"Longevity," her mother had said, blending the word with a sigh as if the two together would act out exactly what she meant more effectively than the word alone. "Years. You've no idea what years can do to you because you simply haven't had the experience of those years. To young people today, if a relationship lasts more than three months it counts as pretty serious."

"I am not 'young people'," Katy protested.

Her mother ignored her.

"But try and imagine what it feels like when you are talking about years. About thirty years!"

"There are lots of people - millions of people - who stay together longer than that. And it's not as if Dad's a monster or anything."

"He isn't. Of course, he isn't. He's a wonderful man."

"So?"

The sigh returned.

"But we're too comfortable. I'm too comfortable. Your father's like the nicest pair of slippers in the world; but one day even the best slippers can get a hole in them, and then they stop being comfortable. They irritate; they let cold in, or water in. You just have to take them off."

"And get a new pair," Katy had said with a barb. "A younger pair?"

At this Rachel turned away. She had promised herself she would not get angry. Liam had persuaded her to have yet another try with Katy.

"Have you asked your father?" It was a less well-worn track, but one worth having another go at.

"Asked him what?"

"What he thinks."

"I don't need to ask him," Katy replied suddenly feeling superior, that she had the upper-hand. "You only have to look at him."

"I think he's tired of me too. I think I may have a hole in my sole as far as he's concerned."

"The only hole in Daddy's soul is the one you've put there."

When the boat bumped against the wooden jetty, Katy was momentarily startled, surprised to find herself there. Autopilot had taken her slowly across the lake. Anyone watching from a nearby path may well have been impressed with the steadiness and evenness of her stroke, how she eased the boat through the water as if it were effortless. And in one sense, in the subconscious nature of it, it was. But the shudder of wood on wood had shaken her out of that reverie like the shattering of a fragile glass pane. She looked down at her feet expecting to see glinting fragments of glass, but all she could see was the black of her camera. She sighed as it all came back to her - not just the replay of the argument with her mother, but her recent attempts at depicting water as a barrier - and instinctively knew that the second would prove as much a failure as the first.

She smiled weakly at the man who now held the boat close to the dock with his foot, retrieved her camera, and stepped out of the gently rocking craft.

"I'm not sure there's a word for it"

"You want to hear about her? Really?"
She nods.
"But why?" Liam is confused.

"You're right, actually I don't," she says after a moment's thought. "I want to know more about you, and how you talk about Rachel will tell me more than you realise."

"So you really *are* a psychologist then?"
She smiles.
"Only where you're concerned."

"Well if that's your game or you're going to try and 'rescue' me like some a professional shrink…"

"I am not a shrink," she interjects.

Liam notes that she did not pick up on his notion of being rescued, yet from the vaguely haughty tone in her voice he can't tell for sure if she is offended or not. He plumps for the latter.

"Shouldn't I be laying on a couch or something?"

"Just talk, Buster, or there'll be trouble!"

She had phoned him two weeks after they had met in the hotel; two weeks since their somewhat surreal parting outside room one-one-seven. Liam had filled the intervening time with work - which he had been unable to avoid - and trying to decide how he felt about their encounter. He had been unable to avoid that as well. Like a pendulum, he swung between extremes on different planes: one moment theirs had been an amusing diversion he was happy to write off, the next it felt like the precursor of something as yet undefined and which he was compelled to explore. Alison was either a bossy, self-opinionated busy-body, or she was a spiky, confident and complex woman. And it didn't stop there. Was she inherently attractive or a Plain Jane who made the most of what she had? He couldn't help but admit he genuinely liked her - but that too was to find himself becalmed in the middle of another pendulum's arc, a position that forced him to make a choice. Underlying all that came the nagging voice that told him whichever position he chose to occupy on any spectrum, she was 'too young' for him. Unfortunately Alison didn't make him feel any younger; rather she reminded him how old he was.

It being a label he had deliberately and premeditatively chosen to apply, not surprisingly the question of age bothered him most of all. The nature and scale of their relationship - indeed, whether there was even the potential for them to have one of any kind - seemed moot and nebulous, and so it should have been pointless to worry about it. But age was a thing definable, measurable and tangible, and that seemed paramount. Unable to avoid it, or finagle his way around it, Liam tried - without conclusion - to confront it head on.

Immediately after their encounter, his being unable to resolve his 'position' to any satisfaction left him in a state of paralysis. Unable to bring himself to call her, he sacrificed their meeting, consigning it to history, choosing to take a fatalistic line, determined to make the best of it, whatever that meant.

"You realise," she had said as her opening gambit on that phone call, without any kind of welcome or small talk, "that I have absolutely no idea where you live."

"Where I live?" He had recognised her voice and that direct tone of hers. It transported him back to the bar.

"The hotel's not far from the M4 which can only mean you live much further south or much further north. East or west, I've no idea."

Liam had wanted to ask why she needed to know, why she had called him. Somewhere he felt as if invisible hands were turning keys that made pendulums swing.

"Unfinished business," she had said, interrupting his train of thought.

"Sorry?"

"In case you're wondering, we still have unfinished business."

"We do?"

"I think so, don't you?"

He had let the question hang before Alison took over again, and they played a little game of geographical cat-and-mouse before confirming that she lived in the north of the Peak District and he on the border between Yorkshire and Lancashire; she in Hope, he in Settle. The place names struck him as profound.

"Not that far, as the crow flies," he had suggested to see what she made of a distance of some eighty-odd miles.

"If you're a crow. Where's half way?"

"Bradford or Blackburn," he replied somewhat provocatively, the thought of which triggered a laugh - a sound he hadn't realised he'd missed.

"No chance!"

"Hebden Bridge is nice," he suggested having scoured his memory for alternatives. "A little 'Yorkshire' for my taste, and striving to be something special and quirky. All the pubs serve Yorkshire pudding with everything - but I wouldn't condemn it for that."

"Hmm," she had said, not sounding convinced. "Let me check it out. I've no intention of driving all that way to end up in some shit-hole."

There had been a brief silence. Liam imagined her (incorrectly as it turned out) checking out Google maps on a nearby iPad to find out what Hebden Bridge looked like, but she had come back to him too quickly for that.

"What are you doing Sunday?"

They had met in the centre of the village and found a tea shop which had occupied them for about an hour with two pots of tea and some Victoria sponge. Liam felt as if they were meeting under false pretences, perhaps as old friends from school might have met at a reunion some twenty years later, trying to remember what they had liked about each other in the first place - and with resigned shock realising that they no longer did. Or, indeed, never had. Their talk had been antiseptic, too banal to generate any real interest or emotion.

In a stilted way, they had flirted with Yorkshire, tourism, politics, a little about work. There had been no Myers-Briggs, nothing about them as people, no re-connection.

Liam had been disappointed. As he drove back to Settle, he wondered what he had been expecting. He stopped on the way home for a short walk in the Dales to try and clear his head.

When he got back home, the light on his answering machine was flashing.

"Call me," was all she had said. Liam's first thought was to wonder if it had been a mistake giving her his home phone number.

"Well that was a bit rubbish, wasn't it?" She said when she picked up the phone. Although framed as a question, it was delivered as a statement designated to remain beyond challenge. Liam could only agree with her.

"Second chance?" she asked.

His pendulums, having been mobilised, had yet to come to rest, so he wasn't sure.

"But no third chances, right?"

The recall of their first encounter made her laugh.

"Good boy!" she said, deliberately patronising. "He's learning."

Choosing Howarth as their second venue had been inspired; it allowed the Parsonage to frame the day. The story of the Brontes gave them a structure within which to work, and took away the pressure of them having to construct something of their own. Exhausting the formal history, they had driven down to the railway station and bought ice creams, choosing to sit on one of the platform's maroon benches ostensibly for the opportunity to watch a heritage steam train pass through. It was as they waited Liam confessed a lack of appreciation for the Brontes, admitting it had been a module at university he had scrupulously avoided. His suffix - "unlike Rachel" - had piqued Alison's curiosity, hence her request: "Tell me about her".

"What is there to say?" Liam starts, buying himself time to work out how to begin, knowing there is no way out of the trap he has set for himself and then obligingly fallen into.

"Everything."

"We were young of course." He thinks about the bookshop.

"Isn't everyone - at least once."

"You know what I mean."

Alison looks at him.

"You need to stop doing that?"

"Doing what?" He is unaware he has done anything at all apart from vacillate.

"Start with age as your waypoint; how you navigate."

"Do I?"

She nods.

"Too often."

He waits for the follow-up but there is none. It is his turn again, time to pick up the thread.

"Well we *were* young. Me especially so, I think. Fresh out of home, raw, green, inexperienced. I know that's how most first year students are, but you can only try and decipher your own relationship to the world can't you? I'd seen her around a lot - we were on the came course, after all. But then I'd seen lots of girls around. And you know what boys and their hormones are like, don't you? Well, no, you don't of course!" He corrects himself.

"What makes you think girls are any different?"

He glances at her, having been looking away down the track. She is serious, intent on what he's saying. He pushes on.

"I liked her a lot, but nothing happened for ages. And then at some grubby party, it suddenly did. She made the move. I was - surprised."

"Boys always are," Alison offers.

"Surprised?"

She nods.

"They have this naïve image of the sexes, their place in the centre of things. They don't expect to be pounced on."

Liam laughs. He hadn't considered himself 'pounced on'.

"Did you 'pounce'?" he asks with a smile.

"All the time," she fires a laugh at him. "Still do."

Her last two words seem to spin around him and then separate, heading opposite ways along the track. He looks up the line towards Keighley, the direction from which he expects the next train to appear.

"It was all a bit - I don't know - giddy for a while. New, fresh. Then we settled into a routine. We never knew how long things would last. I mean, I suppose I had hope but no expectation. I'd seen my friends have relationships of sorts that blazed brightly for a few weeks - sometimes just a few days - and then they'd crash out of them. But we seemed to get comfortable quite quickly. I couldn't believe how lucky I was. I think it helped that we didn't live together at all while we were at college. It gave us space and a certain independence. Not that I'm saying it was perfect, or that it wasn't rocky from time-to-time. And then two and a bit years later University came to an end."

"And you had a choice to make," Alison prompts. Liam looks back at her.

"Funnily enough, not really. Rachel had always said that as soon as college finished she was going to go to Europe for a few months with some of her girlfriends. It was non-negotiable, so I didn't try. She went off, and I started looking for work. By the time she came back I'd found something in London that got me started."

"Started?"

"On a career, I suppose." Liam pauses. "Real life. The normality that follows the hedonism and selfishness of university. You know what I mean? Anyway, when Rachel came back it was a bit like a test, really. And then being given the results of a test. We found out what we really felt and really wanted. If it had been just a 'college romance' we'd have seen that straight away."

"But it wasn't."

Liam shakes his head.

"We moved in together, she got a job, and the rest, as they say…"

"Is history." Alison finishes his sentence for him.

To her left a family with three young children appear on the platform, the two youngest running up and down making train noises, evidently excited by their adventure. Liam's eyes follow them.

"Except it isn't." She says this as she is still looking at him.

"What isn't?"

"History." She glances to where he has been looking and then turns back towards him. "Not all of it. Not all of your history. There's the big chunk that's the normal history most people go through one way or another: marriage, children."

"Divorce," Liam prompts before she can get to it.

"In more and more cases, sadly. But even though it can take up so much of your time, even though it may feel like it's the end, that's not all of it, Liam. We say 'the rest is history' as if that's it; as if the history's been written and the book's closed. That's complete crap. I mean it can be if you want it to be, but it doesn't have to be. And I don't think that's you. A chapter's closed, that's all. Okay, it's a pretty big chapter, a chapter that will take up most of the volume - and why shouldn't it? But it's just a chapter, after all. Haven't you started writing the next one already?"

He tries to allow the notion to permeate, thinking he knows what she means. And he wants to agree, to say yes, but he struggles, unable to penetrate the fog which for a while now has seemed to have descended over his future. Unable to see anything that would approximate to it, he has begun to wonder if there is one hiding somewhere.

A whistle forces them both to turn. A large steam engine appears a little distance away, heading towards them. It is strangely silent until it gets up close, and then there is suddenly the confusion of sound and steam, of noise and smell. People along the platform stand or walk towards its edge. Liam sees smiles break out, children hopping with excitement. With a screech of old brakes, the train comes to a halt and there is a great confluence of comings and goings, doors being opened and closed, shouts and cries: "Michael, here's one!"; "Come on George!"; "Abigail will you put that down!"; "Sorry, after you."; "Is this for the Brontes?" Inevitably there are Oriental tourists trying to capture the moment - their moment - in mega-pixelated form in order to prove something to themselves later on. Liam is suddenly content to have just his memory to rely on, and he tries to fix the moment as best he can, not wanting to lose it.

He feels a hand on his arm. Alison is looking intently at him.

"Why so serious?" she asks.

"Serious?" He tries to smile and feels his face breaking away from the cast into which it had settled.

"Almost frowning, as if you were remembering something, or concentrating really hard."

"Concentrating, yes; remembering? Almost the opposite."

"What's the opposite of remembering, as I'm sure you're not talking about forgetting?" Alison adopts a puzzled look of her own.

"I'm not sure there's a word for what I mean," Liam says.

To their right, the train's whistle blows again, and they watch as it puffs hard, billowing huge clouds of smoke into the air, her hand still on his arm.

"You have to know what you're doing"

Rachel had never considered herself someone who was easily preoccupied. If she chose to think about it, she would have argued for an ability to focus, to keep laser-like vision on a goal. Yet this had brought her - what? Not success, because she had become increasingly uncertain how you measured that; and in any event, her reward, if there was one, felt more all-encompassing. She was not naïve enough to think her single-mindedness was only a blessing. It had won her a first at university, but at the cost of what might then have been considered her reputation; it had given her a career in the media for a while, until she chose to forego it for motherhood; and throughout her life it had also been the rock upon which she had built her relationships.

Liam was the perfect example. She wouldn't say her pursuit of him had been calculated, far from it. Indeed, admitting as much could only demean the love she had felt for him. But ask her if - once she had resolved her feelings for him - her decision to win him over had been backed by an unswerving determination, then she would have to plead guilty. And what was wrong with that? What was the problem with knowing what you wanted and then going out to get it? Life hadn't been handed to her on a plate unlike for some of her friends. Take Claire who always knew one day she was going to run the stunningly successful family business and could therefore skip through early adulthood in a careless, almost reckless way. Or Petra, somehow linked to foreign billions, only having to blink her famous eyes to get whatever she wanted. But Rachel had needed to work at it, to cultivate herself. Ever since she had become a young adult she had needed to maximise everything she possessed: her intellect, her looks. No single ability - or shortcoming! - had missed her microscope, an almost forensic examination of what it meant to be 'Rachel'. Ask her of it had been worth all the effort, and she would have said without hesitation "yes".

But that was not the question currently assailing her. Far from it. The question currently demanding her attention was where was it now: that drive, clarity of thought, pin-point understanding of self, all seemed to have deserted her. It was as if the soldiers in her army had snuck away under cover of darkness to leave her naked on the field of battle with nothing to protect her but an unloaded rifle. The situation was only tolerable when she was with those who knew her best: Liam, Katy, her father. They still assumed those qualities existed in her, so all she had to do was to play up to them, to act as if they were still there. But outside of her immediate and - she had suddenly realised - desperately small circle of intimates, she was merely 'normal', lacking that edge and sharpness which had once upon a time been legendary and had set her apart from so many others. And when one day, as a result of some inconsequential incident during a visit with her father to the hospital, that realisation had hit her, it brought with it further questions: how long had she been like this, and why was it now acceptable to be so?

She could have let it go, of course, but that would surely have been nothing less than admitting defeat, proving she was no longer the woman she had once been. A middle course of some kind might have mitigated any sense of failure; if she spent the time to truly understand what had happened to her, then it was logically possible she might ultimately be able to accept her fate. Athletes became less strong, or fast, or nimble over time, so why should she be any different? Slower, lower, weaker. And even the greatest of intellects saw the diminution of their powers.

But she wasn't a fan of logic; not in this case. It wasn't that she was trying to rail against the inevitable, nor was she attempting to blunder blindly on, all bull-in-a-china-shop, striving to be the person she had been perhaps ten years previously. Indeed, the Rachel she truly identified with may have been consigned to history even further back than that. No, it was rather that she wanted to put up a fight, one last stand - even if it ended up being Custer-like in the face of overwhelming odds. Her motivation was all about proof; proof and demonstration. And even though she was uncertain what she wanted to prove or demonstrate, she knew to whom such evidence needed to be presented: herself. It was this quest, creeping up on her as it had over a period of time, which had settled in her the notion of some kind of material 'shift'.

For a long while she struggled with the nebulous nature of her conundrum; it was a like a vague ache without any localised pain. Over time, however, she began to be able to articulate it a little better, silently and to herself. It was like standing in front of the bathroom mirror and waiting for the condensation to clear. When it did, she saw Liam's reflection and not her own. It was as if she had become defined by him, subservient to him (and thus, by extension, to Katy), and that who she was - indeed, *how* she now was - could only be seen through their eyes. Did she only exist in relation to others? She was Liam's wife, Katy's mother, Ronald's daughter. Once upon a time she had been Rachel, and people had known what that meant.

This realisation had not come to her in one great shockwave; she had not broken down in the middle of the High Street and wept inconsolably. Rachel didn't do inconsolable weeping. Rather it had crept up behind her - almost without her hearing its soft footsteps - and tapped her on the shoulder. When she turned and looked, it smiled back silently. "So" she had thought, as if someone had told her something she had actually known all along.

When she met David, he had crept up behind her too. She had been leaning into the chillers of Waitrose's fresh meat section, debating between sirloin or rump for Liam's supper. Making a choice, she had reached for a pack of the latter at the same time as another hand had done likewise. There had been a brief touching of fingers, some embarrassment. The other hand had quit the field with an apology from its owner who had waited until she had placed the prize in her trolley before he apologised again, allowing her to move on. It had been an insignificant incident without any sway in terms of her personal calculations.

A few minutes later she had seen him again, browsing the cereal aisle. He seemed slightly above average, and she found herself comparing him to a norm that, unconsciously at least, looked like Liam. This man was a little taller, a little younger, his clothes a little sharper. He looked authoritative with an air of success about him, rather than simply solidly professional. There was a tint of grey about his temples which gave a clue as to his age, and his shoes - she always looked at shoes - were not new, but polished as if they were. Yet in all respects except one he was unexceptional; and that one was the fact he wasn't Liam.

On her way home she had tried to shake herself out of a flood of more or less random thoughts and allowed herself to be reabsorbed into daily life and its predictable routine. Rachel let the man slip away from her. Yes, he'd had a nice smile and had been polite, and yes, his hands had been clean, nails well looked after, but it had been nothing. An accident. A trifle.

Two weeks later - two weeks further into the fermentation of her disquiet and on the verge of her finding her resolve and making her declaration - she saw him again in the same supermarket. From somewhere, that old Rachel, the one she had missed yet believed she still could be, came to the surface.

Her trolley full, she had loitered near the tills waiting for him to finish loading his own. Oblivious, he had wheeled past her and parked himself at checkout number seven. She joined the same queue. Ahead of them both a slightly elderly lady was labouring through her packing; the assistant - evidently a semi-retired professional of almost equal age - sat with his hand out, ready for her to pass him cash or some form of credit or debit card. Waiting for the conveyor to move the man's goods forward and allow her space for her own, she analysed the purchases arrayed before her. A moderately healthy mix, she concluded, primarily branded with one or two premium choices such as two bars of luxury chocolate and a bottle of Chablis.

The conveyor having jerked forward, Rachel spoke just as the man was positioning one of the plastic dividers at the end of his provisions.

"How was the rump steak?"

He looked up, plainly surprised that he had been spoken to. Rachel watched as he tried to compute the statement she had made.

His face cleared.

"Ah, yes. Of course. The steak." He smiled. "It was very nice actually. I have a nasty habit of over-cooking steak, but I managed to get that piece just right; pink but not bloody. Caught it before it started to get tough, you know?"

"Absolutely. A minute and a half maximum on each side - twice over - then allow it to rest for five minutes."

"That's the secret?"

"It works for me," Rachel said.

The conveyor jolted forwards and the Chablis clinked against a can of chick peas. As the scanner started to beep, he moved to the end of the line, pulled his bags from the trolley and started packing.

They went through their separate processes of unloading, re-packing and paying automatically, though after he had finished and she was focussed on bagging her own goods, Rachel sensed he had not moved that far away. Usually people cannot wait to get out of the store once they have paid, and gallop toward the car park to transfer bags to their vehicle and then drive off to the somewhere else they would rather be.

The last item put away, Rachel punched her code into the card reader, then slipped the receipt into her purse. She took a breath and turned. He was standing about eight metres away, evidently waiting.

"In return for the tip," he started confidently, "you know, the minute and a half per side thing, might I be permitted to buy you a coffee?"

He nodded towards the entrance and the in-store cafe that lay in wait between them and the exit.

"It was free advice," she offered, now stationary next to him, their trolleys aligned.

"Even so. If you've time."

The question came in the rising intonation of his voice, not in the words themselves. Rachel immediately recognised that it was not a simple matter of 'time' at all; it was a proposition layered with other meanings and nuances. She knew that if she said 'yes', there would be other, unspoken questions being answered too. Some of these she knew or assumed, but she also knew that what mattered most were the ancillary questions that this stranger had invested in the innocent 'if you've time'. She found herself wanting to know if, unlike Liam, he was the kind of man who never said what he actually meant, his words forming lines he expected you to read between. Or not, perhaps.

"These places are normally dreadful," he ventured, once they were sitting at a seat by the window, the comings and goings of the car park in full view.

"Dreadful? And this one isn't?"

"In terms of it being brash and plastic and generally horrible? Yes, I know what you mean. But the coffee is actually quite passable and some days they have really good danish pastries."

"Is today not a good day?" Rachel asked.

He frowned.

"What do you mean?"

"No Danish." She nodded toward the coffee resting solitary in front of him.

"I see. You know, I didn't even look."

There was a slight pause as Rachel glanced out of the window, watching a young mother struggling with a full trolley and a recalcitrant toddler.

"Do you make a habit of this then?" she asked, eyes still fixed on the little drama outside, conscious he was looking at her.

"Of having coffee and Danish pastries?"

"Of luring innocent women into the Waitrose café to ply them with caffeine and iced buns."

He laughed and brought her back to the table. It was a pleasant enough laugh. Rachel liked to use someone's laugh as a measure of their character. His was rounded, confident, and built on experience - she suspected not all of it positive.

"Only…"

A screech of tyres from outside followed by a shout interrupted his reply. They both turned to see the woman dragging the child back to within holding distance of her trolley. Red-faced, she mouthed an apology to the unseen driver who had been forced to break suddenly in order to avoid running her son over.

"Close," he said.

"You wonder whose fault it was," Rachel said, retuning her attention to him.

"The little boy's, of course," he replied as if the answer were self-evident.

Rachel shook her head.

"No?" He looked quizzically at her.

"Either the mother for losing control of him, or the driver for going too fast."

"Or not looking where he was going?" he suggested, trying to ally himself to her argument.

She nodded and reached for her coffee. "Whichever, someone was out of control."

"But not the little boy?"

"You have to know what you're doing - or what you should or shouldn't be doing - before you can be out of control." She felt herself draw two lines of her own for him to read between.

He allowed a slow smile to build. So, thought Rachel, he can see what's not said as well as not say it.

"Would the driver have been a man?" he asked. "I'm intrigued by your theory."

It was her turn to laugh.

"Bound to have been. After all, you're never really more than little boys, are you?"

A sudden image of Liam - of Liam not being a little boy - came to her, and she was forced to look away, down to the mug; white, blue-rimmed, it nestled nearly full in her hands.

"My name's David," a voice said, and Rachel knew he was drawing invisible lines in the air again.

"Some things can't be fixed"

When she came to she was lying naked, legs together, hands at her side, as if she were being readied for mummification. She knew from the hard coldness against her back that she was not lying on a bed but rather a plinth or slab. Yet it was not this individual physical sensation which caused her to panic, to begin to ripple with fear. Instinctively she moved her right hand onto her body, to the small space she allowed herself to create between her legs, and there felt the cold trail of semen. She wanted to scream, to recoil so violently in both sound and movement that she would be able to expel the fluids that had invader her, to turn back time in order not to find herself here, missing a slice from her life, a victim having been stripped of control. But she could not. No matter how hard she tried, no sound came; no movement proved possible other than the shallow trembling she had to endure.

The dream was always the same. Always. And once she had woken from it and reassured herself - her hand nervously brushing across the folds of her nightie or pyjamas - that it was indeed a dream, the urge to cry out tapered away. Little by little she shifted her position in the bed as if testing out segments of her person in turn until she was confident enough to sit up and swing her legs to the side of the bed. Only at this point did she check the bedside clock. When she woke like this she had learned that the time was an irrelevance, that getting back to sleep was impossible, and so had developed routines which allowed her to recalibrate against whatever point in the morning - or night - it was.

Today she was lucky. It had been a little before seven which meant she didn't need to go through the trickery of preparing to go to bed for the second time in one night. Yes, it was early - especially so since it was a Saturday - but she could cope with that; once she had made herself some tea and a little toast there were things she could do which allowed her to resume control. She glanced at Tom as she slipped on her dressing gown. He was sleeping undisturbed, his left leg out from beneath the covers as it so often was. He looked as if he was readying himself to make a getaway.

Katy had never told Tom about her dream. As she waited for the kettle, she wondered once again why that was. It was like an itch she had to keep scratching. She told herself that, even after nearly a year, she didn't really know him well enough to share it with him, to know how he would react. However, as time had passed, not doing so felt more and more like an excuse to hide the real reason. What if he found the whole scenario erotic? What if, turned on by the prospect, one night he got her drunk or somehow drugged her and enacted the absent male part in her dream? What if she woke one morning and found that except for the plinth it was all real, what would she do then? But even as she struggled with that scenario, another possibility always arose. What if *she* found it erotic? What if it was what she wanted to happen? Was there part of her that needed to be violated, taken unconsciously against her will, enslaved and abused in such a way?

In spite of that self-doubt, Katy always came back to the same underlying position: she focussed on Tom, and asked herself why she still seemed to be unearthing questions about him, questions she was unable to answer. That didn't seem right. Weren't such things supposed to go away over time?

They had met at a party. Tabby had decided to make a big deal of the fact that she was twenty-five, as if she couldn't wait for a birthday with a zero in it as an excuse to celebrate. That was true to form of course. Ever since Katy had known Tabitha - "Tabby to my friends!" - there had been grand if shallow gestures, as if that's how she made sense of her life. Nothing was ever mediocre for Tabby; she simply wouldn't let it be. Going on holiday, going shopping for a new dress, even a quiet drink down the pub on a Sunday evening, all had to have a sense of purpose and the theatrical. She was loud and gregarious, and demanded to be the centre of attention.

Almost as much an opposite as it was possible to be, initially Tabby had grated on her. Being the new girl in the office only seemed to bring out the extremes in her, and for a while Katy tried, as subtly as she could, to avoid her. But Tabby was not to be denied; everyone needed to be her friend. And then when her grandmother died, Katy suddenly found Tabby could be a perfect foil, someone within whose orbit she could circulate almost invisibly. Ego-centric she may have been, but Tabby was not naïve. Neither was she incapable of fellow-felling, and more than once surprised Katy by displays of intimacy and tenderness. Almost in spite of herself, Katy came to like her more and more, and as such was an inevitable attendee at the 'bash' Tabby had decided would recognise her non-landmark birthday.

"We'll have it at 'The Lord Butler', or whatever it's called," Tabby had announced at lunch one day. "My flat's so pokey! That way I can invite hundreds of people and get completely drunk. We might even find you a man and get you laid!"

Katy knew her friend was trying to ease her out of the shell into which she had retreated, not that there was anything particularly subtle about her efforts. Yet in spite of all appearances to the contrary, Tabby was a cautious person when it came to her *truly* private life, and it was probably the one single characteristic the two shared. Katy had stumbled a little in terms of relationships over the previous couple of years, and Tabby had - almost officially - designated her role as being the 'fixer' who would solve Katy's 'problem'. Most things Tabitha said came in parentheses. Although she didn't feel the need to be rescued in any way, Katy had gone along with the charade. Attempting to achieve her own version of survival, she had been trying out various pastimes and hobbies, none proving to be a particularly good fit, each of them abandoned as soon as it became evident they were no silver bullet.

"It's no wonder you've had 'man trouble'," Tabitha had declared one evening. "No staying power."

Outwardly Katy protested that she had no such issues, though privately she was beginning to wonder.

Whether all this chivvying, badgering, and prompting had anything to do with Katy somehow settling on Tom that evening at 'The Lord Benbow' she was never really able to say, but remarkably Tabby had been right for once: she *had* found her a man, and she *had* got laid.

"I'd seen you before." He was propped up on one elbow, watching her as she fumbled through some drawers. It was their first 'morning after'. "Though not like this."

Her hand settled on a pair of rolled-up socks that she sent in his general direction accompanied by a playful expletive. As he caught them deftly, she wondered if she ought not have sworn.

"Well held," she said, as if that made amends. Finding a second pair of socks she was prepared to wear, she sat at the end of the bed looking at him, out of his reach, keeping her distance. "When?"

"A couple of times. At Tabby's things, of course."

"Of course."

"In the pub mainly. But you remember that disastrous picnic?"

"The one in Palmer's Park when it suddenly rained and we all got soaked?"

"Yes."

They both laughed.

"You don't remember me," Tom said once the laughter had subsided. "That's ok. I don't think I was very memorable that day."

Katy knew there was no point denying it.

"I wasn't in a good place."

"I know. Tabby said."

"She said?!" Katy was unable to keep the surprise from her voice.

"That you were upset. I think she was worried."

Katy smiled, feeling a fresh flush of friendship toward their mutual acquaintance; it was a sensation which always prompted guilt.

"The previous few weeks had been pretty rough one way or another."

Tom waited, expecting her to elaborate. When she chose not to, he had no alternative but to fill the void himself.

"So she wanted me to try and cheer you up."

"Oh," said Katy, mock enquiry exaggerated in her voice. "How?"

Tom laughed and lobbed the socks he was still holding back toward her. She let them bounce off her arm and fall onto the bed.

"Well she would. I mean, she thinks sex cures everything, doesn't she?"

"But it doesn't," he suggested.

Taken slightly aback, she chose to pick up the thrown socks and return them to the drawer. It bought her time.

"You don't think so?"

"I know so," he said, quietly definite. "Don't you? I mean, it helps, but it's rarely the answer, not in any long-term-fixing-it kind of way."

"Some things can't be fixed," she said.

"Some things can't be fixed," he echoed. It was not a reply for the sake of it, but apparently an amalgam of his own understanding and experience.

And now there they were, months later and the world was moving on.

A sound behind her forced her to turn.

"Making tea?" Tom asked now awake himself and standing not far from her.

"You want one?"

"Please."

As she busied herself with a second cup, Katy could feel his eyes on her.

"I'll bring it through," she said over her shoulder, hoping it would be enough for him to retreat back into the bedroom, glad when she heard him shuffle away.

"There's something wrong, Katy; what is it?"

She had put his tea on the bedside cabinet, choosing to sit at the end of the bed and cradle her own mug in her hands, finding the warmth welcome, the distance from him strangely reassuring.

"Wrong?"

"Yes, wrong. It's Saturday and it's early. You were talking in your sleep and it didn't sound good. Tell me. I can help."

Weighing up whether Tom was part of the problem rather than part of the solution, she was instinctively negative; yet she had painted herself into a corner it seemed. She blamed the dream for abandoning her there, knowing the only way out was to say something. If she left it, protested too much that she was fine, then he would only pester her for the truth; if she wasn't going to divulge the secrets of her unconscious, she needed another escape route. She hadn't planned to share her news with him yet; her voice, slightly tremulous, was hesitant too.

"My parents are in the process of getting a divorce."

"Ouch," he said, sitting slightly more upright. It was a move she could not fail to notice.

"They've been pretending everything's ok, of course, and if you didn't know, you might never have guessed. But underneath the surface it seems they've been struggling. A lot. So." She paused, searching for something more upbeat. "Still, it's all relatively amicable, which is something. My Dad's trying to be very magnanimous about it, saying how it's the right thing for them both; how they have - I don't know - 'changed' I suppose. They keep on about how I am the most important thing, but they've said it so much that it's stopped meaning anything. Or started to mean the opposite. And all the while my Granddad - my Mum's Dad - is slipping away almost without them noticing. Or without her noticing, anyway."

While she was speaking, Tom pushed himself further up from the mattress so that he was sitting bolt upright, back pressed against the wall, a crumpled pillow offering minimal support in the small of his back. Katy was struck by unexpected parallels with her grandfather: how, when she was a young girl, he used to seem ramrod straight to her, and how he used to adjust his posture when he wanted to say something important as if needing to prepare both himself and his listener. She was struck by how serious Tom looked all of a sudden. Liking him a little more because of it, she smiled and tried to find his toes through the duvet with her free hand.

"What?" she asked, hoping to convey that she was alright; that it was ok to talk about her grandfather or her parents.

Tom looked down at the duvet to where her hand had now found his left foot.

"Come on," she said, tugging.

"Come on what?" Tom tried to protest innocence.

"You want to say something. I know you do!"

"How do you know that?" he asked, genuinely bewildered.

"Because of the way you're sitting, the way you look. It's almost as if I can see the words rising up through your chest, just about to burst out of your mouth." She laughed at the notion. "Just like my Granddad."

"I'm like your Granddad?"

"Only in that way, silly. You want to say something, so spit it out. I'm immune."

Tom leant forward and brushed her hand with his own in recognition of her lie, before pushing himself back against the wall and the support it offered him.

"But you were slipping away too, weren't you?" He watched the smile fade from her face and knew he was right. "All the while they've been putting on a show, focussed on themselves, they're in danger of forgetting about more than your

Granddad until it's too late. I'm guessing they've missed the gap growing between them and you too."

Katy stood and walked to the window where she pulled back the curtain a little. Outside it was grey but with a trace of brightness; the kind of morning you know can go either way. A postman cycled by on his way home or back to the depot after an early morning round.

"My Mum has." She spoke to the back of the departing anonymous postman. It seemed safer. "Not my Dad. I think he's trying to hold on. He's certainly never forgotten me. Lately we've become closer than ever I think; I'm probably as close to him as I've ever been. And you know it's funny." As she paused, she felt Tom's arms enclose her. He had risen from the bed and was holding her in a gentle bear-hug.

"What's funny?" He whispered.

"In a way I think that, with all the shit that's happening, he may be the one who actually ends up growing more than the rest of us. Properly growing, I mean. I think Mum's just going to change the scenery; that's about it. But, hey, I'm not sure I care any more."

"I think you do."

"Well, Mister Smarty-no-pants," she said, turning and giving him a brief kiss, wanting to have spoken enough for now, to be able to move on into the day, "you can't be right all the time, can you? Toast?"

"We take steps; little ones, big ones"

"Is that how you see it, a risk?"

Liam's question is delivered to Rachel's back, the path having significantly narrowed at this point to force them to walk in Indian file. He has needed to let go of her hand at the very moment he wants to hold it the most, as if being able to do so will allow him to transfer his thoughts and feelings more directly. He wants her to understand - this perhaps more than anything he has ever shared with her - but instead feels as if he is balancing on a tightrope with no safety harness.

The walk had been his idea. They'd had nothing planned, and given the weather had finally turned its back on the unseasonal wind and rain from the previous few days, it seemed an ideal opportunity. Camped in the house for too much of the long weekend already, they had been getting under each other's feet, the inclement weather leading both of them to eschew any suggestion of venturing outside. Shopping was out of the question as the city centre would be busy and they had no desire to venture further. There was nothing they needed to buy anyway. Surreptitiously, Liam had checked the programme at the local cinema, but there was little of interest on offer unless you liked science fiction or were under the age of seven. Once or twice he had tried to broach the subject, the topic on which he needed closure, but the conversation had bounced around, first in the kitchen and then in the lounge, with no prospect of getting anywhere. Indeed, in doubling back on themselves, the words only succeeded in creating a cacophony inside him, and Liam knew clarity was needed if they were to reach a conclusion.

Rachel had been reluctant. The idea of a walk so soon after the rain had not filled her with enthusiasm, and she had sited poor underfoot conditions as soon as it became evident that Liam was not to be put off easily. "We'll keep to the paths," he had promised, and then pointed out that the hoi polloi tended not to invade National Trust parkland in quite the same way they descended on everywhere else during a Bank Holiday

Monday. To an extent he had been right, but the car park was still pretty full and the paths dominated by buggies, children, and mongrels yapping at all and sundry. His subsequent suggestion that they cut through the Pleasure Grounds and go round by the small lake in order to get to the café had been readily accepted.

Eyes more or less fixed on their increasingly wet boots, they had walked on in silence for a while before he had ventured that they really needed to come to a conclusion about whether or not they should try for a family. He had felt Rachel's hand tense in his own, but at least she had not let it go until the path had forced her to do so.

"Well perhaps not a risk," he hears her say, "at least not in the sense that I suspect you mean it."

"In what sense then?"

"In the sense of how much will change. We've worked so hard, both of us. We have a life now that is settled, sorted; we're on an even keel, aren't we? And we have freedom. We can go where we want, do what we want. Do you want to give that up?"

As a brief patch of longer grass clears, Rachel waits for him but keeps her hands in her pockets; they had retreated there to ensure she avoided any encroaching stinging nettles.

"I don't see how we'll be giving anything up."

"What about last year and that wine-tasting weekend we did on the spur of the moment? Or that trip to Italy? We won't be able to do any of that, not for a long time. Not until it's too late, until we're too old."

"And that's your risk?" Liam asks.

Rachel nods, then slips an arm through his. He presses it to his side.

"But isn't there an even greater risk?"

She says nothing. It is an argument she has heard before.

"Isn't the risk that if we don't at least try we may end up regretting it for the rest of our lives? Or that in a few years you'll suddenly find yourself wishing you'd been a mother, maybe seeing your friends with their families. Then it will be too late. Doesn't that worry you, Rachel?"

She sighs.

"Of course it does, you know that. But it seems such a throw of the dice, such a gamble."

"Having children?"

"What if we can't? What then? Or what if I'm a useless mother? Right now I'm not sure I'm feeling what I ought to be feeling if we were going to make that decision, so isn't that some kind of clue? And my job. What if they won't take me back? Or what if our child were to be - I don't know - disabled or something? What if I became fat and ugly and you left me?"

He laughs gently.

"As if you could ever be fat or ugly."

"Actually, you were supposed to say 'as if I would ever leave you' - but second prize is good enough for now." She unhooks her arm and lets it swing by her side.

"There are an awful lot of reasons why not," Liam says, slowly. "I suppose there always will be."

"And not enough reasons why?" Rachel suggests.

"Not enough logical ones, perhaps. But since when is having children logical? At least these days? Once upon a time having a big family was all about self-protection for when you were old and grey; it was about having someone to look after you when you became decrepit."

"That's not selling me the idea!" She laughs.

"You know what I mean." Liam pauses. In the distance, down by the water, three children are paddling in the shallows, shouting and spraying each other with water. "Wanting kids is about something more than that. It's about proving things. About proving how much I love you, and about how all I want is for us to be together, always. It's about celebrating all of that. And the chance for us to have something even more special between us. It's about sharing that magic." He lets the words hang for a moment. "Or it is for me."

Ahead of them, a little further downhill, the path becomes visible and with it the strolling traffic. A shout makes its way up to them from somewhere. Rachel stops.

"But aren't you afraid?" she asks.

"Afraid?"

"Forget all that risk stuff if you want to." She allows the sounds of the day to intrude for a moment, knowing that what she is about to say is at the nub of her argument, its real heart. "Aren't you afraid? Deep down, in amongst all that idealistic, dreamy, Hollywood-style imagery, doesn't the reality of it frighten you? Just a little bit?"

Liam puts an arm around her shoulder but says nothing, knowing she has not yet finished speaking.

"Because when you start - when 'it' starts - there's no going back. It will be like jumping off a cliff and hoping the water's deep enough to save you."

"That's a strange analogy," he suggests.

"But isn't it right, though? One minute you're standing safe on the ground, and the next you're falling through the air. There's no in-between. And there's no parachute either; once you're falling, you're falling. And even though it's such a small step, it just changes everything."

He knows she is right. As she waits for him to reply, he knows he cannot argue against her. And it is clear Rachel knows that too.

"Once," he begins, more slowly, "I took a small step. I was standing next to a beautiful girl in a bookshop and I spoke to her. That changed everything. Everything." Although he is looking towards the path, the tree-line beyond, anywhere at that moment rather than Rachel, he can sense her smile. He has always been able to do that. "And we do that all the time. We take steps; little ones, big ones. And after each and every one of them our lives are changed irretrievably, irreparably, irrevocably. And not always for the better, I'll give you that.

Who knows, one day one of us might take such a step that pulls us apart; or someone else might. Who knows? Take a job, don't take a job; buy a house, don't buy a house."

"Like that awful place in Putney!" Rachel says suddenly laughing.

"Yes," Liam looks at her now. "That was a step I'm really glad we decided not to take!" They both allow a gentle chuckle its place in their conversation before Liam goes on. "And now I'm standing on the edge of your cliff, if you like. And I think the water's plenty deep enough. But it isn't the kind of step I want to take alone. Or rather, it's a step I want to take with you, and with no-one else."

She takes his hand and they link fingers automatically. Then she nudges them forwards and down toward the path.

"Trying to solve an impossible puzzle"

Tabby had once told her that she lacked staying power, that she never finished things off. It had been late and they'd been out to the pub together, had one drink too many. They were the kind of 'soft drunk' that loosens the tongue enough for you to say what you really want without being out of control.

"That's a bit rich coming from you," Katy had protested, but then found herself unable to back-up her retort.

The difference between Katy and Tabatha was that her friend never declared an intention to complete anything, her aim seemingly to float through life bouncing off things and people until she finally stuck somewhere. A counterpoint, Katy was surrounded by half-finished projects - something Tabby was happy to point out in support of her argument. Among her remnants were unglazed pots from the pottery class she had kept up for five weeks; the forlorn sports' gear in her bedroom drawers that were allied to an under-used and now expired gym membership; the novel she had tried to write. Her main proof - though here Katy felt they were on level ground, although for different reasons - was in her inability to hold on to a man.

"I don't pretend *I'm* looking for Mr Right," Tabby had said. "Not even in my plans. One day it may happen, and that's fine. But you…"

"What about me?"

"That's the one thing you really do need. And want - if you're honest with yourself. But you'll never get what you want if you don't recognise it - and you don't let yourself go."

Tom had been the focal point of the argument. Having progressed to the status of boyfriend - or, as Tabby had crudely put it, "made all the bases *and* hit a home run in record time" - their relationship had normalised somewhat.

"Stalled; that's what I'd call it," Tabitha had said, ungenerously.

From Katy's perspective they had reached 'a certain level'. Things had progressed quickly, she admitted, and because of that - and because she needed time to evaluate - it was only right and proper that she take her foot off the gas.

"Is it wrong of me to want to do that?" Katy had offered in rebuttal. "I don't see why things should continue at such breakneck speed. That's not how I work."

And indeed it wasn't. Yet Katy was obviously well aware that in Tom's case it was exactly how she *had* operated, thereby giving the lie to her defence. Her problem - and the challenge she had posed to herself - was two-fold; firstly to try and understand why she had allowed herself to be so cavalier where Tom was concerned, and secondly, to decipher what the future might hold. Of the two, it was the second of these conundrums which occupied her the most, the primary problem being that in accelerating through the gears to the point where they had quickly become lovers, Katy had yet to establish whether or not she actually liked him.

She was well aware that this was tackling things the wrong way round, but had deliberately refrained from sharing her analysis. Tabby friend would, she knew, simply use it against her in some way, most likely as a means of being able to demonstrate that *she* was a paragon of semi-virtue; after all, she would never go to bed with a man if she didn't know whether or not she liked him in the first place. And Katy knew that for all Tabby's faults - and for her considerable catalogue of very short-lived relationships - this was indeed true.

It seemed a strange thing to contemplate, whether or not she actually liked the man with whom she was regularly sleeping. Tom had made vague comments about them moving in together - or more specifically, she moving in with him - using loose references to saving money as the primary argument. Although she was hardly poor, money was tight, and Katy would have welcomed not having to spend nearly half her income on her little flat. But money was a secondary consideration, especially if she lacked the certainty to move - in all senses of the word.

In concert with her inability to process exactly how she felt about Tom was something even more nebulous. Sometimes she had looked at her mother and wondered how much she liked her too. Katy found herself trying to deconstruct her mother's character, and then rebuild it in such a way so as to see if she could find herself in it. In what way was she like her mother - not now so much, but rather as she imagined she must have been at her age? The reservations Katy had about her - past or present - lacked definition, but reservations there were. Sometimes they surfaced in a glance, seeing her mother in a certain profile, in a turn of phrase, or in the way she occasionally spoke to her husband. "Am I like that?" Katy asked herself, simultaneously wanting - and not wanting - to know the answer. All of this uncertainty (Tabby would have called it 'insecurity') contributed to the difficulty in knowing whether or not she liked Tom. Had she liked any of her previous boyfriends? If you weren't sufficiently self-aware, then how could you possibly know? Under those circumstances, where is the mirror true enough for you to hold up and judge? Katy might well have extended that thought and used it as an excuse for her unfinished projects too. The pottery experiment had been just that: an attempt at discovery, to find an answer - however partial - to the question 'is this me?' She might well have countered Tabby's accusation with a riposte that "when I finish something I will have found myself", but that would have sounded too vacuous.

Wisdom - or lack of naïvety - was one of the things she liked about her grandfather the most. As she had grown older, she appreciated how Ronald had endured all the standard personal challenges and sorted himself out. An increasing awareness of how little she knew about herself, made *his* self-knowledge all the more alluring; being in his presence offered her a degree of comfort neither of her parents could match. There were glimpses of it in her father and she relished those, but in her mother she saw something else; it was wisdom and self-knowledge to a degree, but of a different order, even of a different dimension. For all this affinity with her grandfather, she was obviously unable to ask *him* if she liked Tom. It would have been a ridiculous question. So whichever way she looked at it, she was on her own; and being on her own, a pause seemed the only sensible approach to buy her time to find an answer.

"What's wrong, Katy?"

They had settled on going to the cinema, but daunted by the size of the queue for a film they were ambivalent about seeing in the first place, they decided to abandon their plan. Two hundred yards from the Odeon was a new gastro wine bar Tom had been keen to explore for some time, and in order to ensure the evening didn't prove a complete wash-out, Katy had agreed to try it out. Although she had been wrestling with her question about him - that fundamental assessment - for the previous couple of days, she had convinced herself it was suitably compartmentalised, secure under mental lock-and-key, so as not to get in the way. Because of that, his own question genuinely surprised her.

"Wrong? Nothing. Why?" She tried to strike an upbeat note, and smiled as she raised her glass.

"You seem a bit preoccupied. You weren't disappointed about not seeing the film?"

"Of course not. You know I wasn't that sold on seeing it."

"Me neither." Tom changed tack. "It's not this place is it?"

"What about it?"

"I don't know," he paused to take a look around as if doing so would give him a clue. "Too noisy, maybe?"

Katy scanned the room too. She did so as if noise might be visible - and she had the power to see it peeping out from behind the bar or under the tables of diners.

"No; I don't think it's too bad. It's certainly not as loud as that Italian place on the corner, or 'The Pumphouse'."

Tom nodded in agreement, even though his face said something else.

"What?" Katy said, trying not to sound as if she were accusing him of something unstated, but fearing she was failing miserably.

"I don't know. You've been kind of quiet. Not like you, I suppose. I just wondered, you know? If there was anything the matter."

From behind the bar came the sound of breaking glass and, just like everyone else, they turned for a moment to locate the sound. They saw the heads of two of the staff disappear as they bent down to clean up the mess.

"It's my Granddad," she said, still looking towards the bar. When she looked back at Tom he was already staring at her. It was her stock answer and a card she was concerned she played far too often; but at least there was an element of truth in it.

"Not bad news?"

"No, nothing like that. I just worry about him, you know? I mean, I know he's not well, but he always brushes it off. And my folks never seem that concerned. Especially my Mum."

"Time-wise, is it getting really serious?"

She shrugged her shoulders. There was a question akin to that she had been asking herself about Tom: was it getting serious? Unsurprisingly, thus far it had proven to be a question without an answer. Or rather a question which provoked others. She couldn't help but recall the conversation with Tabby - 'home run' and all - and the fundamental poser, did she like the man who was sitting opposite her? And if she didn't know, what kind of a person did that make her, given the relationship they now had? Fundamental uncertainty about him had progressed to suspicions about herself, and so if in consequence she had become distracted, absent, should it have been a surprise that Tom had noticed it?

She tried to retrieve the thread of the conversation from which she had abdicated responsibility.

"Who knows? No-one tells me anything." She wanted to add "not even myself", but that was a different tack altogether and not one to which Tom was privy.

Letting it go, he glanced away and back towards the bar where order had seemingly been restored, the full complement of staff now attending to customers. Katy watched his profile, his face turned, attempting to be as dispassionate as possible in her assessment of how he looked; surely that might prove a means to uncover how she felt, or perhaps how she should feel.

When he looked back at her, she was rewarded with a slow smile.

"You look like you're trying to work out a Rubik cube in your head," he said. "You've got that kind of frown people have when they're trying to solve an impossible puzzle."

"Do I?" She laughed in spite of herself and allowed the frown to be chased away. His was a nice smile. "Difficult, maybe," she offered, "but not impossible."

"Are you going to let me in on the secret?"

"I don't think so; not yet anyway." She drained her glass and pushed it across the table. "And a Rubik cube *can* be solved, of course."

"Yes, but not in your head!" With an upright palm, Tom gestured towards her glass. "Another?"

Katy, knowing he would offer, had her answer ready. There was nothing wrong with the bar, but it would probably be better on another night with some of her other friends. It was the kind of place Tabby would readily adopt.

"I don't think so; I've got a puzzle to solve, remember?"

Following her lead, Tom stood up, willingly taking the hand she presented to him. Giving it a squeeze, she couldn't help but wonder how many of her unspoken messages got through to him - and how many were misinterpreted, falling wide of the mark.

Outside, it had started to rain again and they were greeted with the remnants of that unique smell of freshness when the heat and the dust of the city gets washed away. Tom pulled her close to him, and they hurried away, destined for his flat.

"There are lots of reasons to be positive"

There are some questions you should never answer while you are angry. How long Liam has known this life-lesson he is unable to say. Indeed, he may not consciously be aware of it, rather steering himself by an automatic pilot which has kicked into gear without his knowledge. Perhaps it is wisdom; the kind of wisdom that one accrues through age and experience - even those experiences one would rather not have had.

It doesn't help that Katy is the one who has asked the question; asked it in innocence, out of concern. Liam knows people will challenge you for a whole host of reasons, and not simply because there is something they are seeking to uncover. They need to be seen to be asking, or they are making mischief; they want to pretend concern, or demonstrate superiority. Most of it is play-acting. Liam is certain none of which applies to Katy - and not just because she is his daughter. They have tried - he and Rachel - to raise her to value honesty and fellow-feeling. When she was a child and inevitably exposed to those less pleasant characters and characteristics that come to the fore with self-exploration and self-development, they would try and explain people, the world, and how it all worked. He had never been entirely sure how well they had done until she was in her late-teens and they suddenly realised they had bypassed the trauma of the 'difficult years' most other parents railed about. Ronald helped too. He was almost the arbiter, the judge who assessed the tie-break question. If ever Katy needed confirmation, she turned to her grandfather.

So when she asked him "How are you?" she did so because she truly wanted to know the answer; the enquiry was not borne out of self-interest, but of selfless concern; it was not an end in itself, but one that might lead to help and assistance if she found herself in a position to offer it. Beneath the surface of such a simple question lay a panoply of meaning and inference, a minefield even. Katy might have prepared him with a whole substrata of context and qualification, removing obfuscation, clarifying that she meant 'A' and not 'B', that she expected his answer to be specific, laser-sharp, even though her query was as vague and generic as it was possible to be.

Liam saw all of that. The evidence of it, this context, existed all around him, not just in the concrete, but in the subtle inference from his demeanour or the words he now used when he spoke. Whether aware of it or not, he had adopted a new lexicon, and had taken to describing things in a changed way, from a revised viewpoint. The stack of unpacked boxes he was gradually working through, opening and emptying, spoke most eloquently. They were neatly piled in one corner of the room that now doubled as both lounge and study. Given those in the old house had been in-built, he had needed to purchase new bookcases, and had gradually assembled them into something approaching 'a wall', hoping that his mass of books would overwhelm the stark and crass melamine and submit 'Billy' to an almost invisible supporting role. He had been confused by the name, how 'Billy' might have been arrived at as the moniker for a range of bookcases. It didn't matter, of course, but he had recently found himself more inquisitive as far as language was concerned and had taken to a greater interrogation of words. Face-value had betrayed him, he had decided. Perhaps this was why he found it so natural to deconstruct Katy's elemental question.

The books were proving problematic, however. Assuming his task would be one of simply unpacking and arranging, enforcing sequence and order upon them, Liam had found less mechanical considerations getting in the way. As he lifted a book from a box, he had been unable to do anything else other than forensically challenge it, finding he needed to understand its presence, to reestablish his connection with it; he wanted to recall where it had come from, when he had bought it, the circumstances of that purchase. Only then was he able to decide where it belonged. Or, indeed, if it belonged at all. Without shock, occasionally he came across a book that was out of place, as if overnight it had become flawed or scarred, contaminated in some way, even traitorous. Beyond the boxes was a small but growing pile of those that had failed to make the cut and were most definitely *not* destined for his new shelves. Most, though not all, had been gifts from Rachel. Perhaps it had been these - Katy noticing them for the first time as she stood in what he jokingly called "his bachelor pad" - which had triggered the question. She knew he seldom threw books away, and yet there they were, destined for some charity shop. Or worse.

And how is he? It is a question of some merit, and one he does not rush to answer. A few weeks have passed since he vacated the house, choosing a tactical if not entirely gallant retreat from the field of battle. He had put up some resistance initially, but then caved in, suddenly too weary for the fight. Work had been something of a godsend, occupying him for most of the daylight hours. He had fitted in slices of time for house-hunting, quickly settling on the third rental he had seen. Having chosen the edge of The Lakes as a suitable landing site, a Settle location had been fine, the house a little small but not too expensive. But best of all, it had been available, furnished, ready for him. He had asked permission to add bookcases to the lounge. The agent had liaised with an invisible landlord and assured him he could do so. He was, he discovered, an ideal prospect: solvent and long-term. He had kept all non-essential details well away from the tenancy application form.

Katy had been his yardstick. It was unfair to use her in that way he knew, but he wanted a second opinion to ensure the house passed muster. She seemed most pleased that there was a second bedroom should she ever want to stay. When she had helped him move in he had dutifully asked after Tom, just as any parent was supposed to do; and now, two weeks later, she had returned and was asking after *him*.

"I seem to be coping reasonably well," he says after a moment's reflection, two volumes of Fielding in his hands. "So far I've managed to feed myself adequately - if not fearlessly and, on occasion, experimentally!" Katy laughs on cue. "I am keeping myself clean - though I fear the house slightly less so - so probably eight out of ten."

"That's good," she says, dipping into the most prominent box and retrieving three volumes of poetry by people unknown to her. She watches as Liam locates the Fieldings in their new home then reaches for the books she is now holding. He seems strangely regimented.

"I'm busy at work, of course, which is good. And I'm beginning to build some kind of a routine. You know how I like my routine!"

It is a line delivered as if he were stating a well-known fact, but it is one Katy struggles to assign to her father. There had been routine at home, yes, but it always seemed to be driven by her mother, as if that was what *she* needed to get her through the day. She wonders if everything is now turned upside down.

"So I think the short answer to your question is 'good', all things considered. I'm trying to stay positive. There are lots of reasons to be positive."

If Liam is thinking of elaborating, the first book of the three Katy has just handed him stops him short. Most of his books bear an inscription on the inside of the cover, usually his name and the date the book was acquired. In this instance, he doesn't even bother to look. He passes it back to Katy.

"For the pile I think, don't you?" He says it as if she is in on the secret.

She takes it from him and places it on top of a duplicated copy of Keats' collected works. There is no questioning involved; she is happy to be subservient to the certainty he displays.

"Shall we have some tea?" Liam asks, dropping the remaining two books he holds onto a nearby chair. "I might even have some of those rather indulgent florentines you so like!"

Said with such a flourish, Katy knows her father has bought them especially for her; a treat for helping him out this Saturday morning. She is happy to do so having left Tom still half-asleep in bed, driving the twenty-five minutes across town before the shoppers came out in force, and then away north.

Liam has always been an early riser. While the rest of the house was still asleep, he was most often found pottering in the garden, especially when it was fine. He liked early spring mornings the best: light enough to be useful, but still with a jagged chill in the air, the kind of benevolent stabbing that made you feel alive, open to the promise of everything. His new house sits on a small plot in a neat cul-de-sac. Each of the nine or ten houses owns a small rectangle of front lawn and another slightly larger plot at the back bounded by bright orange fence panels. It was the only time he had let his guard slip when he had first shown the place to Katy.

"Bookcases they will let me have, but sadly not a garden I can truly call my own."

He had asked permission to cultivate extensively and been refused. The agent had been sympathetic, but the rebuttal - "who will look after it once you've gone?" - was not to be denied. Liam had wanted to answer that the next tenant would, that the landlord could insist upon it, but he was conscious how feeble such an argument sounded. More significantly, the exchange had made it crystal clear to him just how temporary and transient he might be. A refugee. He had been used to permanence and rootedness; the garden at his old home had been testament to that, acreage that was his and which he lovingly tendered month after month knowing he would always be there to do so. Except now he wasn't. He felt as if he had become a statistic. As he stands by the kitchen window waiting for the kettle to boil, conscious of Katy sitting at the small breakfast bar behind him - complete with florentines! - he looks out at the plain lawn, the garden with limited potential, and suddenly feels exactly what he is: a man alone. More than that, however, there are adjectives - perhaps many adjectives - he can choose to apply to Liam-as-man, and few of them are positive. He plays with the good ones in his head: 'free', 'independent' - the kind of words Rachel had used when she had been pleading her case. Or their case, as she had professed to see it. But those words were soon trumped by others: 'bereft', 'solitary', 'rejected', 'old'. It was the last one which caught him by surprise the most. He could do something about being alone if he chose to; he could try and turn some of the others around, even to the extent of finding a tenuous way to make Rachel's appellations apply. But he could do nothing about his age. And suddenly, out of nowhere, there was a new foe; one that had been waiting in the wings for him, lurking, skulking about, only now to show its hand as the boiling kettle switched itself off with a resounding 'click'.

How was he now? Perhaps four out of ten.

"At some point I realised I needed something else"

Other women, perhaps the more reckless ones, would have taken the opportunity to completely re-vamp their wardrobe; and whilst doing so had been appealing to Rachel - the ensuing blitz a tangible manifestation of her new-found station in life - she had not entirely lost her sense of the practical. There was no need for a purge on the grounds of space. She had waited until Liam had departed - a leaving so pointedly thorough that she found herself unexpectedly surprised - and then migrated any newly relegated clothes into the dead wardrobe space he had left behind. It was as close to throwing away as she could manage. Elsewhere about the house, odd reminders of him remained: an old mug or glass; the two prints in the hall he had paid handsomely for but which she had never really liked; that old chair of his in the now rarely used study. Rachel was happy enough to leave these things in situ. She did not know if her action - or lack of action - was down to fondness, the desire to keep memories alive, or as some kind of trophy, a reminder of that from which she had escaped. Perhaps it was an insurance policy of some kind. But then again, if she could not find the source of her motivation it was probably because she gave it no concerted thought at all.

Not unnaturally she had reflected on her clothes a great deal, even more so since she had met David. Her refusal to splurge was governed by two things to which she *did* give some consideration. The first was money. Without Liam around, she already had evidence of how much tighter she would have to control her purse strings. She was far from poverty-stricken, but quickly realised greater financial prudence was called for. The second factor to dissuade her from any form of unnecessary excess was her age. It is not unheard of for mature women to look in the mirror searching for the person they once were. Indeed, in all probability men will do so just as much - and reach the same vain conclusion: if you dress as you feel, or as you want to feel, or as you once felt, well, wouldn't that do the trick?

Rachel was wise enough not to fall for that. But she also knew she had the advantage of not looking her age (people had always told her so), and the day-to-day clothes to which she was already accustomed was - and had been for years - suitable for someone five or ten years younger. Attempting to push back the boundaries even further would, she saw, risk crossing a line, a frontier from which the inevitable future return could only be painful and humiliating.

There was no mawkish sentimentality in her not wishing to throw things away. She had always been reserved when it came to material possessions, not in their acquisition, but rather in their retention. More than once there had been incidents with Liam when they had clashed over the need to keep some insignificant item or other. He had seemed happy to sweep away even those things once held precious. "Everything has a lifespan" he had told her once; if that were true, then she allocated durations against many things which far exceeded his own. She took the barb that she was a "hoarder" light-heartedly enough and pointed to his pathological attachment to his books. Once she had jokingly pointed out that she hadn't thrown *him* away.

That there was no material external stimulus in play made her decision not to act on wardrobe expansion, to perpetuate the status quo, an easy one. But from where would such a stimulus have emanated? Liam had never been much of a sounding board, so his absence made no difference; and her father's opinion on the matter - if indeed he held one - would have carried scant weight with her. It was entirely possible that at some point someone else might step into that particular void, but it was far too early to know if David might be that person. His compliments had, thus far, been safe and superficial. Rachel suspected he was operating according to some inter-gender playbook that gave instruction on the what, when and how of compliment-giving. An assertion one day that he "liked her shoes" had only succeeded in making her suspicious.

Her obvious sidekick for anything sartorial should have been Katy. However, they had seen less of each other since Liam had moved out; a consequence Rachel found somewhat surprising. She had assumed, once the dust had settled, the two of them would be able to cultivate a better mother-daughter relationship, in part because the man who linked them was, to all intents and purposes, out of the way. Not that her ex-husband had been a barrier. Indeed, Rachel was not so naïve as to fail to see Katy's heart was biased towards him, but she had hoped that this new circumstance - of independent girls together - might strengthen their bond. Any evidence suggesting such a hope was at best optimistic Rachel chose to downgrade in significance, as if her doing so made a tangible difference, one which would cause Katy to instinctively respond more positively toward her.

"What do you think?" she had asked, twirling dutifully in the hallway one day when Katy had arrived, as bidden, for tea. Rachel had taken half an hour to choose something to wear that was suitably chic and just young enough, as if she had a point to prove.

"What am I supposed to think?" Katy had asked, moving past her. "This is tea not a fashion show, right?"

Rachel had been stunned by the brusque nature of the response, and it had taken a couple of seconds for her to regain her composure before following her daughter into the kitchen.

"I'm sorry," Katy had said immediately. "Rough day."

"Work?"

"Not really."

Having the good sense to leave it there, Rachel busied herself with the tea things. She pulled a Victoria sponge from the fridge.

"I'd like to claim to have made it, but I can't. Or rather, I won't, because you'd see straight through that."

"Are you supposed to keep it in there?"

"The fridge?"

Katy nodded.

"I assumed so, because of the cream..." Rachel allowed the uncertainty to hang until she was rescued by the boiling kettle demanding her attention.

As she poured water into the teapot, she was conscious of Katy's eyes on her; and then, as its lid clinked into place, sensed her moving away and into the lounge. Turning back, Rachel noticed the cake and attendant plates and cutlery had gone with her too. "She's making an effort," she thought, softening.

Katy had already sliced the sponge and taken her first forkful by the time Rachel joined her.

"It's not too bad actually," she said.

"Bad?"

"I mean, the sponge isn't too cold. I think cold sponge tastes - I don't know - not right somehow; but this seems good."

Rachel put down the cups of tea she had just poured.

"More by luck than judgement," she suggested. It was partly a test, to see if Katy, having been given the opportunity to do so, would be tempted to criticise further. She did not, her attention dedicated to loading her fork with a second mouthful.

"Nice." Katy glanced up at her mother, knowing a comment of some kind would have been expected. "This isn't just any Victoria sponge," she began, then paused.

It was an old joke, one started by Liam. Rachel knew her punchline was "this is an M&S Victoria sponge", but she chose not to deliver it, hoping that her smile was all the recognition needed. The last thing she wanted was to find reasons for them to talk about Liam. This wasn't what the afternoon was supposed to be about: it was for the two of them, a chance to connect, to be a pair, a discrete slice of a family. Rachel didn't want that contaminated.

"How's Tom?" she asked, her tone attempting to suggest genuine interest at best, neutrality at worst.

Katy glanced up then loaded her fork again. The question had been teed up from the moment she had walked through the door, and she hated herself for not simply saying "yes" when her mother had asked if work had been the cause of her rough day. Now she would have to lie and concoct something plausible; after all, exposing the truth - the ongoing uncertainty over whether she even liked Tom or not - was too horrendous to contemplate. Some relationships could operate at that extreme level of honesty, but Katy now doubted whether her mother had ever been in one of those. She wanted to ask her father if the two of them had been totally candid with each other about anything and everything; but she knew the answer she would be given was unlikely to be trustworthy - and that felt like the benchmark for the situation in which she now found herself.

"He's fine. A bit grouchy. Maybe we both are, you know. I mean, work's been a bit of a challenge recently. Long days for him. Sometimes it's like that, isn't it?"

Rachel looked at the plate bearing her untouched slice of sponge. She knew Katy wanted her to say "yes", and to give examples, to demonstrate that she understood. It was the response most parents would have given. But she struggled to reconcile such a situation with her own experience, her life with Liam. Yes, they had both worked hard from time-to-time, and there had been stresses and strains, especially in the early years. But she had stopped working when she became pregnant, and although intending otherwise, never returned. If there were parallels with Katy's 'rough day', they were too far back for Rachel to recall, even if she wanted to. There seemed, all of a sudden, something serene and untroubled about her passage through life - especially the last twenty-five years or so; yet rather than be grateful for that, more than anything else she found herself annoyed by it. Whilst most people would have been glad to have had such a smooth ride, Rachel now regretted hers. She could not definitively say that she wanted to experience again the kind of difficulty and mild trauma Katy was so obviously in the midst of, but she would have liked the *choice*. Living, she now understood, was all about challenge and new things, and she resented - almost afresh - the fact that Liam had made things so easy for her. It was another slant on the charge laid at the door of a man already tried and convicted, so from that perspective the complaint was essentially worthless; but it did serve to justify afresh the decision she had made, the action she had taken. Her untroubled passage had become a further catalyst. She wanted to be in Katy's shoes for just a short while, to see what disquiet felt like. Feeling anew; that was her mantra now.

"I suppose we had our moments," she offered, prepared to compromise having had her strategy unexpectedly vindicated by her daughter's simple question, "especially when we were about your age." As soon as she had uttered those words, Rachel regretted them; not because they were superficial or disingenuous, but because they opened the door for Katy to prod and probe. "But things are different these days, aren't they?" Rachel's question was an attempt to slam shut the door she had just opened.

"In what way?" Obligingly, Katy leant against it.

"Oh, I don't know. Aren't expectations different? Isn't there a different kind of pressure? Everything seems to be faster-paced, more immediate. Do young people really play for the long game any more?"

"By 'long game' you mean…?"

"You know: one love, two-point-four children - or whatever the number is now - the forever-home, the car, the good job. Till death do us, and all that. Isn't that a cliché for people your age? Lives seem to be led in soundbites, so I assume relationships might be the same."

Katy's face made it clear to Rachel she was wide of the mark.

"Do you think we're that shallow?" she asked with some heat.

"No, dear, not shallow. That's not what I meant at all. But everyone seems in something of a hurry. It's all 'instant'. Click, swipe, like, don't like, move on. Or am I being unfair?"

There was a short pause. Rachel looked at her piece of Victoria sponge again, subconsciously waiting for it to reach room temperature.

"There are some people a little bit like that," Katy confessed. "Tabby - you remember Tabitha? - I think she's a bit like that. 'Fail fast'; that could be her motto."

"I like that," Rachel laughed. "'Fail fast'!"

"But you don't think I'm like Tabby, do you? Not really?"

Rachel allowed herself a moment to draw the mental parallel.

"No, of course not. You've never been like that, and I didn't mean to suggest you were. 'Fail fast' indeed! You're much more measured and thoughtful, considered. Don't you think that's right?"

"I guess so. Which means that rough days are harder for me, because just trashing what's causing them and moving on isn't the way I work. It's not the way you brought me up, so you should take some credit for that."

Smiling, Rachel allowed herself to spear some of the cake onto her fork. It was a mother-and-daughter conversation, finally. Mission accomplished.

"But what about you?" Katy said, instantly preventing Rachel's fork from leaving her plate.

"Me?"

"What are looking for now, Mum? If you've ditched all those things you said - the home, the forever-love, and all that - what are you looking for? I mean, when you're younger..." Katy stopped seeing a gaping hole appear before her.

"Why should it be any different? I think I'm looking for pretty much the same things I always have been," Rachel tried to sound as sincere as she could, but the term 'ditched' had riled her. "But what do you mean, 'when you're younger'?"

There was no way Katy could retreat.

"Just that you've more time, I suppose. You know? You can afford to make a few mistakes along the way because you've got time to put them right. Well, most of them anyway." She added the last phrase knowing people who had made some dreadful mistakes - bad relationships, children too early - from which there was no coming back. It was one of the scenarios which played constantly in her head, one reason why deciding whether or not she liked Tom was so crucial.

Rachel allowed the fork to resume its journey to her mouth, determined to make the pause uncomfortable for her daughter. The shop-bought sponge was better than she had expected it to be. Katy waited for her to finish, confused how her mother could be looking for the same things she had already found with her father. How had they become devalued, invalid?

"But I'm not young any more, am I?" Rachel said. She was trying to smile as she said it, but her face was rebelling against her. It almost hurt to remain calm and benign. "You're wondering what my approach is going to be or what my goals are given I haven't got enough time left to afford to make mistakes. Is that it?" She left another gap, Katy's expression making it clear she had no intention of filling it. "Well maybe I shall have to learn to 'fail fast'. Perhaps I should take some lessons from Tabitha."

"Mum!"

The shock on Katy's face surprised Rachel. She assumed it was because her daughter was amazed that she could be capable of such 'young thinking', but actually the phrase had compelled Katy to overlay the behaviours and social mores of people like Tabby onto her mother. It was the incongruity of the combination, the picture of how that might make her mother behave, how she might 'look', which had stunned her.

"Is there anything wrong in wanting to live a little before I'm too old? Or before I qualify for my bus pass and zimmer frame, and you have me committed to some institution or other?" Out of instinct and experience, Rachel tried to capture the moral high ground.

"No, of course not."

"Then what, Katy? Because there's something there; I can hear it in your voice."

"Maybe I just don't understand."

"Why I feel the need to embrace life?" Rachel laughed. She hadn't meant to, but it had escaped before she could smother it.

"No, not that." Katy, trapped in a corner - by her own words as much as anything else - had nowhere to go. "I guess I don't understand what was missing in your life - or why you had to sacrifice Dad in order to do so."

Rachel pushed the plate bearing her half-finished sponge away from her as if she was making room to expand or explode. She did the same with her cup.

"Sacrifice?" The word trembled as it left her mouth, as if it was afraid of being launched into the world. "You'll see one day." She paused. "No, I hope you don't see one day; I hope you never find out. Sacrifice? The only person who has made the sacrifice is the person talking to you now. Me. Not your father. What has he given up? He built a life on his terms, driven by what was important to him. It was his framework, his ambition, his rules. The house, the job, the safe holidays, the normality of it all. The shed, the garden, his precious vegetables. Those stupid pictures in the hall, the crockery and cutlery I hate. You wouldn't have seen that, Katy, how could you? But I was surrounded by what he wanted. The things that made him happy constrained me." Rachel paused and shook her head. "Not always, of course. Not always. For a long time it was wonderful, gave us stability, set our course. It made us - made you - safe. But at some point I realised I needed something else. Don't ask me what triggered it because I can't tell you. And if I knew, I still might not be able to."

Katy wanted to say something but could not. A new emotion was building inside her and she had no reference point for it, no name.

"Perhaps it started when you left home and became independent, this burgeoning feeling of entrapment." Not meaning to be ruthless, Rachel could not help but cast her net wider in order to catch in it all those who had been holding her back. "Once you had left, maybe some of those knots were loosened. I didn't have to worry about you any more. Perhaps that allowed me to see how empty my life had become."

Unable to recognise the person talking to her, Katy put her hand to her mouth as if to stop something escaping, something harsh and uncultured.

"I had become a slave to routine. I asked myself when was the last time I had been really happy. And I couldn't remember. I asked when I had last done something new, had a new experience, was excited or stimulated. And I couldn't remember." Rachel saw that Katy was about to react, and although she had no idea how that reaction would manifest itself, was compelled to finish answering the question. "And I realised that I wanted all those things again; the happiness, the novel, the stimulation. And that no-one was going to gift those to me on a plate. I had to take responsibility for myself again. It was as simple as that."

When Katy stood up, silently and without comment, Rachel made no effort to coax her back down. She had wanted a connection, and had only succeeded in achieving the opposite. Even though she had said nothing, it was clear all Katy's goodwill towards her - what little there had been - was now lost. Rachel knew she should feel regret over what was happening, remorse that she had caused it, harbour a desire to make amends; but she did not. If anything she felt more resolute, as if she had been through a trial - of her as a person, and of her strategy and course of action - and as a result she was stronger, more likely to successfully pursue her goals, whatever they were.

"You ask me how I am," this to her daughter's retreating back. "I'm good, thank you. And for the first time in more years than I care to remember, I feel free."

Katy's footsteps echoed through the tiled hall, past Liam's pictures, to be followed by the sound of the front door closing quietly.

"Only others can see it in you"

He looks across at his wall of books and tries to remember how his old study had looked. This new view is no longer tainted by boxes waiting to be unpacked, and - as he had hoped - the white edges of the Billy shelves are narrowed and disguised, providing little rectangular frames that, if he is honest, he actually quite likes. Their discrete sections gives his collection structure, and with structure some kind of meaning. Not for the first time his eyes settle on his meagre collection of poetry, and he reminds himself that he needs to read more. Recently he had picked up some Auden and Yeats for the first time in many years - something of a random event as he was unloading the boxes - and found himself stunned by their verse, how they were able to condense so much insight into so few words, such confined spaces. Poetry had always been something of a struggle for him - especially Eliot! - and he recalls being told by one of his old professors how he would be ready for it "one day". The arrival of that day, at some point over the previous year, had surprised him. But it hadn't surprised Alison, who, when he mentioned it to her, simply said "well if you weren't going to get it now, when where you?"

They had been back in Hebden Bridge.

"Look, I'm no poet," she had said, that usual certainty there in her voice, "but I've always thought you need to have lived, been through a lot, have a sufficient and meaningful depth to your life in order to understand the poetic."

"'Sufficient and meaningful depth'?" He had been struck by the phrase.

"You like that?" She fired a low laugh at him. "One of my own - or at least I *think* I just made it up!" Another burst. "But you know what I mean, Liam? Only a good chef can appreciate the subtleties in a great recipe or a great dish; only a skilled craftsman - like a silversmith - can understand what goes into to making something extraordinary, like an exquisite silver dish."

"But you're not saying I'm now a poet?" Liam had teased.

"Of course not! How could you possibly be a poet?"

"How indeed?!"

They had both laughed.

"But you do see what I mean?" she had pursued, her voice softened. "You've been through so much - *are* going through so much. It all adds a richness, a complexity to who we are; and all of those experiences not only shape and influence us, but they mean we can see and understand so much more. I think poetry is a great way to measure that. You see beyond the surface of the words to what's underneath."

"And can you?"

"Can I what?"

"Read poetry? Understand it and get beneath that surface? I suppose I'm asking if you've been through enough - pain, pleasure, whatever - to see what's buried there. Because I don't know. And actually it feels a little bit wrong that I don't, because I feel as if I should, given how much you know about me."

"You want to know more about *me*?"

Liam had been unsure whether Alison was trying to smile or not. There was something slightly contorted about the expression on her face which, unless you had been studying it for a while, you would undoubtedly miss. And he *had* been studying it. Each time they had met it seemed as if he was always the default focus - Alison saw to that - and so he had been forced to try and unravel her by deduction and subterfuge, two skills he simply did not possess. Now there was a new yardstick, introduced by Alison, against which he could try and measure her. It was a simple enough question.

"Yes, if you like. And to know whether or not you can read poetry. I mean, properly read it, just like you're suggesting. Because if you can then your life has depth enough too, doesn't it?"

"I can't flaw your logic," she said, looking around to catch the waitress' eye in order to get the bill. It was as if she were looking for a way out. She turned her attention back to Liam. "I'm not sure I'm the one who's truly able to say. I don't think it's something you can recognise in yourself; I think only others can see it in you."

"But?" Liam had wanted some semblance of success from the exchange.

"But, if you're pushing me, you brute, then I think the answer is 'yes'." She paused to open her purse and remove a credit card. She saw he was about to protest. "My turn."

There was a flurry of activity involving the waitress, the bill and a credit card machine, then they were alone inside their bubble again.

"So what do you think?"

"Me?" He paused. "I think you can read poetry, of course. In fact, in spite of your protests, I think you may be a poet."

The rocket of her laughter shot around the small café, turning heads in the process. Alison threw back her head a little, unable to curtail the explosion. After a few seconds, she looked back his way, then, just as she was about to rise from her chair, leant forwards conspiratorially.

"That," she whispered, "was very naughty!"

Recalling that exchange - prompted by his somewhat vacant contemplation of the bookcase - Liam finds himself blending it with his overall experience of her. It is a concoction which leads him to ask the same question of Rachel; how does she fare against Alison's 'depth' test?

He finds himself smiling, not at anyone in particular other than himself. If he had been challenged to answer whether or not Rachel was 'a poet' - or at least 'poetic' - two or more years ago, he would have unhesitatingly answered in the affirmative. But now he can be more definite. And entirely negative. She is not. If he wonders why his view has changed so radically, then he does so for only a very short time: it is because he has had the qualification criteria newly rewritten. And Alison has done that. It has not affected his self-perception in any way, apart perhaps, for hardening his instinctive sense - a gut feeling - that, in spite of what she said that day in Hebden Bridge, he is not a poetic person. He may be able to see and appreciate more now than he once had, but would prefer to view that as a combination of maturity, of having time, of having the inclination to fill a gap in his reading which has been gnawing at him for over thirty years. He is flattered that Alison chooses to interpret this in such a romantic - no, poetic! - way, but he regards himself, either by nature or nurture, as too literal a character to meet her threshold.

Without hesitation he understands that with Rachel his starting point would have been to gift her the quality of being poetic; she would have earned it that very first day in the bookshop. But he now knows such an award would have been influenced by desire, naïvety, raging hormones, the flash of her midriff as she stretched upwards to that high shelf. On reflection, he guesses that over the years, unobtrusively, he would have gradually discounted the poetic stock she held in his eyes, like an ever-declining value of shares over a prolonged period of time. Not exactly junk stock, but by Alison's measure, Liam suspects Rachel would no longer qualify - although it is entirely possible that her current course of action may well rewards her with the necessary credentials. At the moment, hers seems to him a veneer far too easy to peel away.

Sensing this, Liam is embarrassed. Were he in a room with others, he might actually blush, shamed by a sudden realisation of something so obvious - and by the recognition that he had failed to see it for so long. But perhaps that should come as no surprise to him if, as Alison suggested, he is on a journey too. Can you only see something in others - or the lack of something in others - when you either do or don't have that self-same thing yourself? Do you need that dichotomy to arrive at the most accurate and informed perspective?

There is another conclusion too. It is one he is about to articulate when the phone rings.

"Next Friday I'm up in Carlisle, for my sins." It is Alison.

"What are you doing in Carlisle, of all places?"

"Oh, the usual; sorting out the poorly functioning male of our species."

Liam laughs as he is supposed to; it is one of her standing jokes. Before she next speaks, Liam knows she has not called just to tell him that.

"I was wondering what you were doing next weekend. Well Saturday, at least. I thought I might break my journey home in Settle. It's about time I saw you on your home turf."

He allows a moment, just to give her the merest hint that he is thinking about her suggestion.

"That's sounds just fine. I'll have the place disinfected and the red carpet hoovered."

"You'd better!" She laughs. "You know, I don't have your address… email it to me."

"Okay."

"Great." The merest pause. "Must dash."

And then Alison is gone, leaving Liam to finish reshaping his theory about the nature of poetry.

"Flooding the market"

It was, in many ways, exhilarating to be the object of pursuit once again. Still level-headed enough to know that, when analysed in the cold light of day, one coffee in a supermarket café didn't really amount to very much, Rachel tried not to get carried away. The evidence, however, was incontrovertible. Had he not loitered at the end of the packing station even after filling his bags? Did he not then pick up the threads of a conversation left hanging like a worm on a baited hook? Had he not suggested - perhaps even forced her - to have coffee with him, to exchange names, and then, when the encounter was nearly over, did he not calmly share his phone number? Not demanding hers in return had, from Rachel's perspective been something of a master stroke; it left her with the onus, the responsibility, but also the guilt if she did not call him. She stopped short of regarding it an arrogant move, preferring the softer label of 'confident'. It had possibly been a mirror of her own intrusion into what for him had also started out as an innocent shopping expedition.

She had wondered - as they sat talking, and just after the near-miss outside - whether he might be married, but had concluded not on the basis of three pieces of evidence. The first was that they were sitting there at all; hardly standard operating procedure for a married man. Secondly, he wore no ring. And thirdly, he had been completely wrong about the responsibility for the almost fatal accident outside. Might he have wondered the same about her? If so, she would have passed the first two of the three tests, her response to the third merely proving that she knew what it was to be a mother; hardly surprising for a woman of her age.

But however she chose to look at it, the fact that they'd had coffee and that she was now in possession of his phone number was as much evidence as she needed to give her ego a timely boost. What it also did, of course, was to pose a further question, demand from her the interpretation of a new set of circumstances. It was as if she had been able to master one level in a computer game and, as a result, had been automatically and somewhat ruthlessly promoted to the next. Although likely to be equally short in terms of playing time, her next move required a little advanced thinking. There was no room for happenstance in her play this time. If she called him - and she was already sure she would - she knew she had to do so with a strategy in mind, if not a fully thought-through plan. Receiving her call would set off an entirely new train of thought in David's mind, and recognising this Rachel also saw how the game had become more sophisticated, with a whole suite of moves and counter-moves possible. She had graduated to emotional chess.

Yet even as she stood in the kitchen two days later looking out over the garden, absentmindedly playing with his business card in her left hand, Rachel remained uncertain as to the objective of this particular game. Unlike chess, it was fluid, ambiguous, with undefined rules; and she suspected the winning criteria was different for each combatant. If she had no idea what she wanted, then she knew she could only play to lose. Having just established herself in the game, having gone through some trauma and upheaval to give herself the freedom to take a seat at the table, the last thing she needed was to find herself back at square one. Perhaps it wasn't like chess at all; perhaps it was more rudimentary than that. She wanted a few ladders before she encountered the dreaded snake. And was David a snake? There was only one way to find out; she had to roll the dice.

When he failed to answer the phone she was instantly relieved. It was a response that told her a great deal. As she listened to the answerphone message, his voice transported her back to the café - which was also illuminating. At the beep she simply hung-up. Having always felt such action to be rude, doing so was not her normal tack; but the fact that she seemed compelled to do so merely confirmed that she hadn't yet established a plan. She half-turned and flicked the card onto the kitchen table. Treating it with a degree of off-hand disrespect was another useful test of how she felt, teasing herself, pushing at her limits, as if doing so was the only way to find out what she really wanted. Obscurely, she recalled times when Katy had been a young child and occasionally alighted upon a thing she protested she must instantly have, and how she and Liam had included that item with at least two others and then given her the choice of three. Only by doing so could they really test exactly what she wanted, and often it was not the sweet or toy or book originally lusted after.

A somewhat specious parallel which hardly applied to her present dilemma, yet it was telling it had come to her at all, and the notion that she had a decision to make was a novel one. In many respects the conundrum said as much about the past as it did the present. Rachel found herself wondering when she had last needed to make such a choice in her life with Liam; had there been a time when she had protested her need for something and then been forced to validate that need in the context of other equally attractive opportunities? She could recall none. On reflection it seemed as if her life had become one without choices, one where she said 'I want this' and nine times out of ten she would have been gifted it without any obligation to challenge herself. She knew in many respects that said a great deal in Liam's favour, how much he cared for her; and she knew there would be many, including some of her friends, who would argue - privately, perhaps - that she was lucky to have a man who looked after her in that way, someone who was so devoted. But perhaps that had been part of the problem. Perhaps she had suddenly arrived at a point in her life when she wanted to be challenged, to *have* to make choices; perhaps she was tired of being the object of routine affection. Whilst wonderful in its own way, it was also mundane. Since the day they had separated, Liam leaving so completely in the way he had, Rachel found herself making all sorts of decisions. Most of these had been without real consequence, like what she wanted for dinner; but some more so. Even puzzling over an evening meal came as welcome relief to her; being able to choose - being *forced* to choose - was a smaller scale encapsulation of everything for which she had been striving. Obviously questions about David, though still embryonic, were on a different plain entirely to 'chicken or lamb?', but they were not unrelated.

"Anyway, I'm glad you called," he had said.

He had only been able to play his unremarkable opening gambit once Rachel had recovered from the shock of hearing his voice when she lifted the receiver.

"But I didn't give you my number," she had protested, unable to suppress her anxiety.

"Indeed. But I had a missed call - and no message - from a number I didn't recognise. My phone logs all calls in and out. In fact, don't all phones do that these days?" He hadn't waited for her to respond. "So, intrigued, I called back. As soon as you said 'hello' I recognised your voice."

Attempting to regain some kind of equilibrium, there had been a small delay before she had been able to reply.

"Well, now you've found me out."

"Why didn't you leave a message?"

It was a question to which she didn't feel entirely prepared to respond - or rather, one where he had yet to earn the right to hear the honest answer. So she said nothing.

"Doesn't it annoy you when people do that?" He tried a different tack.

"Do what?"

"Call, but not leave a message."

Having ducked the last one, Rachel felt duty bound to reply to this one.

"I know. I'm sorry." It was hardly an answer.

"Anyway, I'm glad you called."

"You are?"

At the other end of the line he laughed. Although it reminded her of the café, it was a sound she had difficulty assessing.

"Of course. If I hadn't wanted you to call, I wouldn't have given you my number, would I?"

"Surely that depends," she suggested vaguely, regaining a foothold in the conversation and beginning to feel suitably combative.

"Oh? On what?"

"Probability, or flooding the market."

"I'm not with you," he said, his voice still relaxed.

"Well, if you gave your number to, say, thirty women, then isn't it almost inevitable that at least one of them would ring you back?"

He laughed again.

"I see what you mean," he concurred, obviously going along with her joke. "Your point being that I hoped someone would - and that I couldn't care less who it was…"

The fact that she was smiling delayed her response just a moment.

"The case for the prosecution rests, m'lud."

"And is the defendant allowed to respond?"

"You mean you actually want to defend yourself?"

"I do," he said. "I need to plead my innocence."

"You have proof?" Rachel was warming to the task.

"The only evidence I can offer is that I only gave my phone number to one person."

"And there are witnesses? After all, this is a serious charge you're facing."

He allowed a suitably sombre tone to enter his voice.

"I recognise the gravity of my situation. But I do have a witness."

"And are they of impeachable moral standing and scrupulously honest?"

"I am."

At this she laughed, satisfied that something had been achieved, even if she were unable to define it.

"Then the case is dismissed, and the accused is released."

"We should celebrate my liberation, don't you think?" he asked, his banter flirtatious once again.

"And how do you propose we do that?"

*

He was only the second naked man she had been alone with since she had married Liam. About a year before Katy was born, Rachel had been attending an art class, ostensibly striving to 'find herself' but really seeking an argument with which to rebuff Liam's pressure to start a family. During a life drawing session, the tutor had said that the model was open to private engagements if any of the class wanted to spend more time honing their skills. Rachel had been first in the queue, not specifically to nurture her talent, nor because the model was a fit young male student trying to earn some money to help him through college, but because she was increasingly concerned about what she regarded as her 'plight'. When, about half an hour into that private session her model became aroused, he was only half apologetic; the other half trying to get the message across that if Rachel felt like taking advantage of his predicament - 'helping him out' perhaps - then he would be happy to oblige. No extra charge. Although flattered, she had left him alone for five minutes, sufficient time for her to make some fresh coffee and for him to calm himself. As she had waited for the kettle to boil she wondered why she hadn't just thrown him out - or why she hadn't accepted his offer. Both trailed in some way behind her primary objective, though which she would have chosen to come second she had always been unable to articulate.

Ultimately the session had been unsatisfying for her (and, she assumed, her model!) as the sketches she produced were clumsy and static, and her perennial problem with joints - especially knees and elbows - refused to go away. She abandoned the class soon after.

The second scenario was a completely different affair altogether. As she stood in the en-suite examining her face in the mirror, she was reminded of that earlier episode; yet it was recalled without humour or any meaningful reflection. The differences were extreme: the figure concerned was not that of a young toned student; she was not seeking a way to avoid motherhood (nature had taken care of that now!); and neither she was attempting to free any latent talent she may - or may not - have possessed. More than that, however, at this point there was no background consideration to be given to Liam. This was all about her; selfishness on a completely different level.

Rachel was unsure, as she stood staring into her own eyes, how much she had engineered the situation, and how much she had been manoeuvred into it. She was concerned that the sense of control she had felt ever since their phone call was no more than illusory and that she had been 'played' by David, expertly so. If that were indeed the case, then it raised other questions, as much about her as it did him. And she knew, if she were to return to the bedroom now and conclude the sequence of events to which it seemed everything had been leading, then she would be doing so without any concern as to what the answers to those questions might be. If she did not, if she begged a pause, a halt in proceedings - a stay of execution, almost - then how she did so would be crucial; if she was as clumsy in her approach as she had been to drawing knees and elbows, then she might not get another chance.

Perhaps that was the equation she was trying to solve: take a stab at it now and accept that half of her answer was guesswork, or churn through the problem logically and show all her working but risk running out of time. Her eyes failed to give her any clues, and somewhere in the back of her mind came what she could only describe as a dull ache; the sensation that told her David had already assumed which path she would take.

"I despise her already"

On a quiet day you can hear the trains as they slow down on their approach to the station, and if you were standing out in Liam's back garden, half way between the house and the shed at the far end, and looked up towards the embankment, you can see them too. Most days were unexceptional, but when there was some kind of heritage steam event it was like having a private front-row seat. Not that such an attraction played any part in Liam's choice of home. He had never been much of a railway enthusiast even as a child, but now, as as result of this proximity, his interest has been elevated to that of an admiring - if not especially knowledgeable - spectator.

Distance had been the greatest consideration when he was choosing where to live. Distance *from* Rachel primarily, because if he was going to be forced to make a break with her then he needed it to be a meaningful one; the thought of her living just around the corner from him and possibly bumping into her in the supermarket was a risk he was not prepared to run. That Cumbria was far enough away from Shropshire and yet close enough to other things was equally important. He wanted to be in or on the edge of a community, but not a large one; close enough for him to be able to walk into whatever 'centre' there might be - a few shops, a pub, a take-away. He also wanted to be not too far from Katy now living in the embrace of Greater Manchester. Access to reasonable transport links was important should he ever find the need to go further afield, a work-related excursion into London perhaps. All of which gave him a large enough area to consider, from the Derbyshire Dales, through most of Yorkshire, and - if he was being expansive - even up to the edge of Scotland.

In the end fate played a hand. Driving north to meet an old friend who had retired to Keswick, he had chosen to eschew the motorway and found himself going through Settle. It seemed like a good place to break his journey. Two doors along from a café - where good coffee and an excellent slice of carrot cake had revived him - was an Estate Agent, and one of the properties in the window, a rental new to the market that very morning, caught his attention. He arranged to view it on his way back from his friend's three days later, and, finding his love of the Lakes revived by his brief sojourn, a geographical tie-breaker kicked in and the deal was sealed within the week.

Once he has managed to come to terms with the dimensions and constraints of his study, it becomes a move he cannot regret. His work being primarily home-based means he could live anywhere from Portsmouth to Aberdeen as long as he has a reliable internet connection and is never very far from a motorway, airport or railway station. Considering his new location, he finds it ironic he has rarely taken the train to any of his client meetings, the car still proving to be the workhorse of choice. He is also surprised how quickly he has been able to establish a new balance in terms of travel, with the odd long haul down to the M4 corridor being the worst incumbrance. There are other compensations: the chance to see old friends, the potential to offer them a bed in the Lakes if they feel like a few days away from the grind. As with many such things however, potential is often of greater merit than its execution. Indeed, when he pauses to consider it - tending his small vegetable patch after a long and inconclusive conference call with a prospective new client as he does so - Alison's imminent arrival is the outcome of the first time he has actually made such an offer. Not that she gave him very much choice, of course. How could he say no? Teasing at a stray weed between his burgeoning courgettes, he wonders if he would have wanted to decline anyway. In fact, would it have been a matter of time before he made the suggestion himself? Hebden Bridge was all very well, but it had always felt to him like a stop-gap, a stand-in, as if it were a place they both knew was interim, merely second best.

Being twenty four hours away from her arrival has done more than focus the mind. Routine, practical things - like shopping and cleaning - have come immediately to the fore, and he finds himself fussing over fresh sheets and towels for the spare room and doing double-duty hoovering. He has a menu planned - indeed, several menus - which will allow him to cater for whatever she might feel like eating, rationalising away his over-preparation by telling himself what they don't eat at the weekend he can have himself during the days that follow. He remains acutely aware that one of the most obvious questions he has not actually resolved is exactly what Alison had meant by "Saturday at least". Planning to leave Carlisle around four, he knows she will arrive late afternoon Friday, but that's about it. Did "Saturday at least" mean just Saturday morning, or into early afternoon, or all of Saturday? Was she being scrupulously literal and meant exactly what she'd said i.e. all of Saturday and therefore by default into Sunday too? The extra thirty five pounds spent over and above his average weekly shop is testament to his determination to cover all bases.

Hearing a train leaving the station to begin its journey south, Liam straightens - the offending weed still between his fingers - and watches it appear into and then pass through his line of sight. His looking has become somewhat compulsive, engendered by various surprises during his early days in the house when, expecting to see a run-of-the-mill two-car DMU, he was rewarded with an historic diesel locomotive from the sixties or some massively long goods train struggling northwards. He smiles to himself, remembering how he had fretted about finding a suitable location on his literary bookshelves for the three tomes on the Settle-to-Carlisle railway he'd felt compelled to buy from the local bookshop. He is still unsure if he has managed to persuade Gill, who runs the shop, that his interest is merely superficial.

The train, having disappeared to his right, leaves him with the vista of an empty embankment and a large unanswered question. It is, he is painfully aware, the question that has been hounding him in one form or another ever since he and Alison had spent that first evening talking in the hotel bar - and since their rather strange parting outside her room, something she has never mentioned. Perhaps, Liam thinks, she has forgotten all about it; perhaps it was of no consequence to her. But for him, it - and what it may have signified - sits between them like a haunting spectre.

He glances down at his fingers, walks to a compost pile slowly growing inside its slatted wooden confine, and drops the weed in. One final check of his watch and the house beckons - it is three o'clock after all! Having taken off his gardening shoes, Liam first returns to the kitchen and flicks on the coffee-maker, pausing by the sink to look out of the window and down the stretch of lawn he has just left. It is not a large expanse, easy for him to keep under control and vaguely fulfilling, even if he can't reconfigure it as he would wish. He knows that fulfilment is akin to what he gets from his relationship with Alison. They have become good friends, and she has been, on occasion, something of a confidant. He wishes he had known her earlier; it would have been useful to have someone to consult when things were difficult. Liam tries to persuade himself that such an arrangement would have been good for Katy too, that in consequence he might have been able to protect her better; but he knows this is a phoney argument, and that the person he was most looking to protect was himself.

It would not have been that simple, of course. Having had Alison in the background two years ago would only have complicated matters - or, at the very least, made his position more ambiguous. Perhaps under such circumstances he would have willingly aligned himself to Rachel's proposition and her aspirations. But that would have depended on his understanding whether or not he and Alison might become more than friends. It is still 'the big question', suspended above him like the netting over his meagre raspberries. It is a light netting, the patch it protects is modest; but it is netting nonetheless, as is the question which envelops him.

Although he has not explicitly told himself this, Liam has a profound sense it will be answered this weekend, one way or another. It has to be. The fact that Alison will be staying under his roof somehow means there can be nothing to stop its being asked, implicitly or explicitly; and nothing to prevent an answer. He cannot believe, being the intelligent, sophisticated woman she is, Alison does not see that too. Perhaps she has asked to stay simply for that very purpose; perhaps she already knows the answer - has known it for a long while - and has decided it is time to tell him. She has been in control after all. And all of the time.

Liam's mind races ahead and he foresees a scenario where she places a hand on his arm and says "Liam, you've very sweet and I like you dearly, but...". It is the inevitable conclusion, of course, and the one for which he most needs to prepare himself. Indeed, just having it front and centre in his mind is like an internal litmus test, an experiment to gauge exactly what lies beneath the surface; his ageing surface. But he doesn't need to apply laboratory conditions to know this is the outcome he seeks least of all. "As long as when she leaves we are still friends" he says silently - and then tuts internally, shaking his head at himself. As he lifts his recently-filled cup from the machine, he is attracted to a reflection in his peripheral vision. He turns his head and is confronted by a man in his early sixties preparing to drink coffee. It seems an intelligent enough face, and - if first impressions are anything to go by - a face which is telling no lies. It looks as old as it is, and - if he is being generous - the head boasts more than the average volume of hair for a man of such maturity. There is something professional, distinguished, trustworthy about the face, and in the eyes the suggestion of honesty. This honesty is not, he believes, simply a reflection of the reliability of their owner, but rather symbol of what the face has been through. There is a depth about them which cannot disguise they have seen their fair share of both pain and joy, and in them, as well as in other aspects of the visage perhaps, traces of recent trauma. Liam looks for the sign of a spark, for some hint of vitality. Perhaps it is impossible for him to recognise these; perhaps such translation is best left to others. The one thing he cannot deny, however, is the age of the face, and he recalls Alison's - not without its own signs of longevity and experience, of course - and strains again at the chain that holds him back: hers is a face with fifteen years fewer miles on the clock.

"I was going to ask you if you wanted coffee, but I can see you need something stronger than that."

Liam, having opened the front door on hearing her pull up outside, is standing on the threshold smiling, but her half-hearted wave as she hauls herself out of her car tells its own story. He moves quickly to retrieve her luggage from the opened boot, pausing for a moment to allow her to peck him on the cheek.

"You're a life-saver," she says, and simply walks into the house leaving him to it.

Her coat and shoes already off, she is standing in the hall awaiting instructions as he returns with a small overnight bag and laptop case.

"Don't you want to lock it?" he asks, nodding through the open door.

"It's very clever," she says. "It takes care of itself."

As he puts her bags down and moves to close the front door, he hears an obedient 'beep' from the car's alarm and can't help but smile.

"Drink first?" he asks somewhat unnecessarily, not bothering to articulate what the alternative might be. "Gin or wine?"

"What's open?"

He smiles.

"Follow me."

Liam leads her into the lounge, refraining from inviting her to sit anywhere in particular knowing she is perfectly capable of making her own choice.

"Is Sauvignon okay?" he asks as he heads towards the arch that leads into the kitchen.

"Break fluid would be just fine at this point in my day!"

The anticipated laugh not following, when he opens the cupboard he selects two of his largest wine glasses, then, having retrieved the bottle from the fridge, pours healthy measures, Alison's larger than his own.

He returns to the lounge and finds her sitting in one of his armchairs, having turned it slightly so that she can better see out of the closed French doors and into the garden. He offers her a glass. She accepts it wordlessly then immediately takes a healthy sip.

"I've been thinking about that since Penrith!"

"Rough day?" He sits in the adjacent armchair, manoeuvring it to face her.

"I've had better. And then some idiot decided to ram the central reservation just in front of me and I - along with a number of others - had to take avoiding action."

"Really?"

"It could have been worse," she says, adjusting her position a little better. "I mean I don't think they were hurt, and I got through. I suspect they may have ended up closing the motorway for a while to recover the car, so at least I wasn't permanently stuck behind it."

She drinks again, then looks at him - properly, he feels - and smiles.

"I can feel my humanity returning already!"

They talk about her day, a loose conversation which allows her to replay its events and unwind herself from them as she does so. The client had been challenging, sceptical; it had taken her hours to get him to accept her methods. Then to make up for lost time she had needed to embrace a greater level of risk than usual and be a little more forthright in her views about him and his team - the latter based on an exercise she'd only managed to get them to do grudgingly. Already worn out, the accident on the motorway had almost been the final straw.

After the first glass of wine, Liam shows Alison the spare room, then leaves her to get changed while he returns to the kitchen to prepare dinner. They have settled on a little chicken with some salad and a tahini dressing. Fifteen minutes later when she reappears, she is wearing jogging bottoms and a loose sweatshirt. It is difficult for Liam to disguise his surprise. He has never seen her dressed like this. If she were someone else - if she were not Alison - he knows he would walk over and hug her. As he stands somewhat artificially fussing over the salad waiting for the chicken to finish cooking, she opens the fridge and retrieves the wine, refills her glass and tops up his.

"Smells good," she says.

"And you've been looking forward to this too since Penrith, right?" he suggests.

"I wouldn't go that far!" And she laughs.

It is a suitably relaxed version of the laugh of which he has become so fond. He smiles, more to himself than to her, and turns the chicken in the pan once more.

They meander through dinner. Alison asks him about Settle and his life there. At one point he mentions the railway, and when she expresses an interest, he tells her what he has learned of its history and the fact that from the garden he can see the trains when they pass. She teases him mercilessly and calls him a trainspotter.

A locally-produced baked cheesecake christens the opening of a second bottle of wine, and they return to the armchairs just sitting and largely saying nothing, looking out into the darkened garden, watching for the occasional bat to flit by. He is reminded of the past.

When she excuses herself to use the bathroom, Liam starts tidying, clearing the dining table and loading the dishwasher. It has been, he concludes, a thoroughly successful evening, not simply because he has enjoyed himself, but because he has given the Alison the opportunity to unwind.

He is still filling the dishwasher when she returns to the kitchen, and when he stands up, closes its door and turns, he finds her standing behind him, watching him. She moves forward and slips an arm around him and rests her head on his shoulder.

"Thank you," she says, "that was lovely,"

There is only one place his arms can now go.

※

He wakes around seven-thirty, a little later than usual. He doesn't need to look to feel Alison lying next to him, and he wants to pinch himself to make sure he isn't dreaming. There is something mesmerising about watching her sleep, the rise and fall as she breathes. He tries to remember everything that happened since she arrived the previous evening, but finds, paradoxically, that he can remember both everything and nothing. Trying to imagine it as a movie he has watched, replaying it in his mind, doesn't seem to help no matter how hard he tries.

"You're frowning," her voice says.

Liam realises he had been looking elsewhere, focused on nothing other than recall.

"Was I?"

"Yes." She moves closer and puts an arm across his chest. "Was yesterday such a dreadful experience?"

He knows she is joking, but it is suddenly too important for him to simply play along.

"I think I'm going to have to start calling you something else."

"Why?" she says, her interest piqued. She lifts herself up a little in the bed.

"Partly because when we first met you said you didn't like your name very much; but mainly because yesterday I met this new person, someone even more wonderful than Alison, and I think she deserves her own name."

She laughs and pinches his arm lightly.

"And what do you intend to call this miraculous woman? Though I warn you, she may prove to be mythical. Or monstrous, and lead you to your doom!"

Now he can't help but laugh too.

"I thought 'Barbara'." He allows the name to settle between them, as if he is serious, as if he really is going to start calling her that. "What do you think?"

"There are worse names," she says. "It's a bit like a weekend name, isn't it?" She pauses and allows the smile to slip a little. "And tell me, this Barbara you've just met; what kind of a woman is she, would you say? And I recommend you think carefully before you answer."

If he were tempted to offer lazy romantic platitudes her warning stops him short. Liam knows very well the kind of person Alison is: the day-to-day professional, a no-nonsense woman. The sort of individual who dives straight for the truth. But there is another side of her too, the jogging pants and sweatshirt person who is allowed out occasionally.

"She's intelligent and funny, of course. And has a wicked sense of humour. And when she's relaxed - and Barbara is at her best when she's relaxed - she's warm and caring, sensitive, considerate. But she's also a little vulnerable too, not in a weak way, you understand. For all her outward show, I think she wants what we all want; to feel like she belongs, and to be loved a little bit."

Alison looks at him unflinchingly for a few moments, and Liam wonders if he has gone too far; gone too far, too soon.

"I think I despise her already" she says, then smiles. "Barbara indeed! Now go and do something useful and make some tea!"

＊

They spend the first part of the morning in Settle. As soon as Alison had seen a train from the garden - standing alone in the middle of the lawn cradling her second cup of coffee - she had insisted Liam show her the station and the bookshop. As if evaluating them, she seems content with the small Market Place and the High Street though Liam is unable to say whether she is satisfied on her own behalf or his. They hold hands occasionally, and she seems to subtly flit between being Alison and Barbara. Having had the notion, Liam is unable to let it go; it seems a convenient way of defining her. He finds he can tell the difference between the two almost instantly, largely by her tone of voice but increasingly throughout the morning in the way she moves or even looks at something.

"What's wrong with you?" she asks him at one point as they pause outside a shop.

"Me? Nothing. Why?"

"You haven't stop smiling all morning. It's as if your face has been paralysed!"

He laughs.

"I can't imagine," he replies, making a show of giving his answer some thought. "Perhaps I have been bewitched."

"Bewitched, is it? That damn Barbara," she says with a show of force. "Just you wait until I get my hands on her!" The threat is momentary.

With the weather set fair for the remainder of the day, Liam suggests they make the thirty-minute drive west to visit Levens Hall. It is, Alison confesses, a place she has heard of but never visited. She says she has always thought of it as "the house with the hedges" which makes Liam all the more pleased with his suggestion.

He has never been sure whether the reality of the gardens meet expectations raised by the photographs of them; it is as if there is a battle - or perhaps an uneasy truce - between those second-hand interpretations and how they really are. He knows of people who - having previously seen almost impressionistic images of yew hedges and sculpted trees - have been disappointed with the place, and others so taken with the physicality and texture of the garden that they give up trying to take their own photographs. "What's the point?" they might be asking.

As they turn through a gate and take the path which leads along the side of the house and into the main gardens proper, Liam wonders which of these two types of respondent Alison will prove to be. In spite of his attempts to promote conversation, she had been largely quiet on the drive over, and they had made the last ten minutes of the journey in silence. It was not, Liam believes, a 'bad' silence, just a little unexpected.

He tries to explain it to himself, attempting to settle on tiredness after a long working week as the most likely reason; her 'giving in' to the mental break he and Settle have offered her. After all, at this moment she doesn't have to think or worry about anything. But a second voice in his head - one with a superior and abrasive tone, the one most able to cut into any thinking moment - suggests with increasing persuasiveness that the reason for Alison's silence is regret: regret about the previous evening and what happened last night. She wishes she had never come, the voice tells Liam; she has made a mistake and, what's more, both he and she know it.

It is a notion Liam tried to bat away as he drove those last few miles, endeavouring to counter-argue with images from their walk earlier that morning, the things she said, the way - only once or twice it's true - she looked at him. Surely that proves the lie to such an argument?

Only a few seconds are needed for it to transpire that Alison is one of those people on whom the real Levens can work its magic. She pauses inside the gate to do no more than simply look. Liam, two or three paces ahead, stops, turns to capture her as she stands there, framed by two small hedges, the overhanging branches of a tree, the gate through which they have just come behind her. He smiles.

"It's quite something isn't it?" he offers, a little unnecessarily.

Initially she says nothing, then moves forward to his side, interlocking her hand with his. And then: "Simply stunning".

They walk slowly between trees and hedges, each of them quietly pointing out things for the other to take in: a peacock, a swan. They make inane unoriginal touristy comments, wondering how such-and-such is achieved, how long things must take to grow, admiring the skills of gardeners. When they come across one intent on the meticulous trimming of a small box, they wish him "good afternoon" and compliment him as if he were responsible for the entire plot. As they walk on, Liam wonders how many times the man must have heard the same praise - and whether he has ever tired of doing so. To his relief, the negative voice in his head has ceased nagging, and he feels free enough to relax, to revel in the wholly unexpected moment; twenty-four hours ago he had been concerned about how clean his house was and how neat and tidy the spare room appeared, concerns which seem almost irrelevant now.

The tea room is a dark panelled affair more in keeping with the house, and Liam can't help thinking they should find a way of creating a greenhouse or some kind of 'garden room' for their patrons with a view out onto the gardens themselves. There are pictures of the exterior on the walls and the odd horticultural item on display, but nothing that does justice to where they are. Whether it matters or not, Liam is unable to decide. Perhaps they have seen enough and are brim-full of the experience, or perhaps there are more important things for him to consider, the taking of tea being the bookend to their visit, an event which heralds the transition to the next.

Although they are keeping up a conversation easily enough, Liam can't help but pose more questions for himself, as if answering one simply moves you on to the next. And there are many more branches to this particular tree than he might have expected - or perhaps they are all just variations on one single question: "what now?"

"Do you do that a lot?" Alison's voice breaks through his thin veneer of thought.

"Do what?"

"Frown when you're thinking."

"Was I frowning?" he asks, genuinely unaware he had been doing so.

"Were you thinking?" she counters with a smile.

It is a smile that reminds him - suddenly, obtusely - of how much younger than him she looks. How much younger than him she is. He realises that particular itch will never stop testing him.

"I know you were," Alison answers her own question. "Well, just in case you were wondering when I was going to abandon you" - she sees a flash of panic in his eyes - "I mean, when I was aiming to go home…"

"Ah," he says, unable not to sound grateful that his instant interpretation of her words was incorrect.

"I confess to not having worked that out in advance."

"You, not having a plan?" He tries to sound jolly and back on her wavelength.

"I came prepared for every eventuality. One idea saw me going home about now, another tomorrow morning, another a little later."

It is a clue, and Liam is suddenly in need of a clue.

"And have you decided?"

"Tomorrow morning?" There is a note of question or application in her voice. "That is if you are free until then."

"Luckily I am," he says. "I don't have to be anywhere until I go into Leeds on Tuesday, so until then I'm all yours." There are layers in his words neither is minded to explore.

"Oh, I don't think I need all of you," she says with a laugh, squeezing his hand as she does so.

"Tell me then, these ideas of yours, the options you gave yourself."

"Yes?" She is clearly curious.

"Did you have a 'Plan A' at all?"

She frees her hand to wag her index finger at him, scoldingly, as if he were a naughty boy.

"You should know by now, never ask a lady if she has a 'Plan A'."

"Really?"

Alison nods.

"For two reasons. First, there's a possibility that you might not like the answer if you knew it. And second, if you did and could work out what Plan B might have been, you might not appreciate the lady quite so much as a result."

They both laugh. Delivered lightly enough, her logic is flawless. And as much as he wants to know - is desperate to know - what she had in mind when she pulled up to his house around twenty-four hours previously, there are too many risks in doing so, too much to jeopardise. Such knowledge can only be counter-productive. He decides to let it go.

"Then," he says, completely aware of what he is saying, "I am entirely at your disposal."

"There comes a point"

Katy had long held a theory that time did not pass in a linear fashion. Her argument, borne out by sometimes painful experience, was that it chose to vary its pace usually to suit other unseen forces. Many weeks might seem to fly by in an instant, yet at other times a single day could drag on forever. And it wasn't just weeks which chose to defy her in this way. Worryingly, months and years were beginning to follow the same pattern. One minute it was April, the next nearly the end of August.

Faced with such rebelliousness, she knew she needed to navigate time via some other method but was struggling to settle on one. The devious blending of weeks and months into a homogenous mass only served to absorb other things into it, smudging their edges until they started to lose their definition too. In doing so they also became indistinct, slippery, difficult to get hold of. Her relationship with Tom, for example, had taken such a turn; it had become normalised, just something she was 'in' or belonged to. She had been shaken the evening he arrived at her flat carrying flowers and announcing it was their anniversary - a surprise replicated with Tom equally taken aback by her failure to celebrate the date in the same enthusiastic and conscientious way he had. A year? Or two? It was, if nothing else, a conspiracy; a plot to undermine her control over her life, her hold on it. She had been able to rescue the situation well enough, however; Tom remained pliable if she applied pressure in the right places, and soon she found herself forgiven - and embarking on their next year together. It had been the path of least resistance.

It had been pretty much the same with her parents' divorce. One minute all was well, then they were talking to her in a Shropshire pub garden, and now - in a flash it seemed - not only had they been divorced for innumerable months, she had fallen out of favour with her mother and her father had moved. Perhaps it would have been more accurate to say that her mother had fallen our of favour with her, but Katy maintained an innate degree of vulnerability and self-doubt which, from time to time, insisted on laying the guilt for such failures at her door. And then these same months had conspired to become nearly a year. She understood her mother had begun to 'see someone' - though she was being unusually coy about the particulars - and her father was living a reclusive life on the edge of the Lake District. During her visits to see him (sadly infrequent, and for no good reason given his relative proximity) Katy had been unable to sense any kind of progress on his side. Her mother seemed to be making an effort, to resuscitate whatever it was she felt needed breathing new life into, while her father apparently remained static.

"What are you doing, Dad?" she had asked a few weeks previously during her last visit, an impromptu overnight stay at very little notice.

"'Doing'?" He had replayed the word back to her, largely to check it was what she had said, but also as if he didn't really know what it meant.

"Yes, 'doing'? Apart from work. Here? New life? New friends? That kind of thing."

He had delayed, briefly, before replying, but she had read nothing significant in that, nor in the fact that the house seemed strangely ordered, clean, under control. She had put it down to nothing more than him finally coming to terms with what it meant to live on your own, a life lesson still fresh enough in her own mind. Had he needed advice, it was one area where she felt she had the edge on him; she would have happily shared her wisdom - if that's what it was - but unlike her mother she was only inclined to share it if asked. He remained her father, after all.

There was little in his response to which she could apply significance or meaning. It seemed his life was routine and dull, largely comprising of work and his books. He confessed that he was getting out a little more at the weekends, and was able to talk about some local pubs and eateries with what appeared to be first-hand experience. This, at least, was something for her to cling to in relation to her concern for his well-being. He seemed relaxed enough; indeed, she might even have said carefree - if only she'd had a meaningful point of reference for the comparison. But she did not, and the recent recognition that over the previous few years he had been increasingly dealing with domestic cares of one kind of another had come upon her as something of a shock. It was less her own negative contribution (though that was another source of any guilt she might feel), but rather the awareness - in hindsight - of the strains her mother had been gradually and almost invisibly overlaying upon him. If ever she mentioned it (and she did try once or twice) her father was typically forgiving, reminding her that Rachel had been under considerable stress because of her own father and, what was more, such pressures had been growing incrementally. That her father was prepared to cut his ex-wife some 'slack' was, for Katy, typical of the man; he had never, to the best of her knowledge, held a grudge, and now, given the most comprehensive opportunity to do so, still publicly refused to apportion blame.

"How's your mother?" he had asked that weekend, on the eve of her return to Manchester. They had been sitting in the lounge drinking coffee after a short post-breakfast walk.

"The usual," she had replied, somewhat automatically.

Her father had looked at her as if she were speaking a language he did not understand.

"You know," she tried to elaborate, "doing whatever she does. She seems busy, if that's what you mean. I think she sees a lot of her friends - well more than she used to - and she's talked about doing some volunteering in the local Cancel Research shop or Oxfam or something." She chose not to expose her mother's new 'friend'.

"Really?"

"Are you worried about her?" Katy heard her words almost in playback as if an echo after she had spoken them, and they seemed strange, stolen from another conversation.

"Not worried, no. I just want to know she's all right. You can't sweep nearly forty years of relationship away just like that."

Katy watched her father for an expression she could layer over the top of his words, as if at face value they only told part of the story. She could find nothing to provide any further clue as to what might lie beneath them.

"And your grandfather, how is he? I haven't spoken to him in a little while."

"I don't think very good."

"Why do you say that?"

"Because Mum's said nothing to me in a while. Not about him anyway. I think she tries to remember to keep me posted. It's nearly always our first topic of conversation."

"Because you ask?" Liam clarified.

"Or because she knows I'll ask," Katy said, clearly less than comfortable, nervous of the small void in knowledge she sensed may exist. "When there's been some positive news in the past she's rung me just to tell me that."

"But you've heard nothing recently?"

Katy shook her head.

"Has she said anything to you?"

Now it had been Liam's turn to be vague.

"It's been a little while, if I'm honest," he said loosely, repeating himself. "The last time we did speak - must have been over a month ago now - she didn't mention him. It was a quick call anyway," Liam added, trying to dispel any growing concern that might be building on Katy's part. "You know, more business than anything else. Well, not business exactly; money, really. Anyway, if there had been any material news I'm sure she would have told one of us. I don't think you should assume there's anything amiss because you haven't heard."

Katy tried to smile.

"You're probably right. But it's not knowing, isn't it?" The rhetorical question sat between them for a moment. "That and the certainty that at some point there won't be any more good news. I mean, that's inevitable isn't it?"

"You grandfather's a fighter," Liam tried to reassure her.

"I know. But there comes a point doesn't there, even for him?"

It was a fight Ronald was destined to abandon soon after that visit to Settle. Though she had tried to be reassured by the line her father had taken, the attempt had been a futile one. Over the years she had learned from Liam the skill of being prepared for the worst, early examples coming from holidays and nagging doubts about some plane or train being late. He usually had a plan, a way of turning a disaster into little more than an inconvenience. It was an attribute that fostered confidence, and as that confidence was proven to be well-founded time and again, perhaps later it turned a little to complacency on her part. Nevertheless, the lesson had been learned and comprehensively so. As a young woman, having been 'disappointed in love' on a couple of occasions, Katy turned to her father's modus operandi and began to devise alternatives, a 'Plan B' in case 'Plan A' didn't work out. She found such a tactic took the pressure off, allowed her to relax. Thus when 'Plan A' inevitably failed it proved no calamity; when it succeeded, it was a pleasant surprise. She adopted the approach more and more, even applying it to mundane things, and in consequence it gave her a degree of stability where just a few years previously there may have been none. She wondered if all women worked that way.

Tom had, of course, been something of a case in point. Her never expecting 'Plan A' to succeed had made their anniversary all the more alarming. Indeed, she found herself trying to remember if staying with Tom had indeed been her first option; what if being with him had actually been the fallback position? What did that say about her? And more alarmingly, what did that say about *them*?

❄

"I want you to tell her."

There is something steely in Rachel's voice that tells him she is not to be denied. When she rang him to say they needed to talk, his mind had been performing somersaults trying to fathom reasons for her request. There were a few, all of which seemed bad.

Not surprisingly though, his first thought was that she had changed her mind. Although a significant amount of time has passed, Liam can't help but wonder if she has come to her senses. However, no matter how much of him may have wanted that to be true - for it to be the ideal outcome in many ways - he is wise enough to be cognisant of the volume of water that has flowed beneath their respective bridges in the last year. In their own ways, each of them has moved on too far. It had taken him longer to do so, of course; the required shift of mind-set had been germinating in Rachel for a sufficient amount of time for her to be getting on with her new life quickly, but in his case months of nomadic emotional wandering had ensued. It had been an exodus brought on by banishment, and the altered landscape in which he had found himself had initially been harsh and unforgiving.

Once Liam has dispelled the possibility of a recall, a plea for him to return home, all other options seem bleak or of limited potential. Whether it were uncharitable or not, Liam's next thought is that she wants more money from him. They had previously been able to settle on a figure amicably enough, and, because he has heard nothing from her in that regard since, he can only assume she has been able to adjust to slightly straitened times as adequately as he. But he knows there will always be something on the horizon to require funds. He thinks of Rachel's car - the most expensive 'ask' he could imagine - and tries to remember how old it is.

He wonders if she might be ill, or on the verge of some other life-changing event. It is impossible for him to contemplate her doing anything romantic, in spite of her protestations relating to freedom and adventure; she had become too much a creature of comfort. So emigration to South America or Australia seemed highly unlikely, as would news that she was going join some religious sect. He knows there have been stresses and strains as far as Katy is concerned, having been able to divine as much from his daughter - though she, in turn, had been reticent to share too much. When Rachel had said "It's about Katy", her voice slightly broken not by tension but due to an inadequate phone signal (she was probably calling from somewhere near the 'black spot' in the garden), he prepared himself for a request to act as intermediary and mediator.

Of the two, only the former is needed, and not as a representative of Rachel but rather as the bringer of news.

"It's about Dad."

"Ronald? How is he?"

"Not good, Liam." Her voice is even, almost unemotional. Others might be surprised, but Liam knows her well enough; she has always possessed an uncanny ability to keep herself detached from the difficult. "He had a fall last week. A bad one. His Help said that he'd been complaining about his joints aching and getting migraines. So they arranged for him to go back into hospital for some tests."

There is a space Liam is expected to fill.

"I thought he was looking a little pale the last time I saw him, but I just assumed he was tired."

"He probably was," Rachel confirms. "Anyway, the doctors have told him that the cancer has spread. It has happened rapidly and mercilessly. They were surprised, I think. You remember that nice young doctor, Walsh isn't it?"

"Doctor Walsh, yes."

"He was very understanding. Waited until they'd got Dad back onto the ward for a rest before he told me. It's just days, Liam. That's all he has left. He said that there's no point keeping him in hospital if he doesn't want to be there; far better for him to be at home."

"I'm really sorry."

In the background Liam can make out the sound of the wind rustling through the trees. He guesses Rachel may have set-up the deckchair away from the house, into the sun about half-way down the lawn.

"They're updating his drugs," her voice fades back in, "but that's just to keep him comfortable. The nurse will come in three times a day now, and I'll make sure I'm over there as often as I can be. Oh, Liam, he's so thin now."

For a moment, Rachel herself sounds fragile, almost broken, and Liam wishes he were there just to be able to fold her in his arms, to give her some comfort, a shoulder to cry on should she need one.

"So I don't want Katy to see him." Suddenly she is businesslike again. "It would be too hard on her. It would be better if she remembered him as he was. Don't you think so? I mean, I suggested it to Dad, to see what he thought."

"And?"

"He cried. The thought of never seeing her again, he said. In a way that more than anything else seemed to hit him hard, proof it was the end this time."

"What do you want me to do?"

It was an offer Liam knows he has to make, and he can foresee the answer he will be given. He will acquiesce as he must, but he will do so for Katy first and Ronald second.

"I want you to tell her. She'll listen to you. You can make more sense of it for her than I ever could. And no matter how hard I try we'll end up fighting, and it will all be my fault."

"It's been hard?" Liam asks, trying to sound as sympathetic as possible.

"She's never forgiven me," Rachel says, the phrase delivered in a strangely loose way, as if the fact of it has become so inevitable, so self-evident, that it can be treated in a casual, off-hand manner. There is nothing to be done about it, is what Liam hears - and because of that, Rachel isn't even going to try. He doesn't know if that's right or wrong.

"She'll want to see him, you know that."

"But she can't, Liam. She really can't - for both their sakes." Rachel pauses. "Anyway, maybe by the time you tell her it will be all over. I hope not, because then she'll blame the both of us." Another pause. "But, you know, part of me thinks that might be for the better."

He words trail away. Liam can imagine their sound being picked up by the breeze, thinned and spread about the garden until they become less than a whisper, an insignificance that brushes past the variegated hebe, the box, caresses the petals on the roses, the buds on the dahlias, and then floats away never to be heard again.

"Of course," he hears himself saying. It is a duty. He does not contemplate whether or not that duty should be his, but he is willing to take on the burden. He tries to imagine the pain that would be generated if Katy visited her grandfather one final time - he tries, but finds himself unable to do so. There is no scale against which to measure it, no words to describe it. Avoidance is the only acceptable route now. Merciful release for both of them. "I'll try and call her this evening."

He waits for some kind of acknowledgement, but none is forthcoming. Listening for any kind of clue, he wonders if the call is at an end, or whether, unable to marshal her feelings any longer, Rachel is now weeping silently, her head in her hands, the phone by her side.

"Rachel?"

"Yes?" Her response is immediate, her voice level, unwavering.

"I'll call her."

"I heard. Thanks."

"And you?" Liam wonders if this question is uttered out of a sense of duty too, or whether it comes from something deeper. Perhaps it is a recognition of their past. "How are you?"

"Probably as you would expect," she offers, leaving him to fill in the blanks. In recent years it had become a technique of hers to answer a question either with another, or by implying that he should know the answer already. Either way, Liam had only ever been able to see it as evasion. Most of the time - or at least until the last eighteen months or so - it had been innocent enough, but now he knows that during the time building up to her decision it had been representative of something else, carrying a different meaning. Under the present circumstances he is prepared to let it ride, even if the picture he paints for himself is an inaccurate one.

"Of course," is all he says, and then, in a heartbeat, the call is over.

As he stares at the receiver, he knows there would have been a time - perhaps not so very long ago - when he would have finished such a call with "if there's anything I can do...". A standard offer for sure, but a genuine one nonetheless. But those words remain locked up inside him, waiting for another day. Probably waiting for another person.

*

In spite of her regime of self-preservation, Katy was still knocked off balance by the call when it came from her father a few days later.

"I've been trying to work out how to tell you," he had said, both trying to be kind and trying to sound kind, "but Granddad is really rather ill."

"How ill?" Katy's first question was a plea for dimensions, some kind of measure by which she could navigate. There could only be one. Time.

Her father's silence gave her a moment to prepare herself - but it wasn't enough.

"Dad?"

"Probably days."

"Days?" It was an exclamation delivered like a parting kiss, poignant, quiet.

"It's all happened rather quickly," Liam rushed into the void. "They took him back into hospital about a week ago. More tests, they said; but he'd clearly taken a turn for the worse. Your mother was there when they broke the news. He was typically stoic, of course; more concerned about her than he was about himself. And about you."

"What did he say?"

Again there is a silence. Katy knows she has asked a question her father cannot possibly answer.

＊

As soon as she had finished the call with her father, she rang her mother if only to confirm the news.

"But what about you, Mum?"

"Me?"

"How are you?"

"Oh, I'm alright. When you've seen something coming for this long - well, it gives you a chance to prepare, doesn't it? I could be in pieces, but I'm not." Rachel takes a breath. "That was something your father was always very good at."

"Being prepared?"

"In his own way."

"Can I see him?"

"You father?"

"Granddad."

"We'll see," Rachel said. Katy couldn't fail to misinterpret the code. "He's very weak just now. They've got him on some pretty powerful drugs, so he sleeps most of the time. The rest of the time… Well, he isn't really himself."

"Can I see you?"

It was a request that surprised both of them. The words had slipped out, prompted by a concern ingrained through years of unquestioning child-parent love; a concern that is only ever undone by the most severe of treachery. Whatever her mother had done - not so much to her, but to her father - it was not yet enough to rupture Katy's instinct.

"Me?"

"Yes, Mum; you."

"Look, I'm going to see him again in the morning. Let me call you after that and then maybe we can make some plans."

After she had put the phone down, Katy knew there were no 'Plan Bs' this time. There was only one outcome, the one that told her she had seen her grandfather for the last time. So she cried. Safe in her solitude, she gave in to her lack of preparation, and as the tears flowed, she hoped Tom would not come home soon.

"The things you find out"

The weather proved nondescript, failing to align itself with either being appropriate or inappropriate, the two ends of a sliding scale. A cultural link between funerals and the climate demands the latter be dark, wet and stormy when in companionable mourning, or bright and sunny if in celebration of the life recently passed. For Ronald's day the sky was filled with scudding clouds and spots of rain, the odd patch of blue breaking through. Nothing seemed destined for superiority.

In spite of this, Rachel looked up and wondered if the blend was somehow fitting, as if it were possible to translate what she saw into a metaphor for her father's life. It was, she knew, a pointless exercise; the kind of endeavour where you can - if you try hard enough - concoct an interpretation to suit not just the person who had recently died, but your present mood. And she was sufficiently self-aware to know that in such cases the latter would always hold sway.

At least she was warm enough. Standing outside the church sharing comments with mourners as they hovered uncomfortably, waiting for the coffin to arrive, she could be satisfied that she had judged the temperature perfectly. It had not been a question of which dress she would wear - she had a very limited selection of black - but which coat would prove the most appropriate. He one true black coat was a little too wintry, and she had been concerned that its fur collar might be deemed showy in an uncalled for way. In consequence she had resurrected the charcoal grey overcoat that used to be her autumnal workwear. It was a garment which had stood the test of time, and - having been recently cleaned - scrubbed up well enough to look almost brand new.

When Liam arrived it was evident he recognised the coat before he registered her.

"I haven't seen that in quite a while," he said, placing a hand on her shoulder but refraining from indulging in a more intimate greeting. "It brings back memories," he concluded vaguely.

His comment was a little obtuse for Rachel's taste.

"My professional outfit," she tried to laugh it off, "not that today is in any way related to that."

She watched as Liam scanned the small crowd.

"She's not here yet," Rachel said.

"Who?"

"Katy. That's who you were looking for?"

"Yes. Of course."

"I had a message from her. She's about five minutes away."

It was a minor untruth. Katy's text had merely given an approximate arrival time, and Rachel found herself only really interested in having Liam cease what she saw as fidgeting; there were a few people there he knew, and she wanted him to go and talk to them. His immediately putting her on edge had been annoying, partly because in doing so it drew her attention away from the event and her role in it - and partly because she did not understand why he should make her feel that way. It would have been different if either of them had arrived at the church with a new 'significant other' in tow; such a circumstance would most certainly have made things more awkward. But it couldn't be that. Indeed, Rachel had no idea whether there were someone new in Liam's life or not, as much as he could have no insight into her present emotional situation. And then she remembered Katy, the natural conduit, a go-between. Perhaps because Rachel had heard nothing interesting from Katy about her father, she had assumed messages going the other way would have been the same; but this was, of course, a ridiculous assumption. However unfounded her concern that Katy might have proven to be something of a gossip, she was immediately annoyed with her daughter, and layering that on top of a growing restlessness brought about by the waiting and Liam's slightly awkward arrival, the result was Rachel feeling suddenly grumpy, wanting the whole thing to be over and done with.

As he stood talking to two of Ronald's oldest friends - a couple her father had met decades ago when he had been a civilian working for the MoD - Rachel managed to manufacture a little distance between herself and the trio and tried to take in her ex-husband afresh, as if she were seeing him for the first time. She wondered if doing so would fill in any gaps, bridge the information omitted by Katy, allowing her to decipher any clues Liam might be sending out, clues that only she could interpret, a byproduct of their years of close proximity.

On the face of it he seemed little changed. Insufficient time had passed since their separation for there to be any material physical difference, and it wasn't as if they hadn't seen each other at all over the past year. Even so, there was something about the way he was standing - now that he was relaxed, talking, knowing that Katy would soon be there - which seemed different, altered. Surprising her, it nagged at her too. His overcoat she recognised, and based on the trousers visible beneath it, Rachel knew the suit he was wearing. Although she had not registered it a few moments earlier, she was also confident his shirt would have been white and his tie black - the one black tie he possessed, purchased some fifteen years earlier when his mother had died. If there was no manifest difference either in what he was wearing or in anything superficial - he hadn't (thank goodness!) grown a moustache or anything like that - Rachel knew she was looking for something deeper, more subtle. This only annoyed her even more. By and large she hated mysteries and puzzles, especially when the evidence sought was so subtly hidden away.

The need to unravel had on occasion caused her problems at university when it felt as if the interpretations her tutors were seeking from her were buried too far in the substrata of the text - or sometimes not even in the text at all, but many steps removed as if the target were only visible via a number of precisely aligned mirrors. On a more prosaic level, this distaste for conundrums had seen her adopt an almost pathological dislike for the murder-mystery and Agatha Christie in particular. If pressed she would claim multiple reasons for not taking to Poirot or Marple: the first and most highbrow was that the writing was not very good (not that she had ever read any), and that it did not therefore qualify as great literature. At University they taught Austen and George Eliot, not Christie. If harder to define, the second reason was a penchant to dismiss popular culture; she would, at all costs, resist demeaning herself, and thus avoided the soap opera or hit comedy show. Her one concession was quiz shows, but these had to be serious like 'University Challenge' or, at a push, 'Mastermind'. But her third reason, and the one she had most difficulty articulating (to herself, never mind anyone else!) was this general discomfort with puzzles. Yet it was an unravelling of Liam in which she was now engaged, an activity the only result of which was, as far as she could see, to suggest that he may have been standing a little more upright than he had in the recent past - but no subsequent deduction followed on from that.

In the end, she allowed this futile exercise to divert her for no more than a few seconds, her attention taken away by the simultaneous arrivals of Katy through the churchyard gates and her father's hearse coming down the drive. The low rumble of heavy tires on loose gravel suspended all conversation and forced heads to turn. There was a moment of paralysis - for not more than a second or two - after which movement suddenly commenced: mourners drifting into the church; those officiating appearing from nowhere as if they had been hiding in plain sight; and Liam - his movement caught in the corner of Rachel's eye - moving away from the melée to intercept Katy. She watched him rather than observe the hearse coming to a halt, and it was only when gently prompted by the undertaker that she herself turned toward the solid wooden doors of the church and the relative stillness beyond. They would be following soon enough, and then they would find themselves at her side, in their rightful place. She wondered if Liam would still be adopting that new gait of his, and whether or not Katy - who was bound to have been in tears by now - would have stopped crying.

❋

Doing her duty and playing the role demanded of her, Rachel navigated the hour or so that followed. She had put her arm round Katy on cue, sang when she was supposed to, prayed when asked. Unsure if she wanted to cry or not, she found herself refraining from doing so. It was not a question of fighting back the tears - and anyway Katy had more than enough for the pair of them! - but rather rationalising their non-appearance. Preparation was the key, she told herself; she had been prepared for this day for too long for it to spring any surprises on her. Emotionally, her father's illness had led to something of a drought, a barren spell that left her with the vaguest memories of when she and Liam had first heard the news and how she had cried then - and subsequently how they had struggled to know what to tell Katy. It was a recurring theme it seemed, how to tell Katy things.

"I'm not here today to say goodbye to my father. That happened a little while ago as he started to slip from me. There was a point - perhaps three or four weeks since - when I could not longer see the man who had shaped me and tutored me through life. No, that's not right. Perhaps it would be more accurate to say that was when the last fragment of the real Ronald vanished. Does grieving start then? I don't know.

"He didn't like funerals, even though one of his last jokes was about getting the chance to finally be involved in a ceremony in which he had a starring role. I'm sure that one wasn't original, of course. Perhaps those of you who knew him well enough will recognise what lay behind that joke: a man who tended to measure himself through others, never through himself. Which is a shame. Although his was an ordinary life - probably as all our lives are - it was also *extra*ordinary too. His CV may not be glittering in terms of achievements and celebrity, but what he did he did with honesty and passion. There was a special kind of integrity about him. And latterly an irascibility that I'm sure some of you will recognise."

There had been a small ripple of laughter at this point. Rachel had taken a pause to glance round the church. Most people were not looking at her but rather sat with their heads bowed, focused on the floor or the pew in front of them, as if removing as much external stimuli as possible gave them the space, the capacity to remember their friend. Liam was one of the few staring hard at her. He gave an almost imperceptible nod of encouragement.

"He said that when the time came he wanted no fancy eulogy, no-one reading 'Stop all the clocks'. He hated Auden anyway." Another ripple. "Yet that is, perhaps, the greatest gift he gave me; an enquiring mind and a love of literature. There are myriad poems that could be read, not just Auden; each of them might hint at something about the man but inevitably only scratch the surface. You might read them all and never get to the nub of him.

"So I simply ask you to do what he asked of me. Pick a moment, an event from somewhere in his life that encapsulated what he meant to you and just remember that. Hopefully it will be a moment that will make you smile or laugh, but if not it doesn't really matter. As long as it's a true reflection of him. If we all do that... Well, I think together we'll have a more complete picture of the man than any poet could offer."

Everyone had been watching her at the end, as if they needed to be attentive in order to understand and then execute the request.

"What moment did you choose, Mum?" Katy had asked later, after the service was over and they were loitering - the three of them - waiting to be taken to a local hotel where the wake was being held.

"Me? I don't think I can tell you really," Rachel said. "It would seem trivial, insignificant to anyone except me, and take far too long to explain." She glanced at Liam.

"Mine?" he said, responding to the unasked question. "The time he took me fishing, of course. Do you remember?" Both Rachel and Katy smiled; it was a story they knew well and one they were happy to recall again. A square in the quilt of Ronald's life. "Gradually, as the afternoon wore on, he became increasingly frustrated by my sheer incompetence. I couldn't get the worm on the hook, I couldn't cast properly, and managed to get the line tangled in a nearby bush more than once. And when I did finally catch something it was so small we threw it back in - only for me to catch the self-same fish about ten minutes later! He spent so much time trying to help me out that day he hardly had any time to himself."

"Which in a way is what fishing's all about isn't it, being selfish, solitary?" prompted Katy.

Liam nodded.

"But it was typically Granddad," she continued, "helping out."

"When he wanted to," Rachel qualified. She remembered when she told him that she was going to divorce Liam; it was an odd choice perhaps, but that was her moment. "I don't think you ever really saw him when he disagreed with you and wanted to let you know it. Oh, he was never an unpleasant, violent, shouty kind of person, but you always knew when you were on a different side of the argument to him."

"Did you see that, Dad?"

"Of course he didn't," Rachel answered before Liam had the chance to speak. "Your Dad was always Ronald's 'blue eyed boy'; he could do nothing wrong as far as Granddad could see."

"I'm not sure that's entirely true," Liam said, laughing a little.

"He was so grateful to you for taking me off his hands."

"Now *that* is entirely *un*true," said Liam with suitable emphasis.

＊

During the day, when she came across people she did not recognise, Rachel tried to navigate through them by era. If they were her father's age she assumed they were once work colleagues, or old friends from years ago, or people connected with the Rotary. Most who fell into this category were more practiced at farewells such as this and often made her job easier by suffixing their condolences with "I worked with your father", or "we studied geography together". Occasionally they surprised her, uncovering a history she didn't know he had -

like a tall, incredibly lean and frail gentleman who, leaning on his walking stick, said "Ronald and I used to play squash together. For thirty years I tried to beat him." Rachel hadn't known her father played squash, never mind his having been invincible. Indeed, she had always regarded him as the anti-sporting type. And then there was the small woman of less determinate age who confessed to once trying to teach Ronald german.

"German?" Rachel had been surprised; her father had never mentioned it, and as a family they had no tangible connection with the country.

"He was a very poor student," the woman said with a wistful shake of the head, allowing Rachel to catch the slight accent in her voice. "Never studied, never managed his verbs very well." She paused. "But he was an excellent dancer!" And then the woman was gone, back into the now thinning crowd.

"Who was that?" Katy's voice was suddenly welcome.

Rachel laughed.

"You know, I've no idea. Apparently she used to teach Granddad german."

"German?!"

"I know! And not only that," Rachel lowered her voice conspiratorially, "but they used to dance together. I didn't know he danced, did you? Did he ever say anything?"

"Nothing," said Katy.

"The things you find out," said Rachel allowing her voice to trail away a little.

"The tall man over there," Katy nodded towards the man with the cane, "he told me they used to play squash together!"

"I know," said Rachel, smiling. "Isn't it funny: squash, german, dancing. What a dark horse my father was!"

Whether it was this new compound image of the man they thought they knew or the opportunity for release but both women burst out laughing, Rachel's hand for a moment on

Katy's arm. A few faces turned their way unnoticed, smiles their silent accompaniment.

"Should we be laughing?" asked Katy after a few moments.

"You know, I think we should," said Rachel, sounding definite. "We should be celebrating your Grandfather as well as remembering him, and I guess laughing is as good a way as any."

Katy scanned the crowd.

"Where's Dad?"

Rachel followed her gaze, though without much commitment.

"I think he left. Said something about having to be somewhere in the morning. Leeds, I think it was." Rachel waited for a reaction. "Why?"

"Oh, no reason really. I haven't seen him in a little while and just wanted to chat."

"How is he?"

From her reaction, Rachel could immediately tell Katy was somewhat surprised by the question.

"Didn't you speak to him?"

"Yes, a little. But not much. And just in the context of the day, considering all this." Rachel's gesture, which is designed to encapsulate everything around them, completes the sentence. "We didn't really 'talk'. And I'm sure you've seen him more often than I have."

"Probably; but still not a lot." Katy gives the impression of contemplation, not so much of what she should say but what she can say. It is almost a realisation of how little she actually knows. "I've been up to to Settle a couple of times; once for a long weekend. We walked a bit, but didn't really do much else."

"How does he seem?" Rachel asked, keen to triangulate the fragments available to her.

"Well, 'settled' I suppose. Appropriately enough." It is a weak joke with little commitment behind it. "He has a nice house - small, you know? - and seems to have found himself a routine.

I don't think he works quite as much as before; at least he's not on the road like he used to be."

Rachel notes the word 'before'. She is sure Katy meant nothing by it, but she cannot escape the fact that there is a delineation of things now, a dividing event, a line she was responsible for drawing across all their histories.

"Winding down, then?"

"Maybe a little, though I'd be guessing." Katy smiled apologetically.

"And is he" - Rachel struggled for the word, something that could encapsulate all she wanted to know about him; a word someone might choose to measure her by and, if they did so, one being unavoidably layered with deeper meaning no matter how simple it was - "content?"

She saw her daughter trying to apply the notion to her experiences with her father in Settle, remembering their walks together, or chatting over a quiet evening meal.

"He seems so. As I say, he's got his routine and I think that works for him. There's a small garden to tend, and he reads a lot. He didn't talk much about himself to be honest. Why?"

"Why do I want to know?"

Katy nodded.

"Oh, I suppose I just want him to be okay, you know? That he's sorted."

The real reason for Rachel's question was to find a measure between them. Having been the instigator of their divorce - the drawer of that 'line' - it should surely be right for her to be in the better position; more content, more sorted. Katy is the only arbiter she has access to.

"I think he probably is," Katy said, her voice unable to prevent a tone that revealed she wanted to move the topic on; that she wanted, in fact - and all of a sudden - to leave. "Yes; he seems to be in a good place."

If it were an attempt to close the conversation down, it proved a successful one. Rachel processed the words individually, weighing them against an internal scale which eventually seemed to come to rest slightly in Liam's favour. It was not the answer she had been looking for or expecting. At that moment her attention was taken by a small group standing at the far door, wanting to speak to her before they departed. As she walked away from Katy towards them, she consoled herself by knowing the imbalance could have been a lot worse.

"The option of taking a rain-check"

"I fell over."

Liam sends the words into the telephone and out, invisibly, across the ether, to eventually be delivered to Alison. He wonders if there is the most fragmentary delay in transmission as he waits for her to interpret them.

"Where?"

"Near Rydal water. Yesterday morning had been miserable, but I was working so that didn't matter. Then the sun came out after lunch and I found myself ahead of the game as it were, so I decided to go for a stroll."

"But all the way to Grasmere!" Her tone tells him how crazy she thinks he is.

"You know how much I love Ambleside and that walk by Rydal Water. It's not as if it's that strenuous."

"Maybe not." She pauses, and Liam imagines her trying not to get any more cross with him than she is already. "So what happened?"

"Oh, a damp boulder, or an uneven one." He wants to make light of it. "It was slippery because of the rain, but I'm sure it moved as well. It must have."

"Did you hurt yourself?"

Liam shifts uncomfortably in his chair and looks down at his left leg as he adjusts the way it rests on the footstool, trying to get comfortable.

"A scrape."

"A scrape?"

"Well," he waits until he finds a suitable word, "more like a bang, I suppose."

"A bang!" Her alarm tells him the word is misplaced.

"No, more of a scrape; some broken skin. And a bruise. I'll have a big bruise tomorrow, no doubt. Rock can be really unforgiving."

"You've been to the doctor?" Alison has slipped into 'boss mode' and Liam finds himself smiling.

"I hobbled to the Chemist. They've given me something to rub on it - smells foul. And they said if it still hurts in a couple of days then I should go and get it checked out."

There is silence and for a moment Liam wonders if Alison's mobile signal has dropped. Having told himself off more than once over his blunder - the drive home had been excruciating! - he is expecting to be chastised; sympathy is not normally Alison's strong suit.

"Then 'bang' is probably the right word if that's what the Chemist said."

"Anyway, I just wanted to give you the option of taking a rain-check this coming weekend. Since it's seized-up a bit, I'm not going to be that mobile and I can't really see me being able to get out."

The words slip out before he can check them. He has become increasing sensitive to admitting any kind of frailty. Although he is not growing older at a different rate to Alison, he feels as if he is, as if the gap between them is increasing. Unintentionally or otherwise, she has given him a new lease of life, but it is as if he is spending this new-found credit faster than he should be. They are a few weeks into their easy routine now, but as he sits nursing a badly swollen knee and his wounded pride, he feels he has somehow managed to misplace years. As much as he wants to see her - as much as he always wants to see her - part of him, the part that's in pain, wants to be left alone.

"That's sweet of you, but to be honest it sounds as if there's even more reason for me to come up. Besides, I've had a busy week and I'm really looking forward to spending time with someone I actually like."

"It's been a bit like that has it?"

In the splinter of a gap, Liam can imagine her nodding.

"And I'll bring food. Lots of food. So don't worry about going out and shopping - not that you can. Just keep applying the ointment!"

"Yes Doctor." And for the first time in the conversation he hears her laugh and feels just a little bit restored.

Time has passed and they have settled into an arrangement whose terms are vague, unspoken. It is an understanding Liam likes to believe is mutual, almost telepathic, because such attributes make it strong and binding. But there are other times - like now, sitting in his chair with a badly swollen leg - when he fears the opposite, and that the two of them say nothing about the embryonic relationship they share because it is fragile and temporary, and to prod or poke it in any way would see it crumble to dust.

He takes consolation from her still wanting to come up for the weekend. Above all else, it had been commitment to honesty which forced him to offer her a way out, but he had done so with some trepidation. Such a move gave Alison an opportunity to bail out on him at a more significant level, and the demons which occasionally accost him were chattering loudly in his ear, telling him that this was her chance, warning him as soon as their pattern of meeting was broken the whole thing would fall like a house of cards. With unnerving certainty, the voices told him to prepare to be alone again. Consequently, he can only regard her determination to visit for the weekend as something of a triumph, a spit in the eye for his internal doubters. But they are never far away, and soon return with snide observations: that she is only coming up to satisfy her own needs - "some peace and quiet" - and not his; that as soon as she sees how frail he has become, she will remember he is just an old man and then be off, deserting him. Liam tries to chase them away, but the voices are always there, like an infliction of tinnitus become disturbingly articulate.

The rest of the day is a struggle, as is the night and most of the following day. When he moves, Liam endeavours to make the most of the effort and cram in as much productivity as possible before being forced to retreat to the sanctity of his study and the support of his footstool. He tries to kid himself he's feeling better and that another few hours rest will do the trick. The burgeoning bruise - thundercloud dark with patches of yellow like frozen lightening strikes - emerges on cue, and if the swelling is starting to reduce it is scant consolation. With less than twenty-four hours before Alison is due to arrive, Liam cradles the phone in his hand as he looks at his knee. The decent thing to do would be to take the initiative and simply tell her not to travel. He knows they will do nothing but mope around the house and he will be miserable because he will feel responsible - and Alison will leave feeling miserable too because she will have wasted her weekend.

Succumbing to his addiction to her, he puts the phone down, double-doses on pain-killers, and has one more scotch than he ought in the vain hope it will help him sleep, and that sleeping will help him heal.

❋

In the end, the weekend proves to be surprisingly successful. Alison spends most of the time fussing around him, being domestic. At one point she takes herself off into town, shopping for herbs and cake. Together they walk no further than the garden, but it is enough. Although Liam is regaining the ability to bend his knee, he is not yet up to walking far, and has already postponed the two work-related trips he was due to make the following week.

At first Alison had been a little alarmed on seeing the state he was in, but once they'd had the face-to-face debate on the linguistic merits of calling his accident a 'scrape' or a 'bang', she dedicates herself to making his weekend as stress-free as possible.

"There are other words I could use," she says, easing his trouser leg back down to hide the unsightly discolouration, "to describe what I see before me and what I should choose to call your accident, but in the interests of harmony I shall keep them to myself."

It is as close to chiding him as she comes. Given his discomfort and the confession as to how disturbed his previous night had been, they agree to sleep separately, supporting Alison's only demand of the weekend that she be allowed to rest too.

And sleep she does. When Liam struggles down into the kitchen a little after eight on Sunday morning there is no sign of her, and it is not until he has managed to source and then eat a little breakfast she emerges. An hour has passed.

"You never sleep this late," he says, unable to keep a note of bewilderment from his voice.

"And you," she says, gently pinching his cheek, "never fall over!"

The day is sedentary but satisfying; there is a kind of quiet domesticity about it that reminds Liam of other Sundays. Sundays in another life. Alison seems buoyant, enlivened, and Liam assumes it must be the benefit of her long sleep. She busies herself around him again and around the house, reads when he reads, occasionally watches some television. There is an old black-and-white classic they catch half of, missing the beginning and all of the ending. He feels as if they have crossed a threshold, and for most of the day - except when a sharp stabbing catches him out - is glad he fell over and hurt his knee.

As he watches her pack, replacing her things in the taupe travel bag that has already become familiar, he wants to tell her something but is unsure what it is. And even if he did know, he worries he would not have the words. So he says nothing, no observations, no declarations.

She leaves him with instructions.

"Don't try and go into town until Wednesday. There's food in the fridge all labelled up as to when it's for. Don't drink too much. Tomorrow, make an appointment to see the Doctor."

He nods dutifully, knowing - even though the edicts come from her - he is likely to disobey them all.

When it starts to rain just as she is about to leave, she makes him stay inside the house rather than get wet seeing her off.

So he stands at the lounge window looking out, even though he knows he will get nothing but a glimpse of colour through the hedge as she moves away. He stands and listens for the closing of the boot, the opening and closing of the driver's-side door. Eventually, when there is a flash of red, it is accompanied by a brief toot on the horn, and then the house is suddenly quiet. Liam imagines this is what it must be like to be wrapped in silence after a hurricane; a kind of eerie, ghostly emptiness.

And the voices in his head chuckle quietly and remind him that hurricanes always bring devastation.

"You laugh like a hyena"

It may be unusual for a woman but she enjoys being in her car. Whilst most people find driving a bind, a chore enforced by the need to propel oneself from one place to the next - and the most dissatisfying when 'the next place' is somewhere you have no wish to go! - in Alison's case it is completely the opposite. Only in her car can she revel in the freedom choice gives her. At a binary level it is merely left or right, but beyond the micro it allows her to go anywhere she chooses, at whatever pace she chooses, at whatever time. Buildings - especially offices and hotels - are like prisons; walls where the options given you are merely illusory. And so, when faced with no sense of journey, she tries to construct one, to create an illusion of travelling so that, at the end of the day, hopefully she and her clients have a sense of being somewhere else.

It is a lot like story-telling, and she seems to be good at that too. Or at least it is a talent that fits her theory. She once told someone she likened herself to a teacher of braille; a person who helped those who could not see to interpret something that was immediately in front of them. Afterwards - after the lesson, the meeting, the 'session' - even though they hadn't physically moved, she wanted them to believe they were in a different place, and when they were, almost universally they seemed grateful.

Being confined also brought out the 'showman' in her, the ring master - or the Siren that could lure people to their doom. She could orchestrate and cajole, manipulate and guide, and often the people she was with had no idea they were being played. She made the involuntary, voluntary. She wondered if such a skill made her a bad person or, at best, a shallow one. Was this ability of hers to act the part nothing more than a mask, covering up her own inadequacies with bravura performance? She had never doubted she was a flawed and incomplete woman; not in the physical sense - never in the physical sense! - but rather unrounded, missing a core ingredient, a gene. People had accused her of being hard and unsympathetic, which was why she made an extra effort on some occasions. The most unkind - and those who really didn't like her - said it explained why she had never married or had children. She would, they knew, make a terrible mother. There was no doubt in her own mind that she had a hard streak; it was a prerequisite for the job she did and the way she did it. Thick-skinned, she would rush headlong into conflict, thriving on it, always seeing the benefit of resolution before the next person, always one step ahead. It was, she knew, a little like a conjuring trick: keep their attention focussed on one thing - the *last* thing - while you prepared the next. Sleight of hand, or of voice in her case.

"You laugh like a hyena" a client had once said to her. She had solved his problem, but he had not liked the way she had done so, disapproved of her methods, and was not shy in telling her so. "Only over the carcasses of my victims" she had laughed, dropping her invoice onto his slightly substandard desk. She needed to feel superior, and her laugh was important. It was a weapon, a punctuation mark - a trademark, almost. She would fire it when someone got something right - or when they were way off the mark. Often they never knew the difference until she had spelled it out for them, guided their fingers once again over the dots on the paper.

Sometimes she let her guard down, but not often. Very rarely she found herself compromised and in a situation which ran counter to her modus operandi, that inverted the "it's business, not personal" mantra she would incant at the beginning of any working session. Tough days, long days, trapped in a meeting room when she had been unable to find her way out, unable to educate her clients, show them the light, lead them to safety - those days were the worst. She'd had one of those days when she met Liam for that drink in the hotel. And another when she came to stay with him in Settle that first time. Bad work days followed by limited freedom in her car - little time to 'unwind' - left her in a strange midway state when she was neither one thing nor another, neither "business" nor "personal". She was vulnerable then, and she hated being vulnerable. It was an enemy she had spent a lifetime fighting.

She had driven away from Liam's that Sunday afternoon with some gusto, speeding to the end of the road not as if she'd departed reluctantly, but rather as if she had escaped. She spun her little red car (a sports car, of course!) away from the town and headed south on the A65. Having already decided to avoid the motorways, she had left the top down in order to feel the exhilaration of the drive, the wind whipping through her hair, something to blow the cobwebs away. It was not that the weekend had been a bad one; far from it. Liam had been as charming and hopeless as always - especially so given his incapacitation - and she had revelled in the freedom his immobility had given her. The cooking and tidying she had undertaken were, contrary to appearances, essentially for her own benefit, allowing the exorcism of some of her domestic demons in a safe environment. And the walk into town had been a joy, an excuse to simply 'potter'; a mundane pleasure for most, but one in which she indulged so rarely it felt like a treat.

Her spirits beginning to be lifted, the stunning sleep she'd enjoyed on the Saturday night had so recharged her batteries that she felt strangely unstoppable the day after, a whirlwind already chomping at the bit to get stuck in to a challenging week ahead. What also helped was the fact it had been a genuine weekend, devoid of artifice. She had driven to Settle in a state of some confusion, and being worn out by her working day exacerbated the need to keep her guard up.

There had been a time when she had not been so calculating, when she hadn't realised there was a benefit in being so. As she pulled out to make a sharp manoeuvre and overtake a lorry on a short straight stretch, she was reminded of the younger Alison - the much younger Alison - who would have sat and waited for the perfect opportunity to make that manoeuvre; the Alison who had not yet learned that there were such things as calculated risks, and not having learned of them, had no idea when or where to take them. As she shifted back up into top gear and left the truck in her wake, she was reminded that it had been a painful lesson but an undoubtedly necessary one, even if she could not see it at the time. It had also been the moment when she had wanted to leave her old name behind, as if 'Alison' described the person she once was. She had been only partly joking when she told Liam that she disliked her name; something she is reminded of when he occasionally calls her 'Barbara'. Although a joke for him, it is a reminder for her, the warning shot that keeps her on her guard. There is nothing intrinsically wrong with the name 'Alison' and she doesn't really hate it; it is what it represents - the person she once was - that riles her.

Jonny had been perfect. To the young, naïve, impressionable version of herself setting out into the world of work and unsure of her future direction, he could be nothing but. Slightly older than her, he was suave, sophisticated; he had experience - the kind of experience Alison craved for herself - which offered to unlock the secret as to what she should do with her life. Their attraction had been mutual, and - less experienced than he and with just a small number of generally tepid relationships behind her - she had found herself 'all in' before she knew it. The imbalance, so patently obvious to Jonny from the very beginning, only became clear to her later when it was all over. Determined to never again be in the position of the 'old' Alison, she carried that experience around like the wound that aches when the weather gets too cold or damp; it is the barometer that tells her when things are about to deteriorate from 'fine' or 'fair'.

Driving on the A65, she looked up at the sky somewhat involuntarily, feeling the pressure changing once again.

*

She got home a little later than planned. In places the road had been clogged with people heading south after weekends away, and she had stopped for petrol, extending the break to indulge in a service station coffee and a browse through some magazines. In spite of the delay, she arrived back in Hope in good humour, still enthusiastic about the week ahead, looking forward to throwing herself headlong into problems to be solved, putting herself at risk - 'living on the edge' - when it came to running meetings or workshops.

Leaving the old Alison behind had become easier over the years, though occasionally she might still surface. Having been thinking of Liam, she remembered their visit to Levens Hall where her old self had made a dramatic and decisive reappearance, and there had been nothing she could do about it. But now she was back in control, her vision laser-sharp once more.

She had intended to break the news to him over the weekend, but had never quite found the moment. She knew this was partly due to his incapacity making him seem so vulnerable - and she never aimed to kick a man while he was down. Yet obtusely, she also saw her procrastination as a result of suddenly feeling so energised and wanting to revel in that for a few short hours. Driving south she had been steeling herself, trying to decide the exact terminology she should use. Words, she knew, were important; they not only delivered a message but set-up expectations for the future. Even though underneath it all they might essentially mean the same thing, saying 'pause' or 'break' or 'stop' told different stories, had different impacts. And she wasn't entirely self-centred or heartless. This wasn't just about her. In a way it was less what she said and more how Liam chose to interpret it. And she knew full well Liam's history, how he had been treated by Rachel. It was important to her that he didn't end up feeling there was something wrong with him, because there certainly wasn't. Yes, he was overly concerned about his age, but he could do nothing about that, so why not just get on with things? Surely that's what he had been doing with her. Or that's what she had helped him do. It was something to be emphasised.

Because of all that, when she lifted the phone from its cradle, she was determined to be gentle, telling herself that she had to paint the right picture - tell the right story. The notion allowed her to settle. Telling stories. Something she is good at. Something she does every day.

"Barbara!" his voice says unable to disguise the surprise.

She knows what that tone means - and thus how she needs to play her hand.

"Put your feet up"

"I just want to take a few days off," Liam says, the mobile phone pressed to his ear as he tries to pace the garden. As ever the signal is not particularly strong, but for some inexplicable reason he feels the need to be making his excuses outside, unconfined. "What? No, nothing like that; I'm fine. I feel like I haven't stopped for a while, that's all. And I've had an invitation from an old colleague to go and visit him in Scotland. It's where he's retired to; he's some Laird now, I think." The friend is an invention, a spur-of-the-moment thing, but Liam is pleased with it; it's the kind of colour that adds credibility to a lie. He is in no state to go anywhere. "No, I think we're all up-to-date on the deal. Ahead, if anything. And you know I wouldn't desert you if we weren't. Let them stew for a little while; radio silence, and all that. They've got our latest offer, so let them think it's the final one." It is easy to sound more authentic at this point, Liam knowing he is on solid ground. Indeed, the offer he and his client have just made for a small - but growing - retail business in the Midlands is a generous one, and one that should, in fact, be their last. "Yes, I know; these VC boys always want a little more than their pound of flesh. But they're realists too. They know a good deal when they see one - it's what makes them rich!" He laughs at something said. "And I'll keep an eye on the email, of course. If anything crops up, I'll be straight on to it." Another pause. "Alright. See you in about a week, Max."

He has no intention of going anywhere. Or perhaps he has, but simply hasn't made his mind up yet. He has been in something of a tailspin for the last twenty-four hours feeling as if someone has picked up his appointment book and ripped all the pages out; he has no idea what he is supposed to do next.

He recalls sitting in his chair immediately after her call, diverting all his energy into decoding what she had told him. At least this is what he imagines he did, or pictures himself doing. If he were asked to swear to it in a court of law, he might struggle. He would be an unreliable witness. The words were simple enough, the sentences in which she had bound them uncomplicated, the literal interpretation easy to fathom. He had picked up on all the nice things she had said about him, about their time together, and somehow managed to cast them aside as if they were merely noise, the unimportant part of her statement. Now, having applied this harsh filter, Liam is wrangling with what is left and trying to make sense of a subtext of his own invention. He has sought to persuade himself that he is over-reacting, and that what she had said - and the way she said it - was genuine, non-manipulative. He has tried laughing at himself, challenging with questions like "what did I expect?" and "shouldn't I be grateful that she spent any time with me at all?" But these merely play to an undercurrent of negativity.

Having slept badly, he had got up early and gone for a short hobble along a nearby bridleway. It was hardly inventive, but it got him moving and out of the house. What it had failed to do was to stop him thinking; a single line of enquiry which blocked out everything else. And then he had remembered work, and in doing so knew there wasn't a single part of him that could be spared to devote to it. Hence the call to Max. Excluding the injury from his fall, the picture he painted for himself had been accurate enough to justify a short leave of absence, if only to clear his head.

Slipping his phone back into his pocket - and simultaneously hearing the faint tell-tale sound of a train rolling through the town - Liam wonders whether Scotland might not be a bad idea after all. He could avoid the pain of driving and choose to go by rail; "let the train take the strain". Just a night or two; absorb himself in something different, in a place he didn't know. That challenge - of coming to terms with a new environment - has some attraction. Perhaps up to Glasgow and then on, not far; Loch Lomond, maybe. Seeing somewhere new.

It is strange how Alison's retreat seems to be affecting him more than Rachel's did. That, he muses, can only be the result of time's passing; after all, there was so much history with

Rachel, so much to lose. But then he remembers that more than anything else he had been angry with her, at her betrayal. Alison's withdrawal seems more tactical - even, if he is honest with himself, understandable. He knows full well the Liam with whom Rachel fell in love was not the Liam she left, no matter that he actually feels pretty much the same person. Alison's extrication is from precisely the same individual she accidentally bumped into. Or almost the same. Liam likes to think he has changed a little over the last few months, and for the better; if so, he knows that is largely because of her. But has he changed enough? Or are there things impossible to address? He wonders whether the fact he is half-heartedly contemplating a few days away on his own provides the answer to those questions, and not in ways he would wish. Inevitably.

A stabbing pain in his left leg brings him back to reality. He looks up the garden to the house; only a few yards really, yet it seems so much further. It is not just the distance which is daunting, but the going back inside; Liam knows there will be echoes there, fresh imprints from Alison's touch and influence. He wonders if that was why he had slept so badly, and curses his knee because he knows if he were able-bodied he would either be away from here or, by cleaning and tidying, trying to exorcise the place. It is activity he needs, not to be cooped up at the scene of the crime.

It is not cold, but he shivers involuntarily, an action which forces him to glance to the sky. It is virtually cloudless. From an abstract recent memory, he recalls a weather forecast that suggested "high pressure in charge", temperatures rising - even in Cumbria! Against the external kitchen wall, two weather-worn chairs and a small picnic table stand neglected. He could dust those down and bring them out onto the lawn, maybe his footstool too; if he wrapped up warm - enough layers to give him flexibility in case it really did get hot - and then brought out some books, his laptop, perhaps he might make the best of things, being outside without going anywhere at all. He could force himself to walk up and down the garden every hour or so to try and drive some flexibility back into his damned knee. Tomorrow he will need to get some shopping in, so will have to brave the trip into the town one way or another.

Having a plan comes as some relief, and Liam finds the distance to the house shorter than it had seemed. A few minutes later he returns semi-laden and proceeds to brush down one of the chairs and the table, then manoeuvre them out to a central spot on the lawn. He hears - but does not see - a train whistle through; he thinks momentarily of Scotland and knows that would have been a crazy idea.

*

Eschewing the doctor, he relies on the foul-smelling poultice and short enforced marches to get his knee back into some kind of shape. The days of that next week pass in a routine of sorts: bursts of activity followed by drags of boredom. If he could draw his mood it would be a sine wave, a little like the pulsing pattern that might glow from a hospital monitor. And if he were able to hear the beeping, it would do no more than persuade him he was still alive; a factual, non-qualitative sound. Having been enough for the first few hours of this interregnum, the routine satisfies him little beyond that.

By the Thursday he is able to walk with sufficient ease into town, and without too much pain; enough to confirm there is no reason why he shouldn't go back to work. It is easy to know why he has missed it: not because of the work itself, but because of the activity it demands of him. More than ever, he needs to be occupied.

When Liam rings him, Max asks about Scotland. Liam, who has forgotten his earlier lie, bluffs his way through another, saying that he had decided not to go in the end. His line - "apparently the midges are really bad this time of year" - is embarrassingly lame, but it is enough to satisfy Max who, quite clearly, has been chomping at the bit to get his deal done. Liam promises to pick up on the various emails trails on the Friday and then travel to see him in Birmingham on Monday. "We're nearly there" is enough to placate him.

And so the months begin to pass in an anonymous way. Liam forces himself to be busier than he had been planning, taking on a little extra work here and there; he is more diligent perhaps, a little more driven, and he finds projects concluding slightly earlier than he had anticipated and once or twice with better than expected results. He is rewarded with the occasional bonus which he diligently squirrels away in various savings pots and investment schemes as directed by his accountant.

"At this rate you'll soon be able to retire," Will says one day over lunch after a particularly handsome bonus accompanies the satisfactory conclusion of a tricky merger. "You've built yourself a nice little nest egg. Why don't you put your feet up?"

Retirement has never been something Liam has actively considered. He has been increasingly aware of its proximity, of its ever-increasing threat, but it has always been just around the next corner, never standing full-square in front of him. Will's suggestion pops it right into focus, an inevitability Liam finds impossible to ignore or go around. Knowing it is a topic he can no longer dodge, he decides - driving home from lunch - he must give confront it seriously, systematically. If it were a problem with a deal, a roadblock or something commercial needing to be resolved, then he would analyse it, break it down into its constituent parts and simply 'dismantle' it. The prospect of adopting such a methodical approach makes him feel much better, as if he already has the upper hand, and so he sets out the terrain and terms upon which the battle will be fought: his garden that Saturday afternoon, relaxing in one of his outdoor armchairs with a glass of wine or two. Perhaps with a notebook to-hand. Given the choice, he would want to work through it with someone; he knows a good general never rides into battle without a trusty lieutenant at his side. He briefly contemplates calling Alison, but they have not spoken since she freed herself of him. She has called twice, but he missed her both times and chose not to return either call. Unrealistically, he thinks of enlisting Rachel's help, but they haven't spoken for even longer, and, to be frank, why would she care - apart from wishing to protect her share of his income? He settles for Katy, only to find that he cannot get hold of her in time so he must face the enemy alone.

In wishing to deconstruct the question facing him, Liam - once he is comfortable in his chair, already one glass of wine to the good - opens his notebook at a clean page and writes 'Retirement' at the top, then underlines it. Twice. The second line seems to give it gravitas as a word, as if forcing him to take it all the more seriously. He pauses to refill his glass and then tries to isolate the core components with which he has to wrestle. He is trying not to look upon the exercise as one that demands any kind of immediate commitment. Indeed, this is a reconnaissance mission, an attempt to understand the enemy's position. Later he will make a decision. Down the left-hand side of the page he starts a list with several blank lines between each entry for workings and further thoughts. He writes: 'age', 'money', 'time'. Then he pauses. They are small words, insubstantial things on their own; at one level they all represent somewhat nebulous concepts. Yes, his age is an absolute thing that can be enumerated precisely, but to Liam - in the context of what he is doing now - that is hardly the point. Of course, he will need to consider social norms and his legal status of a person of some maturity (he refuses to countenance 'old age pensioner'), but 'age', as he considers it now, is more about how he feels. He may be sixty-four, nearly sixty-five, but what does that actually *mean*?

Leaving that question for the moment, parking it in the 'difficult' column, he moves on to 'money'. This is much easier. Will has already run some numbers for him, outlined various scenarios based on him stopping earning right away, then in one year, two years, three years. Will stopped at three years. That there might actually be an inescapable and finite 'end' hits Liam for the first time. He wants to formulate the question "what about four years, or six, or eight?" but something stops him, a nagging voice returns - the same one that niggled at him when Alison was last there - to ask "who wants a seventy-two year old working for them?"

He takes a sip of wine and then runs his fingers along the lines of numbers in Will's spreadsheet: savings amounts gradually dwindling over time against spend and falling levels of income. All the years of doing deals, working through computations, looking for the optimum position, lead him to an unavoidable conclusion: he can't stop now, but he could stop within two years. He allows his eyes to slide up a few lines to where the word 'age' stares back at him as if it were bating him, asking for a fight. Placing a simple tick beneath the word 'money' to signify that he has it covered, has a plan, doesn't have to worry about it, Liam moves to consider 'time'.

It had been written not as a philosophical prompt but rather to question what he was going to do with his days once he has stopped working. Even so, it is the vague and esoteric which assaults him first; combining 'time' with 'age' is like having two bullies joining forces in order to beat the shit out of him outside the school gates. He puts down his pen and sips again. He has never liked bullies. Divide and conquer. He picks up his pen again, determined to make a list of the things he likes to do, the things for which he wishes he had more time to devote. It is another list: reading, gardening, walking. The last word stops his list-making; involuntarily he looks down to his mending left knee and thinks of his body. There is more than one way to consider 'time', he realises; time has a different metabolism depending on levels of physical and mental ability. Ronald was proof, if proof were needed, that those two particular clocks often tick at different speeds near the end. He knows which is the more important, but shakes off any desire to try and delineate them for himself. This is just an exercise, after all; why not assume 'time' - his remaining time - as being the same for both? "His remaining time." Again the whispering voice; the sniggering.

Reading, gardening and walking - and now he is stuck. Liam thinks for a moment and then writes 'hobbies' as if that were a thing in itself. He hears himself justifying his decision to clients like Max: "and I'll have lots of time for my hobbies". It's the kind of statement most people might accept at face value, surely a reasonable justification for his decision; but what would he say to those who might frown and ask "what hobbies?" Gardening, reading and walking don't seem enough. Worse than that, the words themselves feel superfluous, empty. They were easy for Liam to write; in a professional context he would call them "free hits". There must be more, something new; there must be something he has always wanted to do but never had the time. Isn't that what people say? Isn't that what both Rachel and Alison argued in their own way? 'Travel' is a common ambition, ignoring the fact that older people are often either too poor to too frail to enjoy it. Liam, having added 'hobbies' to his list, puts three dots after it in order to demonstrate that he hasn't finished with that just yet. It feels like a suitable compromise. He waits for the teasing voice but hears nothing.

He once worked with a man - Tony - who, when in his fifties, was assiduously saving for his retirement. He was proud of his plan, confident he would retire early while still young enough to get the benefit of all that hard work. Liam remembers him as an affable, slightly over-weight and florid individual - and he also remembers the shock one weekend when he heard that he'd died of a massive heart attack. The recollection makes Liam question the activity in which he is currently engaged, wondering what the point of it is; does it matter whether he can or can't articulate what 'hobbies' means? And does Tony's lesson tell him that he should work on as long as possible - or perhaps simply stop right now? He suspects it is the latter. He knows - even without the prompting of that intrusive negative voice - he should let tomorrow go hang. It is a logic which, if he follows it, leads him down other avenues and alternate paths. Some of these paths might have included Alison, and Liam can't help but wonder if he had been committed to such a route she might not have walked out on him.

The problem is, of course, one of bravery. Even if he knows he should stop working now - knows it as profoundly as it is possible to know anything - then he is similarly certain that he lacks the courage to take that step. He retrieves his glass and sipping from it again wonders if he has always been that way, the kind of man who takes the safe option, is risk averse or worse. One might observe that the kind of work he does is inherently 'risky', so how can he possibly be risk averse? But Liam combats any professional threat he faces by taking a structured, methodical approach; he de-risks the deals he works on. Has he been doing that for himself for years, de-risking his life? When was the last time he took a chance, personally, on his own initiative? Is that what Rachel did, and is the audacious bravery of her action the single most shocking component of the whole episode? If so, should he have been applauding her all along? Alison clearly took a risk with him, but it was a calculated one, and as soon as it became evident to her that the rewards were - he is unsure of the word - 'inadequate', she bailed. As he sits there contemplating his own inadequate list, he realises the last thing he can do is to blame her.

'Time'. The word stares back at him unadorned, almost as if challenging for a definition. It makes 'hobbies' feel easy. It is the immeasurability of the finite - of the unknown finite - that is defeating him. He could make list upon list of the things he could do with his time - read, write, walk, sculpt, take up pottery, knitting, train spotting, bird watching; it could be never-ending. Yet Liam knows it is all dependant upon one limiting factor, upon one unknowable element: how much time he has. He thinks of Will's spreadsheet, the numbers arranged in an orderly fashion, behaving according to set rules and formulae hiding in the background. If you know the number in one cell, then you know the one in the next, and so on. These are absolutes. For a moment Liam wishes he could corral time in the same fashion, chart it, then choose how to spend it, wisely or not. It is something of a macabre thought, but he cannot shake it. What if he was told he had ten years to spend, or twenty? Or five? He is as certain as he can be that such knowledge would make his mind up for him. "What's the rush?" he might say to himself. The phrase 'take your time' hits him in all its literal accuracy, knowing that he *is* spending his time even as he sits there; he *is* choosing to deplete his stock in contemplation of his stock - the most futile activity of them all. The irony of wasting the very commodity he is suddenly desperate to protect - and to do so willingly, without hesitation - strikes him as exceedingly funny; it is something he wishes to share, but has no-one to share it with. And even if he had, would they understand?

He shakes his head and drains his glass, as if the combination will bring him to his senses. It does no such thing of course, and so he throws his notebook back onto the table and fixes his eyes on the herbaceous border at the far end of the garden.

Two weeks later, another misplaced step, another fall.

"I thought it was what you wanted"

Even though so much time had passed, Katy was still unsure as to whether or not she had forgiven her mother. Preventing her seeing her grandfather before he died may have been stimulated by selfless motivation, an unspoken desire to protect her daughter, yet Katy's decision to forgive her would have been easier to make if this particular need for absolution had been a one-off, rather than another to be added to the tally. Fundamentally, Katy had yet to rationalise whether she would ever be able to forgive the betrayal of her father, and everything else seemed to stem from that. Having to revisit the same old question afresh only made the situation more complex, and no matter how hard she tried - or how hard she *felt* she had tried - it seemed little had changed to materially tip the scales in her mother's favour.

The best Katy seemed able to concede was that a new kind of familial equilibrium had been reached; most importantly perhaps, it was one to which her father seemed reconciled. Unable to find the words to pose the direct question to him, rather than divining his opinion as to whether or not he was happy she could only rely on her own judgement when interrogating the evidence presented during her infrequent visits to Settle. She saw echoes of their old home and of his footprint there: the study, the garden. And he seemed not only at ease but during her penultimate visit months previously there had even been a little frisson about the place, the source of which she struggled to locate. She had been tempted, after this, to finally draw a line under the recent past; it seemed as if both her parents had done so themselves, so why should she be the one clinging to the wreckage?

But something prevented her. Certainly, her mother's reticence to open up just before her grandfather's death sat a little uneasily with Katy, and from her perspective it was significant she had been the one to offer an olive branch. If the attempt to use his imminent passing as a catalyst for reconciliation had failed, it was not for the want of trying. Yet rather than regard that missed opportunity as some kind of closing event, it became negative, inconclusive. Typically, Katy was willing to regard it as a postponement, prepared to book her mother in for another chance. No matter how angry she had been - or indeed, still could be - she did not regard herself as totally heartless.

Her most recent visit to Cumbria, weeks after her grandfather's funeral, proved as surprising as the one before. Not because of the continued presence of her father's new-found joie de vivre, but because of its absence; one minute it had been there and the next it was gone. Not that he seemed tangibly any the worse for it; if anything, he seemed back to the normal, stable, reliable individual she would have previously anticipated encountering. He was the man Katy had known for the last ten years of her life (excluding the period during the divorce) and so there was really nothing to be alarmed about. It might even have been regarded as reassuring. But something was missing; a light which seemed to have shined briefly, mysteriously, was no longer visible. Not that her father appeared perturbed by its absence. Indeed, Katy was unable to say whether or not he noticed anything at all, and not having remarked on his up-beat tone when she had seen him previously, felt poorly equipped to challenge him on that which had burned for a short while but was now no longer there.

Perhaps it was preoccupation with her own version of domestic bliss over the previous few months which had demoted any further reevaluation of her parents' past. Having taken her grandfather's death hard, Katy was as grateful as she was surprised by Tom's proving to be something of a rock. She had lashed herself to him for a few short weeks to ensure fixity of some kind. It was not that she had anticipated any cataclysmic breakdown on her part, far from it; but having a constant point of reference, a Pole Star, was a useful insurance policy even if she never intended to make a claim against it. At least that was her interpretation of events. As she returned to a state she considered 'normal', Tom failed to mirror that reversion, seeming to have changed permanently. He was more attentive than she could ever remember, closer in ways Katy had been unable to describe. There were aspects of this new proximity that - for a time, at least - forced her to look on him and their relationship in a new light: he was more caring and tender; there was a greater consideration in their intimate moments which proved stimulating. That the candle of their sex life should suddenly burn so much brighter as a result of what she still regarded as a tragedy felt incongruous in the extreme; yet it was a byproduct she was happy to revel in for a while. Then, almost as quickly as it had come upon her, Tom's unwavering attentiveness became cloying and stifling. Katy struggled to know if that was because she had moved on and no longer needed his comforting, or because Tom was becoming increasingly intense. Prior to this there had been a few brief days where she had found herself contemplating a never-ending future with him, the inevitability of children. Doing so, although a new sensation, for a while seemed appropriate, apt. Having a positive appreciation of him replaced by something almost its direct opposite was, therefore, a juxtaposition which proved difficult to reconcile. She had wanted to discuss it with her father on her earlier visit to Settle, but that had coincided with his seeming to be in a really good place himself, and the last thing Katy wanted to do was to deflate him with her own concerns.

Inserting some distance between them had been Katy's only available recourse.

"But you don't even like the gym!" Tom had been unable to suppress his surprise when he heard the news.

"Just because you've never known me to go," Katy had protested weakly.

"It's not just that. What about all those times you've slagged off the women you've see in tight lycra, posing around town, too slim for their own good? 'Junkies' I think you called them once."

She ignored his objection.

"I used to go. A while ago. Before I met you. And I decided I wanted to have another try, that's all. I'm feeling a little..." -

she struggled for the word, knowing the one which came most readily to mind in describing how she felt had nothing to do with physical conditioning - "flabby."

It was a pathetic offering, and even though she regarded Tom's reflexive laughter as justification for her signing-up for a month's trial and a few beginners' spinning classes, it still annoyed her. Working on her fitness would not be a bad thing, that was obvious, but going to the gym - *having* to go to the gym to make the classes, to justify any financial investment - was actually all about space, her space, nothing else. When it had occurred to her that she needed to put some day-to-day distance between herself and Tom, to give her the room to re-establish exactly how she felt about him after the roller-coaster of first revelling in their new-found intimacy and then being turned off by it, the gym seemed a pragmatic solution. For perhaps three days a week she had given herself a reason to be away from the house for two hours at a stretch. It was time that appeared on her horizon like a desert oasis. More than that, whatever his observations, she knew Tom couldn't really object. She had worried he might also become enthused and decide he wanted to join the gym as well; after all, if extra exercise was going to be good for her, then why shouldn't it be good for him too? Even so, she had taken a calculated risk, betting on Tom regarding what he would need to give up to do so - very little, on the face of it - would be too high a price to pay for an hour of physical discomfort. She was also gambling that there was a limit to his current pathological devotion to her: it might also prove - this diversion of hers - a litmus test of how *he* really felt too. Even though this analysis led to relatively binary choices, when she gave it due consideration it was evident that there were multiple routes to reach a conclusion. This meant that however definitive her assessment of the situation might purport to be, it could in fact be no such thing. She might as well have pulled petals from a daisy while chanting "he loves me, he loves me not...".

The whole enterprise proved more demanding than she recalled from past experience; the spinning classes were especially tough and forced her into a grudging reassessment of the slim and lycra-clad as they stepped off their bikes at the end of a session to warm-down with a fifteen minute jog on a running machine or a gentle encounter with the stepper. Katy was envious of the warm-down, never mind their prowess on the bike. Although the temptation to throw in the towel after just a couple of visits was remarkably strong, she forced herself to weigh pain and discomfort against what the gym offered her. Having expected to welcome the space, the absence of Tom, the preoccupation with something else, she was not disappointed - even if the price was hard work. What had surprised her most of all, however, was the anonymity. She walked through the door and onto the gym floor and found herself known by no-one; it was almost as if she didn't exist. And because of that, there was no pressure on her, no expectations other than the low ones she imposed on herself. It was this invisibility above anything else which permitted her to relax, and once she had seen off enough sessions for her muscles to scream more tolerably at her, it was the anonymity which allowed her to unwind. The whole combination saw her stamina levels rise, and two months in - the trial period already relegated to history - she was feeling the difference physically.

Tom began to feel the benefit too. Not in Katy's level of fitness - though he couldn't help but notice how much more 'toned' she was - but in her mood. The agitated short-fuse to which she had been all too frequently exposing him gradually became a thing of the past, and their routine seemed to establish a revised datum akin to that enjoyed prior to her grandfather's death. She was not oblivious to this new balance, nor to the sense that Tom had felt it too, so she found herself prepared to give him additional credit for simply not mentioning it. He may have remarked on her looking a little slimmer - safe territory for a man! - but that was as far as he chose to take it. Katy had decided that for once further analysis was not required.

In the end, however, her assessment of the situation - of their situation - proved all too superficial, its equilibrium blown out of the water when one Thursday evening Tom proposed.

Like so much in her life it seemed, she hadn't seen it coming. Her mother's desire for a divorce had been an earthquake; her grandfather's illness a significant tremor. But this. It felt off the scale. Four little words which, in an instant, undid all her hard work. Bizarrely, the first thing she registered was the threat of walking back onto the gym floor no longer anonymous but branded by a small gold ring; she would be a 'wife'. That tie, that belonging, would turn her into something else.

"But you can't be surprised, surely?" Having witnessed Katy's shock, Tom could not help but be incredulous himself. The two of them had stood there - he limply holding her hand - staring at each other as if they were complete strangers. When she failed to reply, Tom could only continue. "I just thought things were going so well. And after all this time." He paused. "I thought it was what you wanted."

From somewhere Katy thought she saw lightning. It may only have been imaginary, figurative, but it meant thunder was coming. She wanted to close her eyes and close her ears, to hunker down under a duvet somewhere and ride out the storm. But she knew she could not, for she was at its centre.

She replayed the notion that Tom thought he knew what she wanted. It was an obtuse idea given, on this topic at least, she had no clue herself. Indeed, until he had said "will you marry me?" the words sideswiping her, tipping her off balance, the phrase might never have been uttered in the history of the world so far was it from her consciousness. But it was worse than that. Tom even *believing* he had sufficient understanding of her was a remarkable notion. As he stood there, she was struck by how little he knew; indeed, did he know her at all? She looked down at their hands, still touching. It was an ignorance which stretched credulity beyond the point at which it snapped. Posing the question disqualified him in so many ways. If he *had* known what she wanted, how different would that have looked? For example, he would have understood why she needed to go to the gym and not questioned her motives. But taking yet another step back from that, had he been in tune with her desire for space and distance, then surely he would have been proactive and done something to mitigate her strife, removing the need for her to contemplate the gym in the first place. What did *that* say about him? And what did it say about time, the value of it, and what they - she - had done with it? Surely there should have been something to show for all that time, all that effort; hadn't she earned something from the relationship? Didn't she deserve something more? Was it not reasonable to assume that time invested should lead to understanding, because the evidence presented to her - "I thought it was what you wanted" - suggested the complete opposite.

Decision-making was the problem, in part because being decisive had never been her strong suit. The double-whammy was that whenever circumstances changed and things shifted, Katy compounded her difficulty by always assuming there was a decision to be made. Tabby had often accused her of being unable to 'go with the flow', and if she had not quite understood exactly what she meant or what that looked or felt like, then "will you marry me?" had suddenly crystallised that notion. She now realised she had moved through her adult life with an increasing sense of self-obligation; she was operating against a default equation which meant every time someone changed one of the variables she was forcing herself to re-solve the algebra. Tabby, in being so much more laissez faire, would simply ignore the implications of the things that seemed to bother Katy, perhaps never even acknowledging there was an equation to solve in the first place. Tom's proposition was, however, one of those interventions to which even Tabby would have needed to respond; doing nothing was simply not an option. In setting this new problem alongside those from the past which she had forced herself to address, she realised her mistake; namely, her failing to recognise that she might simply have let some of her earlier conundrums go and see how life played out. There was a resolution to be made on that front - another decision, perhaps! - but she could come back to that later; there would be time enough.

Obtusely, she had turned Tom down almost before she realised it; even before she had weighed-up all the options. After he had left the flat - "just to get some fresh air" - Katy found herself amazed she had done so. And so swiftly. It had been the biggest decision she had ever faced in her life, and if her track record was anything to go by, she surely needed days - if not weeks - to evaluate the options, all possible solutions. Yet she had taken just seconds, her rejection of him surgical, precise. Standing by the window and watching him walk down the path and then out the front gate, turning right towards the park, she hoped she had been kind, had chosen the appropriate words. That she could not remember them was of little concern. The greatest relief of all was that a decision had been made; one taken quickly, instinctively, in consequence sweeping that particular monkey from her shoulders and passing it on to Tom. For now it was his turn to decide something. His gamble - not that he would have seen it as such - had failed to pay off.

"Now look what you've made me do"

She had known Matthew for as long as she could remember. He was the kind of person who could creep up on you without your realising he was there. Or at least that's how Alison chose to recall him later, when he was no longer around to contradict her. It was a regular occurrence, this not forgetting Matt. Inevitably perhaps, he forced himself on her once again not long after she had freed herself of Liam, prodding and poking at what she had chosen to do, at her history, challenging her to debate with him one more time. She was not fond of rituals - especially intangible ones - but had given in to this one; it had become a yardstick against which to measure the unmeasurable.

If you pressed her, she would have told you they were six or seven when they first met. There are anecdotes to support the timeline though some of these she has borrowed from friends over the years because they suit her purpose; anecdotes borrowed and their ancestry then forgotten. Equally vague is the recollection when she became aware of Matt as a burgeoning adult, a potential foil for her own rather hesitant march through puberty. The event where they first kissed is indelibly etched on her memory, however. It had been the end-of-term prom marking the culmination of secondary school, the herald of another long summer break, precursor to the rigours of sixth form and 'A' levels. During the nine or ten years of their acquaintance they had orbited each other, unaware of the gravity pulling them ever closer. She had been the taller of the two until they were about thirteen when Matt suddenly grew - both upwards and outwards. The passing of a single term was enough to see him become the object of infantile crushes amongst some of her friends, their attempts at grown-up conversations about him as ham-fisted as their clumsy and unsuccessful wooing. Such discourses were pastimes in which she never whole-heartedly participated, and even though she could see the attraction, her appreciation was from a safe, academic distance.

The prom party put an end to all that, of course. Within twenty-four hours she had a boy-friend, her life turned upside down. Although they swore undying love and were inseparable for six weeks until school began again, their studies would soon not cement their relationship but shatter it: Alison was to remain in the same school, Matt moving to a technical college closer to his home. They told themselves it would make no difference. Alison assumed one clumsy attempt at intercourse would be enough to bond them together forever. That it failed to do so should have been no surprise; it certainly isn't when she looks back on it now. But at the time Matt had been her world, and when he began to drift away, not unnaturally subsumed into his new life and his new friends, it felt like a tragedy. She saw herself as a Juliet, convinced that life was no longer worth living.

Two years later another party reunited them. Matthew had quite clearly moved on. When Alison first caught a glimpse of him, she remembered the boy even though she was looking at a dashing young man. He had walked straight over to her, smiling, confident, without hesitation giving her a hug. Years later, she cringes at the memory, at how naïve she must have seemed to him, still the girl from the prom trapped in a life of fantasy. That they became firm friends said more about him than her; it was a role he slipped into easily, adopting it by default without asking permission, as if it was his destiny and the most natural thing in the world. When he asked her probing questions about her own life, begging for the detail on the two years or so he had missed, she was vague, off-balance. He insisted on taking her to the cinema; they met for the occasional walk on a Sunday. Without her realising it, Matt provided her with a framework, a sounding board against which she could explore her own personality. She could be cross, flighty, aloof, preposterous; he would take it all in his stride, alternately laughing or scolding. They were both nineteen, and meeting Matt again was like being introduced to the older brother she'd never had.

Even though they ended up studying at universities a hundred miles apart, Matt remained her rock. They would see each other at least once during term, and always over the holidays. As Alison grew in confidence and began to blossom into an independent woman, he was always in the background, a counter-balance for when she misjudged, an aide when she slipped. She kept nothing from him.

"We're like a sad old married couple," he said to her one Easter evening after they had drunk too much wine and were laying on the sofas in his parent's lounge listening to Keith Jarrett.

"Not sad," she protested, happy to leave the rest of his statement intact.

More than once she had wondered if they should try again, see if there was enough of that juvenile spark left to reignite the teenage flame. But she had always shaken the notion away, certain they had found something in its stead that was too precious to risk.

The only time they ever clashed was later, when Jonny appeared on the scene.

"You know," he said over the phone one day, "that he isn't good enough for you."

The two men had met at a work event; Matthew being in town for a couple of days, Alison had invited him along. She had desperately wanted them to be friends. Feeling as if she loved both of them, surely that would be enough to guarantee fealty? But they had clashed instantly. Aware of their shared history, Jonny's arrogance and superiority over the other man was fuelled by his possession of Alison, of succeeding where the other had failed. Matt's desire to protect her made him aggressive, convinced the other man was not to be trusted. The clash had forced Alison to take sides.

"I think I should be the judge of that, don't you?" Her rejoinder had been biting.

"Well I suppose there's a first time for everything."

With the benefit of significant hindsight, Alison knew there was a version of her - both a pre- and post-Jonny version -

who would have taken his rebuttal in the spirit intended. Instead they fought.

The damage was done. After their row, Matthew refrained from contacting her until it was too late to mitigate the suffering eventually brought on by Jonny; and Alison chose to keep her own counsel until a mutual acquaintance had revealed his cancer diagnosis.

"Look at you," Matthew had said approvingly, the smart, professional, hardened and somewhat battle-scarred Alison standing on the threshold of his room at the hospice.

"Look at you" she wanted to say but could not, because looking at Matthew was suddenly the last thing she wanted to be doing. Clumsily propped up in the bed before her he seemed someone else, an impostor, the pale shadow of the brother she had loved.

In spite of herself, the sight of him had made her cry - and she had sworn she would never allow another man make her cry, not after Jonny.

"You bastard!" she had said. "Now look what you've made me do."

"Well, it's a start," he had smiled, then coughed. It was a harsh, rasping cough; the kind of sound bereft of hope, a predictor of the future.

She had looked around the room while she dried her eyes, conscious he was watching her closely. It was a sterile, impersonal room; suitably transient. The standard gambit of "how are you" or anything akin to that was obviously denied her. In the end she chose to pretend their few years of silence had never happened.

"Well, you were right about Jonny."

"Of course," Matt replied, picking up on her tone, "though it gives me no satisfaction at all. For once I'd hoped I might have been wrong."

"Me too." She slipped off her coat and threw it over the back of a chair, taking the one closest to his bed. She gave his frail hand a brief squeeze. "Unfortunately it took me far too long to realise he was, in fact, Mr Wrong."

"How long?"

"Oh, a couple of years, I suppose. Or just under."

*

"Are you okay?"

Another cough had caused her to pause. Matthew, having turned his head away for a moment, now offered her a weak smile.

"Never been better," he lied.

"I can come back some other time," she offered.

He shook his head.

"You know I don't like cliff-hangers, so you can't just leave the story there, half-told. I'd have to make the rest up for myself and who knows where that might lead?"

It was a statement which implied nothing, although once upon a time it might have been laden with meaning. It was not lost on her, and the cruel irony of it bit. She knew Matt intended the irony, but not the cruelty.

"Anyway, we'd been going out for, I don't know, nearly a year, I suppose. I'd been besotted from the start and still hadn't got over it. For a while it had been hard - I mean after our row and everything - but then I guess I let you go, drift away. There'd been a choice to make, and to be honest, you made it an easy one. And I did too, I suppose. All of which could only mean more space for Jonny to fill, and filling it, he became even more fundamental to me. I hate myself for it now of course, but I was living my life through him: we did what he wanted, went where he wanted. I told myself that was what love was all about, and that me being selfless just proved how much I loved him."

"And not how..." Matthew interrupted, but stopped himself from finishing the sentence.

"It's all right," Alison said quickly, "you can say it; all it proved was how stupid I was. Am I right?" She didn't wait for him to agree. "And it did prove that. In spades. Not that I saw it, of course. I mean, how can you? How are you supposed to *know* that kind of stuff until it's too late?"

Her pause allowed him in.

"You aren't. Not the first time; the time you learn from. You just have to hope you don't get too badly burned. And then hope you're wise enough not to make the same mistake again." He hesitates.

"Say it," she prompted. "I know you well enough, even now; there's something else."

"Well, the Alison I see here has clearly learned her lesson."

"How so?"

"You have an independence and edge about you."

"'An edge'?"

"Pass me that water will you, please?"

She waited as she watched his hand, shaking, take the glass from her then bring it to his lips. One sip, two. He handed the glass back.

"You give the impression that you don't stand any nonsense, that's all. It's a bit like you've built a minefield around yourself and stuck up a sign that says 'Danger! Keep out!'."

Alison laughed.

"Christ! Am I that severe?"

"Not severe. Just someone who's not to be messed with." He paused again, then smiled. "Which isn't to say, of course, that you're not an attractive woman."

"So you still fancy me then, after all this time?"

"Always."

His laugh dissolved incongruously into another cough. Alison waited. There was a rejoinder, but she had no desire to make him laugh again.

"So I thought Jonny was it: 'the man of my dreams'. I was so stupid!" She paused to allow her to corral the story again before pressing on. "I made assumptions about us, about our future. I assumed he would ask me to marry him, that we'd have children and live happily ever after."

"But clearly not."

"Clearly. One day I broached the subject."

"Marriage?"

"Children," she clarified. "I might just as well have told him I was gay or had VD or something. It was something he hadn't seen coming. Or maybe he had, I don't know. It rocked him. And the transformation was almost instantaneous. We hadn't been living together, but he'd been staying at my place so much that we might have been. On reflection he was probably just using me as a cook, a supplier of food." She hesitated a moment. "An easy lay."

Matthew moved an arm across the covers and put his hand on hers. Alison stared at it for a moment then let it rest there.

"He was just taking advantage. He must have been because he started staying away, gradually, then more often. There were reasons he couldn't come round or go to the pub or the cinema. Excuses. And then at work I started to notice the looks I was getting. I'd seen them before; looks reserved for other girls. Looks that were full of pity rather than envy; looks that told you they knew what was going on even if you didn't."

"Someone else then."

"Cindy or Candy or some bitch from Accounts. It doesn't matter." Alison paused. "Why is it that men can be such bastards?"

Matthew offered a wry smile.

"Not just men, I'm sorry to say. But," he said, hurrying past her quizzical gaze, "it's good that you're still angry."

"Why's that?"

"Because it keeps you on your guard."

"Just to make sure I keep the minefield warning signs painted nice and clear?" She laughed.

"Something like that." He withdrew his hand. "Just remember to take them down at some point."

The evening had encroached on her stealthily. She had been sitting reading and then, at a break between chapters, found her mind wandering. A sadness had descended with the decline of the day, and her room seemed bathed with it, her sole companion. Looking at her book, she retrieves its bookmark from the side table and inserts it, then gently tosses the book onto the settee beside her. Across the lounge the silent telephone sits as if it is watching her, accusingly. She stares it down and feels it give up.

They both knew (as if the phone could be personified!) she had been right to make the call to Liam. It is still recent enough to be raw, though; recent enough for her to recall Matt, and for him to inhabit her posthumously as he tended to at such moments, offering her the balance and counterpoint she needed. It is Matt she always missed, and in doing so she feels sorry for Liam.

There had been a time when she had felt sorry for herself, of course; would curse the fact that she had been unable to find a way to dismantle the 'Keep Out!' signs she had erected. Men - not many, but some - had, like Liam, ventured to get close to her. All of them had been defeated, one way or another. Once upon a time she had been amused that the no-go zone on a battlefield was called 'No Man's Land'; the irony of it appealed to her. But as soon as she realised that in her case it was harsh reality and not irony, her perspective changed. It wasn't as if hope had left her - hope that one day someone would come along to sweep the minefield clean - but rather that she had become resigned to her fate. She understood that not only did those mines keep men out, they kept her in too.

It had been a few years since she had come to realise the real reason the mines had been planted in the first place. She'd assumed it was because of Jonny; a defence mechanism to prevent herself being hurt again. To some degree that may have been true - for a while at least. But after her reconciliation with Matthew, that brief but priceless time she'd had to get to know him again before he died, she realised the reason for the minefield was to protect her relationship with *him*. In spite of it all, *he* had been the one true thing in her life; he had been the one man for her; 'Mr Right'. And she had blown it. What was it he had said about learning through those first time experiences? If life was a series of chain reactions - another of Matt's theories, she was sure - then he had been her catalyst, the source. For years she had made the mistake of thinking that Jonny was the person who made her what she was, but Jonny only existed because of Matt; so when she had the chance to recapture him (those brief, painful few weeks at the hospice) then she doubled her efforts not to let him escape again. Jonny may have initiated the building of her defences, but her memory of Matt only reinforced them.

Liam hadn't stood a chance. He had been facing three adversaries, two invisible to him. First, he had to best Jonny and prove he was a good, honest and sincere man. Not a difficult ask given the standard Jonny had set. It was the kind of test most men would have been able to pass. The second bar - Matthew - was raised so much higher. How could anyone supersede such an exemplar? On one level clearly an impossible task, but if you had passed the first test and were close enough on the second, then surely being alive, available, having 'potential' to do more and be better than you were at that moment might just have been a tie-breaker in your favour? But his third foe had been Alison herself. Whether she realised it or not, what could he possibly do if she had achieved a balance she had no desire to change, possessed scales she didn't want to tip? She had accumulated her store of history and experience, ticked off an inventory which had led her to a place of calm, an emotional stasis. If this was where she needed to be and where she had decided - consciously or not - to see out the rest of her days. There was little Liam could do about it.

Matthew challenged her on that decision, brought his big guns to the internal duologue she'd fabricated with him during her last visit to Settle, and which she continued on the long drive home. He had argued Liam's case, pleaded for a stay of execution, but Alison was set on her course. She never allowed herself to ask just how close Liam had been to breaking through those defences - but it had been a near thing. She thought of Levens Hall. He was close there, her hands beginning to reach for those warning signs to rip them from the ground about her. But there was always something else, always another objection to keep him out - or her in. Once reconciled to her fate - and to Liam's - Matthew gave way as he had to, retreating back into her memory, the loyal savant who would always reappear when needed.

"It's about your father"

It would make life so much easier to navigate if news arrived in a managed, coordinated way. Why couldn't it take into consideration your preferences and predilections, rather than barge in or sneak up on you? Katy remembered the way her parents had broken the news about their impending divorce: the trip out for a Sunday lunch, pretending to be one thing but actually being something else, wilfully, deliberately. And Tom's proposal, a declaration so unforeseen that her reaction ended up rupturing their relationship. Surely there should have been a better way to go about that, to prepare her, to lay the groundwork? Sometimes she wondered if the problem lay with her; the fault of some inherent inability to read signs, to see things coming. Tabitha told her that she was, by turns, too trusting, too naïve, too gullible. And perhaps she was, but in Katy's mind that did not excuse 'news' - personified into some sinister cloaked figure who hid in doorways and shadows - for jumping out on her.

If, habitually, she saw herself as a victim, it was something she never articulated, at least not in those terms. Starving and malnourished children in news reports on the television, they were victims; the displaced refugees from war zones, they were victims too. All the while she had a choice - even if she opted not to exercise it - and it was a choice which could have protected her from self-pity. That was her rationale, but the theory was a little limp when measured against history's reality. She was upset when she found out about her parents; to be angry had been her choice. Yes, the news had been a shock, and she would have preferred to have been told some other way (or not at all, obviously!), but being vexed - then and still - had been an assertion of right. Turning Tom down, that too had been her choice; so how could she see herself as victim there, even if Tom had, in exercising his own prerogative and leaving two days later, abandoned her to be alone once more?

There was a part of her which liked to assume that she cared more about others than she did herself. Such a philosophy explained her anguish for her parents - and what she regarded as relative ambivalence as far as Tom was concerned. In the latter case, she had convinced herself that their parting was for the best, going so far as to persuade herself she had been in the process of occupying that position in advance of his proposal and the cascade of events which followed. This was a safer approach, one which allowed her to deploy as much self-protection as she could muster. Such defence mechanisms simply didn't work when it came to the suffering of others. No matter how she might try to beguile herself with internal argument, nothing could compensate for the anguish she had felt with regard her father's divorce or the death of her grandfather. That they had taken their individual fates in such spectacularly mature and stoic fashions only seemed to make her own reaction all the more hysterical, and no matter how hard she tried - at least in the early days each each crisis - nothing mitigated that.

Knowing Katy handled unexpected news so poorly - especially bad news - Rachel might have tried a little harder when she broke the news about Liam.

"It's about your father," had been her opening gambit, delivered in such a fashion as to telegraph that what was to follow could be nothing short of catastrophic. It was news coming once again with so little notice.

No matter how Rachel had subsequently tried to soften the blow with references to "having lots of time" and the fact that doctors "could work wonders", the blow had already been struck. Katy reeled during their brief and all too antiseptic interview, and continued reeling for some time after.

When Liam's first fall - the 'unstable boulder' - had been followed by two more in the space of just a few months, the resultant severe bruising and neck pain had forced him to consult his local GP.

"I'd like to take a scan," Dr Woods had announced.

"For a bruised hip?" Liam had been incredulous.

"No, not on your hip."

Two weeks later it had been confirmed that Liam had a small growth inside his skull applying some pressure to the surface of his brain.

"It's probably nothing," Woods had said with the air of a man who was leaving all his options open, "but it would explain those tumbles you have been taking. Another couple of tests, don't you think?"

Rachel had relayed the story in a perfunctory way, offering just a précis of what had actually happened. Whether this was because she didn't know or because she simply wanted to get the news-giving over and done with, Katy couldn't say. Indeed, she had been unable to process much of their conversation at all until some time later, at which point the specifics of who said what had long since blurred and become irrelevant.

"The Consultant says it's a tumour, and because of where it is and how fast it appears to be growing there's very little they can do about it. In fact," Rachel had continued quickly to prevent any rising of Katy's hopes, "nothing much at all."

She had not intended it to sound dismissive and unconcerned, the hollowness in her voice not a result of a lack of feeling but rather from the effort to control it. But Katy's expression told her she had missed the mark once again.

Later that day, long after her mother had left her and she had cried, tried to pull herself together, and then cried some more, Katy's next reflection was that soon there would be no-one left in her world who she loved. It had been a notion whose arrival had surprised her, and one she tried to bat away as being selfish, telling herself that she was the least important person in all these dramas. But unintentional or not, there persisted a sense of her being the unfortunate one, not in terms of the present situation which was, of course, infinitely worse for her father, but in consideration of how she would be left in the future, where she would find herself. It seemed she had lost so much: a happy home life, a grandfather she adored, and soon her father. If she had chosen to put Tom into the list it would have added further weight, but she did not, a conscious decision which only succeeded in forcing her to ask herself again whether she had ever loved him at all. If he could be dismissed so easily, what did that say about their relationship? And it was also telling that her mother featured in none of her calculations, either in terms of past loss or future landscape. Katy wasn't sure whether she should have been surprised by this or not, or whether it was merely confirmation of what she had known all along. She debated with herself the rightness or wrongness of the demotion of her mother to an also-ran, and although she tended toward the latter eventually decided it didn't really matter. There was no sudden urge to put everything back in order or 'right' the 'wrong' (if that's what it was). Rather, it felt almost confirmatory; recognition of something she had known for so long now. Any lingering desire to offer Rachel one more chance had disappeared with the words "it's about your father".

Having learned her lesson from her grandfather's passing and her mother's preventing one final audience, Katy was determined not to make the same mistake again.

"I expect your mother's either been making the whole thing melodramatic or else underplaying it massively," Liam had said when she rang him the following day. It had taken almost the whole twenty-four hours for her to re-establish sufficient equilibrium to make the call.

Her father's tone had been somewhat dismissive, as if he didn't really believe what was happening and, by doing so, was suggesting she shouldn't either. If it was meant to offer Katy some consolation it failed spectacularly, but it did force her to adopt a more business-like tone. Hard facts - feeling as if she had been deprived of them by so many people - suddenly became of paramount importance, even though their interpretation wasn't her natural metier. She knew her father would not play games with her. So for three or four minutes they played a game of question-and-answer, Katy ensuring her questions were closed enough to force her father to avoid obfuscation.

"Is that it?" he asked when she eventually went silent. "What's the verdict?" It was a weak attempt to lighten the mood, but Katy was too busy processing data to respond.

The facts speaking for themselves, it seemed cut-and-dried with little room for error. All that remained to be answered were the vague, intangible and yet important details that inhabited the periphery.

"When?" she had said simply.

"When?" Her father paused, evidently taken aback.

"When can I come and see you?" Katy adopted the long form of the question, unaware that her previous attempt could have been taken in more than one way.

"Whenever you like, love."

Katy had heard the sad smile in his voice and, for the first time in the exchange felt on the verge of losing control.

"But not in a couple of weekends though," Liam had clarified. "I've someone coming to stay. Barbara. An old friend. You know."

There was something in the way his voice trailed away that seemed to capture all the regret in the world, as if those few words, those very few words, had sufficient capacity to hold everything one ever needed to know.

"Of course not," Katy replied, as if it were patently obvious she was going to avoid that weekend. "Maybe the weekend after."

It was a question without the question mark, delivered in such a way as to give him no room for manoeuvre. Liam allowed his silence to speak for him.

"How's the garden looking?" she asked, her words slipping out as if their previous conversation had never happened, as if they were just catching up and dahlias were the most important topic of all.

"There have been moments"

"I spoke to an old friend about you."

"You did?"

She nods, slowly, thoughtfully; the way one nods when you are taking your time, weighing up your words before delivering them. As Liam watches her, he can imagine the process going on inside her head, the checking of each syllable to ensure that together they do not tip a scale.

"When?" he prompts, after she says nothing.

She looks at him all consideration, taking up her glass as if doing so aids the calculation.

"The last time I was here." She pauses at the inaccuracy. "Well, when I was on my way back to Hope."

The peculiarity of the statement, no matter how linguistically and factually correct, starts Liam's head spinning. The notion of hope as something you can travel to and from is all too familiar. He knows how uplifting the 'travelling to' can be - and how soul destroying it is when you leave it behind. He is sitting across from the very person who last embodied hope for him; the person in whom he had started to invest a future that simply never materialised. Within in himself he cannot help but see the physical embodiment of hope thwarted: his tumour - unexpected, unwanted - being the thief stealing everything from him in broad daylight, not even having the professional courtesy to ply its trade under cover of darkness.

He shifts in his chair, uncomfortable. Because he cannot trust himself - or his thief! - he remains as static as he can, more immobile than he needs to be; even a walk down the garden is filled with trepidation in case there is another misstep. Or worse. Unable to pursue the fight on open ground, Liam has retreated into his bunker even though he knows there is no respite there; his thief has the run of the place.

"I see," he says in a manner which demonstrates he sees nothing at all.

Alison places her hand on his, briefly. It is the touch of someone with whom you once shared a past, nothing more.

"He took your side actually."

Liam looks up at her. He can tell from her expression there is no joking there. The slight playfulness he can see in her eyes, the way the corners of her mouth are rising the merest degree, softens her meaning; it betrays benevolence and tells him he is safe to ask.

"I'm glad someone did," he replies, instantly wishing he had been more circumspect with his own choice of phrase. For a second he wonders - suddenly and unexpectedly - whether it actually matters any more, the words he chooses. Releasing them unfiltered may no longer be as important as it once was, but then Liam reminds himself he has always been considerate and that remaining so is still important; civility is something to which he can still hold fast. "Other than me, I mean."

Unintentionally, he slips again.

"You think I didn't?"

"And what did he say?" Not wishing to answer, Liam knows he has to let her question slide. "And who is he, anyway?"

❉

It had been a momentous decision to call her. Enough time had passed to disqualify everything other than a shared history, and one he felt sure Alison would have relegated down a division in the league table of her memory. Liam could not know how she now felt about those few brief months, though he was certain her perspective on them would be entirely different to his own. He had considered leaving her out of this, his swan-song; leaving her with whatever residue of their relationship she felt comfortable. Perhaps none at all. She had called him three times after their parting; three times when his touch might have still meant something to her; opportunities he had been given to keep the lines of communication open. Uncertain why he let each one slip, he hoped - when he finally picked up the phone and selected her name from his contact list (even though he knew the number by heart) - that his neglect had not been terminal. Liam knew Alison was a 'three strikes and you're out' kind of woman, and, taking a dispassionate view, how could he blame her for being so? But there had been no neat ending after she had told him their relationship was over. At the time if felt more like a business deal that had, in a vague and haphazard manner, fallen through at the last minute.

Choosing to call had been a selfish act - at least that was how he had seen it. Closure was what he needed; the desire to see her one final time (for he had decided on that specific limit) was his signal goal. It had occurred to him Alison might have regarded his invitation as maudlin or even spiteful, designed to make her feel bad, to rake over the ashes of how poorly she had treated him. But there was risk for him too in their meeting again. Not only might the sight of her throw him into a turmoil about which he could do nothing, he was also cognisant that when she saw him in his extended incapacity, she might feel even more justified in having abandoned him. He could be offering her new and indisputable proof that, had they remained together, he would have been unable to keep up his side of the bargain and thus simultaneously demonstrate her decision had been a prudent one. But there had been no trace of that on the call. She had been surprised certainly, but in response Liam removed any likelihood of awkwardness by launching into a brief but factual account of his current unsolvable predicament and making it plain he hadn't called her on the expectation that she might have been able to work miracles of any kind. "You were actually there at the very start of it", he had said. Having made it clear to her that she was entirely free of obligation, it was the only way he felt able to tie her and his illness together. He told himself he wasn't trying to make her feel guilty; he was just trying to lay out the facts.

He put the phone down after she had unhesitatingly agreed to come and see him, to visit Settle again "and watch the trains". He simply didn't know what to think.

*

"Matthew? An old friend from school. Someone who has seen enough of the good and bad of me to be able to express an honest opinion - and who isn't afraid to do so. Someone I can call up whenever I need to. Although having said that, he has been known to barge in when his intrusion was least welcome and tell me what he thinks anyway!"

"He sounds a brave man," Liam says, smiling. "I like him already."

Alison lets the remark pass.

"So what did he say?"

She shakes her head in response to the prompt. It is a subtle gesture, not negative but rather as if she was shooing a fly away.

"He questioned my motives. Asked me if I was sure, knew what I was doing."

"And?" Liam is unable to help himself.

"Oh, he's always doing that, questioning my motives, thinking he knows me better than I know myself, assuming that all the years we've known each other gives him some special insight. Or privilege, or something."

"You never mentioned him," Liam points out.

"No?" Alison allows a thought to complete its journey. "There was no need really. He wasn't relevant; just a friend from the past. I mean, did you tell me about all your old friends? I can't recall you talking about anyone other than Katy - which was most of the time! And Rachel, of course - but only when I pressed you."

"Is that true?"

"Which part?"

"All of it."

She stands up.

"You know me well enough, Liam, not to doubt my honesty." She pauses. "Walk me out into the garden. I want to see it again." Then, sensing he is about to protest, "And I won't take 'no' for an answer. I need to inspect the borders."

He laughs at her in spite of himself, knowing it is pointless trying to argue. From somewhere he feels a stabbing sensation that has nothing to do with his physical lack of well-being.

They walk outside slowly, cautiously. There is nothing untoward in his movement, and if you were none the wiser you might just assume he was a strolling kind of person. But out of fear he has taken to a kind of meandering crawl, to give himself half a chance to compensate should he find his feet disobeying him again. Only the stick upon which he leans hints at the story. He waits for Alison to make a comment but she does not. Her eyes are indeed examining the borders, the vegetable patch, as if she were a Sergeant Major inspecting the troops.

"I'm surprised," she offers as they pause toward the far end of the garden. She notes the new lock on the shed. "It's all very neat; pristine almost. I had expected it to be a little…"

"Neglected?" Liam suggests, to help her out.

"Never neglected," she laughs.

"I have a man now," he explains. "Jack comes in two or three times a week to keep things ticking over. He has an allotment where he grows his vegetables, but nowhere for flowers; and where he lives, the gardens are all managed. So he comes here to play. It seems to work well for both of us."

She nods her approval. From nearby a tell-tale whistle calls her from his side a back toward to house, back to the patch of lawn where she knows she can see any passing trains. Liam reaches her side just as a heritage 'special' chuffs its way out of the station, heading south.

"Every weekend, at least twice a day," Liam says, "more during the summer holidays."

"Isn't it odd," she says as they resume walking, "that we still refer to them as 'summer holidays' long after we have ceased to be children, or our children have ceased to be children. It's like we can't let them go, those months of July and August; as if, providing we still call them the same thing we used to when they represented a special time, a time of sunshine and freedom, that's what they'll always be."

"Very philosophical," Liam says.

She slips an arm through one of his - the one not tensed with his grip on the stick.

"Don't tease," she complains. "You know what I mean."

Liam nods.

"I do. And it is funny, isn't it? There's nothing special about July and August, not really, but those words we choose to give them - 'summer holidays' - invests them with something extra, something magical. The power of words, of course - not that most people would realise it, not consciously anyway." When they are nearly at the house Liam asks "More tea?".

"Are you reading much?" Alison ignores his question.

"Why?"

"Oh, I'm just inspecting the borders!" She fires a laugh in his general direction. Liam feels the stabbing pain again. "I'm interested; what do you do with your time, given you can't be quite as active as you used to be. Surely a chance to catch-up or re-read things perhaps."

"One last time?"

"That's not what I meant, and you know it."

"I have a list," he says, admonished. He holds the back door open then follows her into the kitchen where she has headed straight for the kettle. "A little Henry James, some Laurence Durrell, Eliot."

"Eliot?" Pausing as she is about to turn on the tap, her surprise is evident.

"Yes, why?"

"Isn't that a bit - I don't know - 'hard'?"

"I know what you mean," he says, sitting at the kitchen table, watching her as she goes about preparing the tea with a modicum of movement and maximum efficiency. It sums her up really. "I've always found him hard. But you know, I think there are some things that I am beginning to understand.

Finally. Perhaps you need to have lived a little to unlock their secrets."

"Then," she says, sitting opposite him as the kettle begins its low rumble in the background, "I may never try him again."

"What do you mean?"

"What do I mean?" she echoes. "Only that my life has been too narrow for such insight. Compared to yours, for example."

"Mine?" Liam laughs. "I hardly think my life is that rich or sophisticated or challenging!"

"It's all relative," she suggests. "I've never married, for example."

"Or divorced," Liam suggests, playfully.

"Exactly so! Or divorced. Or had children with all the traumas and joys and stresses and strains that brings. I've never been that stretched professionally, I just keep churning the handle: 'same shit, different day'. Only the faces change."

Her voice trails away and Liam is for once uncertain whether she is being serious or not. The kettle rumbles louder, and Alison stands up to attend it.

"But you've had your moments," he suggests, immediately regretting the last word, worried that it sounds too trivial.

"Oh yes," she says over her shoulder, "there have been moments. Some very good moments."

With the kettle turned off, an odd silence descends over the kitchen, a silence punctuated by the sounds of tea-making: water being poured, stirring, more pouring. It is as if the house is holding its breath. For the first time in the day, Liam is suddenly scared. As he looks at Alison, her back square on to him, he feels overcome but does not know why. He wants to ask her what this feeling is, assuming she can interpret it; but he says nothing, knowing that his words will betray him.

"You go through," Alison says, still facing away from him, "I'll bring these through. I've got to get something from the car."

Liam hauls himself up and does as he is told. As he shuffles slowly back to the study he hears more stirring and then her footsteps along the hall, the front door opening. His favourite chair still sits at an angle that allows him to see his books and, out through the window, his garden. He allows his gaze to settle mid-distance as he listens. Her footsteps again, back into the kitchen. He waits for the sound of crockery but there is none, just Alison's tread again back to the front door.

And then nothing.

Liam waits for a minute, expecting more sounds, specific sounds, the noises that would fit the pattern he has laid out for the next sixty seconds. He realises with a shock that he is now navigating by such small slices of time; it hits him as does an ache that comes unbidden. From somewhere outside the sound of a car. Assuming Alison has gone to the toilet and forgotten to close the front door, he lifts himself from his chair once more. At the threshold of his study he can look along the hallway; the front door not quite closed. And he can also see into the kitchen. There is a box on the table that wasn't there a few minutes ago, a white rectangle of paper screams at him from its surface.

'I couldn't bare to say goodbye', she has written, her usually flowing hand strangely staccato. There is a single 'x' occupying a line on its own.

Liam moves the paper to the surface of the table and opens the box. Books. He finds himself smiling even as a tear falls onto the discarded paper. Poetry books, C.S.Lewis, books about 'great gardens of the world', even a book about trains! There is a Kahlil Gilbran - which he hasn't read for years - and *The Catcher In The Rye* - which he has never read at all.

He sits down at the table and runs his hands over their covers as if acquainting himself with them. He had wanted closure, and here is Alison still trying to open doors.

"Is there anything else you need?"

"Who was your friend?" Katy asks across the dining table, their plates, empty now, pushed to one side. She cradles a half-full wine glass, rotating it slowly between her fingers, its broad foot not leaving the surface of the table.

"Friend?" Liam assumes she is referring to the man she bumped into as she was arriving earlier in the day. It had been a perfunctory greeting devoid of any kind of introduction, partly because his dirty hands had been full of horticultural paraphernalia. "You mean Jack. He just helps out in the garden."

"No, not him," Katy clarifies. "I guessed who he was. You didn't need to be Sherlock Holmes to work that out, Dad."

"Fair point."

"I meant the friend you had to stay last weekend."

"Oh, sorry." Liam recalibrates. "It was only a flying visit in the end. She didn't stay."

"'She'?" Katy tries to load the word with as much meaning as possible. It is a rudimentary attempt and one totally out of character, which is why it fails - but Liam laughs anyway.

"Barbara," Liam says, choosing to use Alison's alternative name.

In the week since her visit, he has started to think of her in this way, as if doing so will help him to create some distance between them. Alison is too real, too close, and so trying to replace her with a fiction has become his way of insulating himself. Barbara was never really there, and so if he focuses on her he naïvely believes it will be harder for him to recall the visit to Levens, the first night she stayed with him in Settle. That person was Alison, the Alison from whom he finds he still needs to protect himself. It is a clumsy device, but unable not to think of her at all, it's the only one he has. It does not work. He wonders if her last visit had concluded in a more conventional way, if she *had* said 'goodbye', whether it might be easier now. But he suspects not. He is caught not wishing to remember, but also desperate not to forget. There is a third state that is neither and both of these things.

"An old friend," he offers. "Well a friend of a few years anyway."

"You've never mentioned her before."

"Have I not?" He feigns surprise knowing full well he had kept Alison's presence a secret.

"No Dad."

There is something in Katy's voice - a stern note, the attitude of a teacher telling off a naughty pupil - that makes him smile. It feels like role reversal. Shakespeare's 'Seven Ages of Man' pops unbidden into his head.

"Really?"

"Really. So spill the beans."

Her phrase makes him recall an accident he had two days previously when he had managed to drop an opened bag of frozen peas, sending them all across the kitchen floor. The spilling had been easy, it had been the corralling afterwards that took the effort.

"We met at a hotel down south somewhere; Newbury or Swindon, I think it was. Somewhere like that. We just got talking the way business people in hotels do when they're on their own, miles from home."

"What was she like, that day you met her?"

"Tired - she'd had a rough day - but still interesting. Feisty, too; you know, independent, confident, professional. And funny, with a really sharp wit." Liam tries to rebuild the image, but it is less clear than he wishes it to be, blurred by other images and events since then.

"There was a connection," Katy suggests, still a little playfully.

"Yes, I suppose so," he agrees. "She lives a fair way from here, so we met up just occasionally; but it was nice when we did."

"This was after you and Mum split?" Katy asks the question as if there is only one potential answer, so Liam simply nods. "And how old was she?"

The destination to which Katy is trying to navigate is clear enough. Liam smiles, recognising it. He has already decided that he will tell her just part of the story, not that there is any part of it he is ashamed of; it is simply knowing she will want a different conclusion and that he will struggle to replay what actually happened in such a way as to satisfy either of them. The piece of paper containing Alison's final words is now a folded bookmark at about the mid-point of the Salinger she gave him. Liam can see Holden Caulfield in himself, in everybody.

"Younger than me," he says simply; then, seeing Katy's eyebrows rise, clarifies. "A little; not much. A bit younger than your mother I suppose - though to be honest I never asked her."

"You didn't?"

"Isn't is supposed to be rude to ask a lady her age?" He laughs. "Anyway, it didn't seem to matter."

"That's a good answer," Katy says, sitting back in her chair and finally lifting the glass from the table.

"Which part?"

"Both."

As he watches her drink, Liam wonders what she will be like in ten years, in fifteen, this daughter of his. And will she, later on, meet a man in a hotel, offer him some temporary respite, some friendship when all seems lost? Or will she be married, a mother, living a stable life, assuming tomorrow will be like today, absorbed in the safe march of time?

"What are you thinking about?" Katy asks. "Barbara?"

"No." He pauses for a moment. "I was thinking about you."

"Me?"

He nods, watches as she leans forward a little, her interest piqued. It is sufficient to see the glass returned to the table top.

"I was wondering what you will be like in a few years from now. What sort of life you'll be leading." He is conscious he could be leading them down a cul-de-sac, but she asked the question and he wants to be honest. At least she hasn't protested that he'll still be around to see how she's doing. That gives him hope Katy will keep them all safe.

"Do you think I'll be like Mum?"

Her question surprises him.

"You know, I don't think that's something I've ever considered."

"Well then. Consider it now."

He watches her as she reaches across the table for the bottle to top-up her glass. There are mannerisms there he supposes, as well as the tell-tale physical resemblance: the distance between the eyes; the slightly pointed nose. And hidden out of sight, the general shape of her - especially around the hips - echoes Rachel.

"Not really," is his superficial conclusion.

"Really? Why?"

"There are physical similarities for sure, but you're just a different person to her in terms of personality, attitude."

"Is that good?" Katy could have loaded the question, but has done well not to do so.

"What do you think?"

Katy lifts her glass and takes another sip.

"It depends. I mean, there might be some things where I wish I were more like her. But not others."

"Such as."

Liam wishes he had a glass in his hand now too. That would represent the natural order of things. But he has had to swear off alcohol, "just for a while" said the consultant. "Just forever" was what Liam had heard.

"I wish I were a little more 'ballsy'," Katy says after a moment's thought. "She's much braver than I am. I wish I had some of that."

"But you're less reckless," Liam interjects, "which should mean that your decisions are more thought through, have some rigour about them."

"You'd think," Katy's words are delivered quickly and without hesitation. They leave an enormous space for Liam to walk into.

He does so gently, wary of a booby-trap, the potential cost of another mis-placed step.

"Tom?" He tries just the single word, partly to keep it simple and partly to give Katy a way out should she choose to take it.

"Ex-Tom." He reply is almost as rudimentary.

"'Ex-Tom' eh? So Tom's a thing of the past?"

"He proposed." Even though it is relatively old news from her perspective, the words still feel fresh on her lips. Apart from Tabby, she has told no-one. It is an interesting experience, this divulging to her father, being the focus for just a short while. "He proposed, and I said 'no'."

The kitchen absorbs the silence for a second or two, creating a vacuum Liam feels compelled to occupy.

"Which was, I assume, a wise thing? Otherwise you wouldn't have turned him down."

"Yes, I suppose so. It must be, mustn't it? I don't think we loved each other enough; and, in the end, I don't think he understood me."

Liam laughs a little; and even though it is a small, sympathetic laugh, it draws a quizzical look.

"If it's understanding you're looking for - and from a man, to boot - well, I suspect you might be waiting a long time!"

"That sounds like the kind of thing Mum would say."

"Believe me, it's the kind of thing your mother *did* say!"

The image breaks into the atmosphere like a pin through a balloon. Liam had intended nothing of the kind, but as he settles back down he is glad he said something that made them laugh. Under the circumstances, a conversation about Tom might easily have taken them down a somewhat darker path.

"In that case, there was nothing special about Tom after all - and I think I'm only on the look-out for special."

It is less funny from Katy, but it is sufficient. Liam can't help but think how, as time passes, one compromises what one is 'on the look-out for'. As each year wanes, another element in the search criteria goes by the wayside; standards slip, and the search for the nine-out-of-ten is reduced to eight-and-a-half, then eight, then seven. Alison pops back into his head. She had been a nine and no mistake; a nine now, next year, in five years. And what about him on that scale? Perhaps he might have rustled up a seven or so when they met at what now seems an age ago; but today? Now he would be lucky if someone rated him a four. Or a three. He wants to counsel Katy not to be too choosy, to know when good-enough is good-enough. No matter what has happened in the relatively recent past, he had been profoundly lucky with Rachel. She had been off the scale - and, however you measured it, was still way ahead of him.

*

"What time's your train?"

"A little after three, so I guess I'll leave about quarter to."

"I won't come with you," Liam says, his smile trying to keep it light, "because if I'd wanted to do that we should have left an hour ago!"

From time to time throughout the weekend he has made fun of his plight, not wanting it to intrude too much and dampen their spirits. Katy has played along well enough, but with not long before she has to leave, Liam senses that particular charade is over. He suddenly sees the value in a small rectangle of paper dotted with just a few words.

"Will it get better?" she asks.

"Will what, love?"

"Being able to get about. You know, the walking."

"Don't let this fool you," Liam says, waving his stick in the air from where he sits. "It's not really walking that's the problem, it's the falling over! I daresay if I really wanted to I could manage to build up a decent head of steam, but that would be - as the doctor said - 'tempting fate'. And so I don't. It's not worth it."

A shadow passes over her face.

"And anyway, where would I go?" He tries to chase it away. "I've walked everywhere there is to walk around here, and I don't need to travel for work any more. I'm quite happy pottering about. As long as I've got my garden, my study, and a decent internet signal then I'm fine."

Although weak, her smile tries its best to accept his tone, though it is soon replaced by another note of concern.

"You're not still working though?"

"No, of course not! Not really. A little advice here and there; a few emails. I welcome it, actually. Nothing onerous, just sharing the benefit of my experience with some old colleagues. The variety is good for me." He points to a small sideboard upon which stand two bottles of whisky. "From a grateful client - but those would *not* be good for me! Do you want to take one back with you?"

Knowing she doesn't drink whisky, the shake of her head comes as no surprise.

"And other than that?"

"And not falling over, you mean?"

She tries a laugh on cue, but hers is an unconvincing as his own.

"I'm mainly reacquainting myself with some old friends."

Another frown; something else he has to explain. He looks at the clock. Fifteen minutes and she will not be there. Fifteen minutes and, though she does not realise it, he may never see her again. He feels something beginning to catch in his throat, preparing to ambush his words on their way out.

"My books." He nods in their general direction. "Something old, something blue... There have been things I've been wanting to re-read for so long. And I'm mixing them in with the new. Barbara left me some books when she was here last week, actually."

"So she knows you well enough to buy you books, eh?"

"Not so fast!" He laughs. "She knows me well enough to buy me books, yes; but not *what* books. It was a bit of a scatter-gun approach, to be honest."

"Anything interesting?"

Liam senses that she doesn't really care, but is keeping up with the drumbeat of their conversation, knowing if she does so the time will go by less painfully. He nods to the little table beside his chair.

"Holden Caulfield," he says with another nod, as if the name is the purveyor of special meaning.

"Aren't you…"

"A bit old for that?" He rushes in and laughs again. Katy reddens. "That's what I thought to be honest. But I'm not so sure. And somewhere there's some C.S.Lewis too. Perhaps she thought I could do with a trip to Narnia."

"Couldn't we all," Katy says, then looks around as if she has misplaced something. It is a final clue. "Is there anything else you need?"

He shakes his head. She stands.

"I need the loo."

Liam walks slowly towards the front door and waits for her at the bottom of the stairs. He figures it will be easier for them both if he treats this departure as he has all of her previous visits. He checks his watch as she eventually reappears at the top of the stairs, having taken far longer in the bathroom than she needed.

"Perfect timing!" he announces, trying to keep a bounce in his voice. "A brisk walk and you'll have about five minutes to spare." He holds out her bag. Not wanting any excuses, any scene, he had been cradling it in his arms ready to present it to her. There can be no hesitation now.

She pulls her coat from the rack and pulls it on, then takes the bag.

"Thanks, Dad."

"Maybe," he says, as he steps forward to open the door, "I should see if you could come and visit next time Barbara's here?"

Katy's face lights up. It is the desired reaction.

"Really?!"

"We'll see. Now," he leans forward and kisses her on the cheek, "run along. And call me to let me know when you get back home, okay?"

"Okay."

She squeezes his arm, turns and is gone, waving over her shoulder once she is through the gate.

By the time he has closed the front door, Liam's tears are flowing.

"I think we're always who we really are"

If you did not know the backstory to the scene in front of you it would not take too much working out.

"It's what we do," Liam had said to them once, but so long ago that neither of them could possibly remember it, a throw-away line uttered across the dining room table on a nondescript Thursday. "We take all of the clues from what we see or hear and recompile them in order to generate a composite picture only we can see. All the time. We interpret, translate, because our brains hate gaps, and we come up with something to fill-in those gaps, a new history. It has to be new, for how can it be the real thing? And you know what? That's what writers rely on. They know that's what people do, and when they write stuff they are plugging-in to our ability to rebuild. It's essential to them."

Later, in the same, short conversation: "I think that's why deconstruction can work, because we're actually very good at *re*construction. Does that make sense?"

Whether it did or not neither Rachel nor Katy could say. As they sat in the silent room, they were each recreating their own slideshow from the past, attempting to relive history within the abstract confines of their minds. Nothing was really being shared, and even if they had been able to recall that post-dinner conversation, they would have failed to remember the exact dialogue. A philosopher might argue that as they can't replay Liam's words, can't unearth that event, then how can they know what he actually meant - and in what way?

If they had been reminded of the conversation, been able to dredge it up from the deepest recesses of their memory, they might have smiled.

"It was," Rachel might have said, "the kind of conversation Liam liked best, especially if he was in the mood: literary, deep, convoluted, theoretical. Even when we were at university he was always pretending he understood that kind of stuff, but he never did. Not really." And they might have laughed, soft, understanding, loving laughs.

If anything, the current scene screams memory at you. That and the fact that Rachel has spoken of her ex-husband in the past tense. It is how they have been speaking of him for a few days now. The rawness of it, the anger at having to do so has passed and they have realised - as they knew they would - that life goes on. The next day they will say their final farewell to Liam, the public show.

The dinner they have recently finished was - appropriately enough - a little like old times, even though it was just the two of them. You get the impression of a ceasefire in force, like Christmas in the trenches, a recognition that there is something more important than a vague and strangely impersonal enmity. They have both done a lot of thinking in the last few days as they plunged to varying depths into what seemed like a bottomless cavern, dark, cold, and full of echoes. They have needed to rely on each other more than they might have wanted, and in doing so Katy has come to realise that part of her anger at her mother is simply the transference of frustration. And Rachel knows she has allowed her personal history - and the fact that she never actually forgave herself for abandoning Liam - to sour her love for her daughter. It is almost an unintended bequest.

Not that either of them will have said as much, nor confessed to what they have seen and felt as they have looked back into the past - and, in doing so, back into themselves. Why would they? They have been focussed on Liam, the common link which joined them. But there it is. And hence the room and its screaming of memory.

The removal of his thread poses questions about the future, of course; but such questions are little more than unformed inclinations at present. There are two answers to the conundrum "what next?" The first is that as individuals nothing much changes: Rachel pursuing her new independent life, financially even more secure now that her ex-husband has died; Katy continuing to cross-examine herself over Tom, pulling apart their relationship to see if she can divine its secrets and its failings. Hopefully she will try and work out what went right too. But the second question about the future relates to the two of them and how they must now function *together*; perhaps it is even about whether they function together at all. It is almost as if the terms 'mother' and 'daughter' only had meaning when they are co-joined with a 'father/husband'. Does Katy feel less like a daughter because Liam is no longer there to bind them? Does Rachel feel less like a mother for the same reason?

They look at each other and smile; a wan, somewhat lost smile which tries to convey understanding of their shared bereavement. It is a gesture that works because the other's loss is also their own. There is no need for words - or there are no words to fit the need. This registers particularly with Rachel who knows such a proposition could have led to a debate in which Liam might have revelled. She can imagine some specious trumped-up theory dressed in a suit of inauthentic literary criticism; and when she does so she can't help recall all those years ago when he left a lecture on Derrida and Lacan and bemoaned 'the emperor's new clothes'. It triggers thoughts about what she will miss the most, ignoring the fact that for the last couple of years she has missed him not that much at all. Or at least that's what she tells herself - just as she tells herself that she *should* be missing him, should be compiling a list of what is no longer there. It will be a useful thing to have prepared in readiness for the conversations that will be forced on her tomorrow.

But it is an endeavour, this list-making, that is immediately problematical. If there was so much she missed about him, then why (one might ask) did she leave him in the first place? Or force him out, depending on your allegiance. So there needs to be a counterpoint, a balance to ensure fair dealing. But this is not fair dealing for Liam's benefit, but for her own; she will be the one who cares how the day plays out, and how she emerges from it, unscathed or not. Irrespective of whether she approves of it, people will judge her; their grief will not stop them. Mutual acquaintances will feel sorry for her for sure, but they are most likely to have felt sorry for Liam prior to that, and how the scales are balanced at the end of the day can have relevance for her alone. It is a calculation which permits her to budget in such a way as to be generous, gracious, happy to leave the scales tilted ever so slightly in Liam's favour, playing the card that in doing so mutual friends might come to see her in a better light. "Paying it forward" Liam used to call it - though apropos of what Rachel has no recollection.

If there is a spectrum for measuring how much you might miss someone, Katy is at the opposite end, her position on the continuum defined by what it means to the individual who remains, the extant half of the partnership. Katy's predicament is entirely different: having now lost both her father and her grandfather, she has been deprived of her two most important confidants, the only two men who truly offered her advice and perspective. She may realise in a vague way that this should make her mother all the more important to her, that there is a role for Rachel to play after all, but on the eve of Liam's funeral this is too early to be considered. It may prove a step too far in any event.

Katy is sufficiently self-aware to know she needs someone to whom she can turn, and that figures with attributes of wisdom, reliability, honesty and caring are increasingly hard to find. Tabby goes part-way on all counts; indeed, in some areas and on some topics she may be the ultimate oracle. But there are things precious to Katy which can only be safeguarded by the exceptionally trustworthy, and both her former exemplars have abandoned her. As she contemplates this void, she finds herself wondering if there could have ever been a circumstance where Tom might have grown to be such a person, as if the ability to fill that role might be the yardstick by which one should measure a man and his potential future in your life. Love and passion are all very well, but they are fragile and dangerously transitory things. And perhaps in terms of being a 'solid sage' they are mutually exclusive too. As her father became more the rock, the stable pivot for her relationship with her mother, did that simultaneously begin to supplant the passion that Rachel had once felt for him? Had he unwittingly become transformed from what Rachel had once needed to something far less relevant? As Katy looks at her now - a surreptitious, sidelong glance, as if she were hoping to catch her by surprise in order to uncover a truth - she attempts to gauge the kind of man her mother might need. Clearly she had coped remarkably well with the death of her own father, and Katy can only surmise that this says more about Rachel than Ronald.

"What is it?" Rachel says, catching Katy out mid-thought.

Katy tries not to blush, unable to prevent the feeling that she has been caught red-handed doing something she intrinsically knows to be wrong, her hand in the cookie-jar.

"Nothing. I was just thinking."

"Thinking?" Rachel turns her body slightly towards her daughter. "About what?"

"Men," Katy suggests.

"Men!" The notion clearly amuses her mother, so much so that Katy can only assume she has immediately grasped the slightly grubby end of the stick.

"I mean older men, mature men, role model men; men like Dad and grandpa." She feels flustered, certain she has blundered from meaning into insinuation.

"What about them?"

It is a simple enough question, but one which seems fraught with danger, booby-trapped almost.

"I don't know," she tries to buy a little time. "How important they are, I mean to us: men to look up to, or consult with, or take advice from."

Rachel lets out a little laugh.

"Shouldn't you be saying 'people' rather than men? Why should it be a man who performs that kind of function?"

"I guess because it's always been Dad and Granddad for me." Katy instantly realises she has left her mother out; surely the most politically correct answer would have been to suggest there was a triumvirate?

"But you were fortunate, dear," her mother says, showing no sign of having been offended. "They were both remarkable men in their own way and they loved you dearly. You were very lucky to have them. I can see why you would miss them so."

"What about you?"

"Me?" Rachel seems surprised to be dragged into the debate.

"I mean, don't you miss them too?"

Rachel remembers the lines she has rehearsed for the following day, but knows they will be of little value here.

"Yes, of course I do. But not in the same way you would; after all, I had completely different relationships with both of them. Perhaps it's also because I'm older, more mature; I have my own wisdom if you like, so I need to supplement it less. Years ago it would probably have been a different story, but…"

Letting it go, she allows Katy to fill in the blanks for a moment, strangely indifferent as to whether she gets it right or not. But then something tells her that this is an important conversation, though in what way she is unclear. She senses that they are drawing lines here, that Liam's passing represents more than just the loss of someone dear to them both. Whether she wants to recognise it or not, there is something at stake which can only be about the two of them. It is an uncomfortable feeling for Rachel, not because she does not know how Katy will respond, but because she is unsure about herself.

"I think your grandfather and I became more like friends over the years. Of course he was still my Dad too, but I needed him less in that role. The ground shifted, I suppose. Does that make sense? It was as if we saw each other for who we really were - or that we allowed ourselves to be seen in that way."

Rachel allows the theory to float between them, replaying it in her head to see if what she has said is what she actually meant, whether the words were doing her idea justice.

"Do you mean that you changed somehow?"

Rachel looks away for a moment. When she turns back, a feint frown is building even though she is trying to smile.

"I don't think so. I think we're always who we really are. It's all about what we see or what we choose to see or show. It may be that there appears to be some kind of seismic shift, but there isn't really."

"Did that happen with you and Dad?"

"A seismic shift?" For a moment the smile wins out over the frown.

"No. The part about seeing who you were, underneath; and about choosing who you were or if you showed it. That bit." Katy replays the words, uncertain if she has either their sequence or meaning correct in her own mind.

"People say 'we grew apart' don't they? I don't believe that at all, not in the way the words mean. I don't think your father and I ever 'grew apart' in that sense. I think it was more that what we needed, what we wanted, gradually changed over time. It's such a subtle transformation it's almost invisible. A tiny bit day after day, like a tap dripping. It seems insignificant then one day the sink's full. Does that make sense?"

Katy nods. She tries to apply the logic to the life she had experienced at home before the divorce, to strip away the filter she had applied to their mutual existence - the model of mother-father-daughter - and examine them all as individual if interconnected people. What her mother says sounds right, even if she struggles to make it compute. And of course it applies to her too.

"So I don't think we grew apart, your Dad and I, or changed, or actually stopped loving each other - not at some really basic level. I don't believe that."

And for the first time Rachel realises that she *can't* believe it; that she can't allow herself to accept their lives, their history, just fell apart. If she does so then what does that imply? That they had been living a lie? And for how long? Or even worse; that she had some level of responsibility she simply hadn't recognised until now? If she had changed - fundamentally and irrevocably - and that change had forced them apart, had been her undoing, then this flies in the face of everything she had told herself about why they had parted, why she had needed to be the catalyst for that.

Rachel feels tears beginning to form in her eyes and, not knowing why they are there, tries to brush them away. But it is no use. As the first one falls, she tries to focus on understanding why she should be crying now, and who she is crying for, as if concentrating on that will stop them; mind over matter. Is she crying for Liam or for herself? Or perhaps for Katy, or even her own father? The sudden realisation that she doesn't know, that there is no certainty behind this unknowable and unnameable emotion only makes things worse.

She tries to apologise, but Katy, clearly struggling herself, tells her that it doesn't matter. But Rachel knows that it does; it is a question for which she doesn't know the answer - and she hates unanswered questions. She has always loved certainty, needed it; her desire to be decisive has been bred from a longing for black-and-white. It is what, ultimately, forced her hand with Liam; and it is now here again, in the room with them both, begging her for an answer to a problem she has not yet been able to articulate. She looks again at Katy as if *she* might know, as if she has the clue to the conundrum Rachel must unlock. Or perhaps Katy herself is the conundrum. And if that is the case, then how on earth is Rachel supposed to resolve that?

The problem is simply too big for her. She feels defeated, beaten by an enemy who has, she realises, been stalking her for years, compiling the evidence against her, waiting for this moment. It is as if, with Liam's death, her last line of defence has fallen away; as if he had been protecting her all this time - even during the separated years. Perhaps he had been protecting them all, quietly, from the sidelines, allowing them all to be who they wanted, to make their mistakes. Illuminated - at least partially - Rachel wonders if she may have stumbled across what Katy was meaning by the men in her life, the roles

Liam and Ronald played for her. And if that were the case, and if it were true, then does it not apply to her too? Is she not now alone in a way she has never really known before? Is that why she is crying?

Katy watches her mother, head bowed, no longer trying to stop the tears, and knows she should move across the void between them, should go and sit by her side, place an arm around her. But she is crying too. It is as if tears prevent movement, and when both people are crying how can it be possible for either person to make the first move? Katy thinks she recognises grief, sees in her mother's slightly shaking shoulders a mirror of how she felt a few days ago. She believes, suddenly, quietly, and not without some relief, as if she is one step ahead; as if her mother's anguish offers a mirror to something in herself. She has lost, felt pain, but perhaps - just perhaps - she is ready to move on. Her grandfather, her father, even Tom; perhaps she *had* to lose them all to do so. What was it her mother had just said about choosing who you were or what you saw or presented to the world? Was it possible that the time had come for her to become someone else and that she needed the loss of these men to do so?

Bizarrely, Katy feels more powerful, more composed, the superior of the two. It is a role reversal she knows will not last, but for this instant, this precise moment, amid the trauma and the heartbreak, it is there, palpable. And although she doesn't want to, she can't help but revel in it, and in doing so remain seated where she is, watching her mother cry.

The Wake

"Alison?" Katy played with the word in her head as if it were code for something, a key that might allow her to pick a long-neglected lock.

"Yes. An old friend of your father's."

Katy had accepted the hand offered and held it briefly.

"I'm so sorry," Alison said.

"We've had enough time to be ready, I suppose, so it's not the shock it might have been." Distracted, Katy tried to run through a list in her head. "I'm sorry, but I don't recall your name on the list. And if you're an old friend of Daddy's then I don't understand why you weren't on the list."

"Then I'm puzzled too," said Alison, falling in step with the younger woman as they walked back toward the waiting cars, "after all, I did get an invitation."

"You did?"

"Of course." Alison thought for a moment. "Is there anyone you expected to be here who has failed to show up?"

Katy nodded.

"A few people; not many. One of Daddy's ex-colleagues, but he's not well. And a nephew who's currently travelling in South America."

"Anyone else?"

"Funnily enough," said Katy, pausing for a moment, "I was expecting someone; apparently another work connection who I also don't know."

"Called?"

"Barbara something. I can't remember the surname."

Alison laughed.

"You know her?" Katy said, a little surprised, unable to see that she'd said anything funny.

"I'm sorry," said Alison, placing her hand on the other's arm, "but Barbara's me. I'm Barbara."

"But you said your name was Alison." Katy was unable to keep the confusion from her voice.

"It is." Alison paused. "It's an old joke between your father and I. When I first met him I told him I didn't care for my name very much and that he was welcome to call me whatever he liked. Which is what he did. He tried all sorts of names out in his head I think, but in the end Barbara was one of his favourites."

"How extraordinary."

"How funny," Alison corrected. "And how typical of him."

"Really?"

Alison couldn't fail but pick up on the tone of incredulity.

"Sometimes he could be remarkably witty. In a dry sort of way, of course."

*

"How well did you know Daddy?"

It was later, and noticing Alison walking alone in the garden at the side of the house, Katy slipped out to join her. It had become claustrophobic inside, and there was a limit on how many times she could listen to the same stories or make the same replies to the same questions. After a while, condolences take on a less benevolent aspect. She had needed some air, and seeing Alison gave her the perfect excuse.

"That's a much more pertinent question than you might imagine," Alison replied.

"Meaning?"

"In many ways you father was really easy to get to know. I felt that I had him off-pat the first time we spent an evening together." Alison notes the slight arch of Katy's left eyebrow. "We were just having a drink in some dreadful hotel bar after our respective work days were over. We'd bumped into each other the previous morning at breakfast. I'd had a rough day at work, if I remember correctly. We just talked." Alison pauses for a moment to allow memories to re-establish themselves. "Actually I probably did most of the talking."

"About anything in particular?"

"About Liam, actually. I'm one of those people who help companies with culture, organisational change; things like that. There are any number of psychometric-type tests we do on people all the time. If I've got it right, your father challenged me to analyse him."

"And did you?" asked Katy, the notion clearly amusing her.

"He seemed so interesting. I got a tremendous sense of a man who was complex and sensitive, but who plainly wasn't happy at some profound level. That should have stopped me, actually. I should have known better."

"Because?"

"Because I played my little game and seemed to get right to the heart of him. Not that I told him that, of course. I mean, I gave him my professional analysis and that seemed to be pretty much spot on. But I felt as if I'd got beyond that; managed to touch something he hadn't planned on me seeing almost. It made me sad because I felt as if I'd betrayed him - and yet we'd only just met."

Katy looked away, down at the grass, the flowers beginning to die back in the borders. She tried to imagine the scene, to place her father alongside this woman in what must have been a strangely charged and intimate scenario. Alison was not unattractive now; back then she would have surely been quite striking. Katy guessed she was perhaps of an age equidistant between herself and her father, maybe fifteen years either side.

"He was flummoxed, I think."

"Sorry?" Alison's voice dragged Katy back. She looked at this person, a new link back to her father about whom she knew virtually nothing, and wondered what their story had been. If they'd had a story.

"He didn't know how to respond, bless him." Alison glanced back at Katy and smiled. "I don't think he knew he needed rescuing."

"Rescuing? From what?"

"All sorts. From his work; from life. From himself, mainly."
For a second Alison seemed to momentarily shake herself.
"I'm pretty sure, for a while at least, he thought I was the one
who could rescue him."

"And did you?"

Alison stopped walking and looked down at the grass. Once
Katy had paused too, Alison raised her head and smiled. Katy
thought it a wistful, uncertain smile; one that seemed strangely
out of place. Alison placed her hand on Katy's arm.

"You know, I've been asking myself that question for the last
little while, and still I don't know."

Suddenly, a late summer butterfly flitted between them,
dragging their attention away as it zig-zagged towards the
fence, then up and out of sight. There were tears in their eyes
when they looked back at each other. Then they hugged,
cementing the moment for ever.

The End

www.ingramcontent.com/pod-product-compliance
Lightning Source LLC
Chambersburg PA
CBHW021320190726
48288CB00003B/895